Praise for *At the Edge of the Haight*
Winner of the PEN/Bellwether Prize

"What a read this is, right from its startling opening scene. But even more than plot, it's the richly layered details that drive home a lightning bolt of empathy. To read *At the Edge of the Haight* is to live inside the everyday terror and longings of a world that most of us manage not to see. At a time when more Americans than ever find themselves at the edge of homelessness, this book couldn't be more timely."

—Barbara Kingsolver

"Katherine Seligman's new novel makes alive and visible the lives of people we often walk past, sometimes as quickly as we can."

—NPR's *Weekend Edition* with Scott Simon

"A terrific novel, half murder mystery, half a tale of growing up. The heroine and her friends are unique in my reading experience—homeless young people living in Golden Gate Park, with their own community and their own rules—and their story is suspenseful and touching throughout."

—Scott Turow

"Memorable . . . Quietly compassionate . . . Katherine Seligman's gripping debut novel, *At the Edge of the Haight*, explores a community on the edge of a historic setting and on the edge of getting by, with a compelling protagonist and an array of issues to wrestle."

—*Shelf Awareness*

"Insightfully looks at the lives of homeless people . . . Seligman's skills as a journalist are evident in the story's realism. Her detailed descriptions allow the reader to imagine the harrowing day-to-day lives of those living with constant housing insecurity."

—*San Francisco Examiner*

"I love Maddy Donaldo. I can't wait for you to meet her. Not since Carson McCullers's Frankie Addams have I seen a character so defined by her deep dualism—an electric desire to be both invisible and seen, free and bonded." —Mesha Maren, author of *Sugar Run*

"Inspires empathy for San Francisco's unhoused. A journalist who has written extensively about homelessness and mental health issues, particularly in California, Seligman is a keen observer of the wealth gap in San Francisco and the challenges facing those experiencing homelessness. Seligman's writing is at its best when it juxtaposes the experiences of living in San Francisco for those who have and those who have not." —*San Francisco Chronicle* (review)

"I loved this novel: its tenderness, its toughness, its brilliantly named protagonist Maddy—these days, what thoughtful person isn't mad? Maddy is a Holden Caulfield for our times, smart, streetwise, a survivor who is not jaded. Seligman's vivid portrait leads us to understand San Francisco's street people not as 'the other' but as extensions of our friends, our families, our neighbors, ourselves. If there is hope for our species, it begins there." —Fenton Johnson, author of *At the Center of All Beauty: Solitude and the Creative Life*

"[An] incisive look at homelessness in the Haight." —San Francisco's *7x7* magazine

"*At the Edge of the Haight* brims with empathy for the overlooked and the underserved. It's a deep, dark, and necessary look into lives often discarded and disregarded—an urgent and important read and a startling debut." —Ivy Pochoda, author of *These Women*

"Through careful observation, author Seligman seeks to humanize a community that is often ignored and misunderstood . . . Winner of the 2019 PEN/Bellwether Prize for Socially Engaged Fiction, *At the Edge of the Haight* is a thoughtful look at modern homelessness."

—*Booklist*

"This book pulled me deep into a world I knew little about, bringing the struggles of its young, homeless inhabitants—the kind of people we avoid eye contact with on the street—to vivid, poignant life. The novel demands that you take a close look. If you knew, could you still ignore, fear or condemn them? And knowing, how can you ever forget?"   —Hillary Jordan, author of *Mudbound*

"An intense, personal drama about wayward lives positioned between redemption and disaster. Putting a human face on those who live at society's margins, *At the Edge of the Haight* is an intimate novel whose young characters struggle for survival and a little bit of dignity."

—*Foreword Reviews*

"A compassionate and probing character study of the type of street kids Seligman knows people tend to overlook or even scorn when they see them begging on the sidewalk."

—*San Francisco Chronicle* (feature)

"Subtle yet compelling . . . *At the Edge of the Haight* not only offers unexpected insights into the daily life of those who are young and on the streets, but into the confusion of tenderness, hurt, fear and fierceness that tumble within the minds of many. An enlightening read for anyone of any age."   —Helen Benedict, author of *Wolf Season*

"Earnest . . . Seligman has a strong sense of the city and of the challenges faced by the homeless . . . Seligman's portrayal of life as a homeless young person is immersive." —*Publishers Weekly*

"*At the Edge of the Haight* is a novel of rare grace and compassion that opens a window onto a world to which we often keep ourselves closed. With a keen sense for setting and state of mind, Katherine Seligman takes us on a journey into the hidden spaces of America, where the friction created between the need to be seen and to disappear, to remember and to forget, sets little fires that help us see better, help us stay warm." —C. Morgan Babst, author of *The Floating World*

"An insightful portrayal of homelessness . . . Heartfelt . . . Brave." —*Kirkus Reviews*

"The most compelling aspects of *At the Edge of the Haight* involve navigating this mode of survival: the danger of living in the Panhandle, the cop-free zones in which to hustle tourists, the effort that goes into scoring food, the prisonlike routine of lining up at the shelter for a shower and a bed. Seligman excels at describing those elements, which shine a light on a community that, at least to the oblivious masses, appears merely another component of the Haight Street tourist experience—a reminder of an ancient hippie dream, now fried to a crisp." —*Alta*

AT THE EDGE OF THE HAIGHT

AT THE *EDGE*
OF THE *HAIGHT*

by KATHERINE SELIGMAN

ALGONQUIN BOOKS OF CHAPEL HILL

2021

Published by
Algonquin Books of Chapel Hill
Post Office Box 2225
Chapel Hill, North Carolina 27515-2225

a division of
Workman Publishing
225 Varick Street
New York, New York 10014

First paperback edition, Algonquin Books of Chapel Hill, October 2021.
Originally published in hardcover by Algonquin Books of Chapel Hill in
January 2021.
Printed in the United States of America.
Published simultaneously in Canada by Thomas Allen & Son Limited.
Design by Amy Ruth Buchanan / 3rd sister design.

This is a work of fiction. While, as in all fiction, the literary perceptions and
insights are based on experience, all names, characters, places, and incidents
either are products of the author's imagination or are used fictitiously.

LIBRARY OF CONGRESS
CATALOGING-IN-PUBLICATION DATA

Names: Seligman, Katherine, [date]– author.
Title: At the edge of the haight / by Katherine Seligman.
Description: Chapel Hill, North Carolina : Algonquin Books of Chapel Hill,
    2021. | Summary: "When Maddy Donaldo, a homeless woman who has made a
    family of sorts in the dangerous spaces of San Francisco's Golden Gate Park,
    witnesses the murder of a young homeless boy and is seen by the perpetrator,
    her relatively stable life is upended"— Provided by publisher.
Identifiers: LCCN 2020034563 | ISBN 9781643750231 (hardcover) |
    ISBN 9781643751153 (ebook)
Subjects: GSAFD: Suspense fiction.
Classification: LCC PS3619.E46328 A96 2021 | DDC 813/.6—dc23
LC record available at https://lccn.loc.gov/2020034563

ISBN 978-1-64375-208-2 (PB)

10 9 8 7 6 5 4 3 2 1
First Paperback Edition

To David

AT THE EDGE OF THE HAIGHT

CHAPTER 1

Root skimmed the sidewalk with his nose, sniffing at food wrappers, a black boot, and a pair of red tights someone had tossed in a perfect Z. I put my hand on his neck and nudged him past. "Not your business," I said. He locked his eyes on me because he knew I had bread and cheese in my pack. They always kicked you out after breakfast, but you could take whatever you wanted if you stayed late to help clean up. It meant splitting from Ash and everyone, but I knew where they'd be, sitting at the front of the park, waiting for things to get started. I should have been there too, but of course I didn't know that until later.

It was too early for tourists to be out. Two men stood at the bus stop, coats drawn up against the fog and whatever else had blown in overnight. Jax was slumped on the corner in his wheelchair, snoring in small puffs, a gray blanket draped over his head. Otherwise, no one was around except for hardcore sleepers twisted in doorways, still too wasted to hear the cleaning truck brushing water against the curb, as if that did anything. You could always see what was left behind.

I kept trying to hurry Root along, but he was taking his time, until the truck churned alongside us and he stopped and tilted his head to the smell like he was thinking about it. Then he took off, racing down the street, his tail flicked up straight. He crossed at the corner and disappeared into the bushes. I tore after him, my pack slapping against my back.

"Root!" I yelled in a frantic voice. I'd taken him to the free clinic downtown a few weeks ago, foam spilling out of his mouth from something he found. They'd pumped his stomach and lectured me to take better care of him, as if I could make him act right when we stayed in Golden Gate Park. They told me I should think about giving him up so he could be adopted and be safe, in a house. They didn't get it. We took care of each other.

"Root, get your ass out of there," I screamed. "I mean it!"

There was no trace of him, but he knew his way around the park. We all did. I reached in and rattled the brush, which was waist high.

"Root!"

He came halfway out, his muzzle crusted with dirt. He looked at me the way he did when he knew he was in trouble. I grabbed for his collar, but missed, and he scrambled back in. I followed him through the brush into a small clearing and I kept talking to him, what did he think he was doing, he was crazy, so I didn't see right off what was in front of me. But Root was looking down, at a kid lying on the ground, perfectly still, his eyes wide open to the sky. His head was turned a little to one side, his arms spread out as if he was making an angel in the dirt.

Root sniffed his face and neck. The kid stuttered in a single long breath and I stood there, watching, holding my own. Root licked his cheek and edged his nose down the kid's chest toward a seeping stain of blood. In the middle, almost hidden, was a tiny slit in his shirt. I couldn't stop looking at the blood, the kid's halo of light brown hair, and for once in twenty years on this earth I couldn't seem to move.

I knew I would see it for the rest of my life. Whenever I closed my eyes, he would be there, his life leaking out on the ground. Maybe it was true what my stand-in of a mother said. *You are going to end up damaged goods.* I couldn't help copying her voice. "You are going to be sorry," I said to Root and pulled him away from the kid. I wanted to put my hand on the kid's chest to see if it was moving, but I couldn't get myself to do it. My heart was banging against my chest. Who was I going to scream for? Ash and everyone else, they wouldn't hear me.

Root startled and growled with his mouth closed, a slow deep rattle he made when he knew he was on guard. We both looked over at a man standing at the edge of the clearing. He could have been there the whole time, waiting, or maybe he'd walked in right after us. He was a head taller than me, his black and gray hair pushed back into a stringy ducktail. I had a sweatshirt hood pulled up over my head so nothing about me stood out, but Root was something you'd remember. He looked like he'd been sewn together, his face soft Labrador, the rest some short, wide pit bull creation.

The man stuck his hands in the pockets of his camo pants and stared at us. I tried to stare back, but all I could do was reach for Root, who moved from a muffled growl to an all-out bark. I didn't usually make people nervous, but the man shifted back and forth, crunching sticks and leaves under his boots, which made Root bark louder. The man lunged toward us, then stopped, like he forgot something. I thought how easily he could come after me. No one would know. I'd be lying there, next to the kid. The cops would think we'd done it to each other.

"Keep a handle on the fucking dog," he said, wiping at what looked like blood on his forehead. I could tell he was used to ordering people around.

It seemed like minutes passed, but it must have been less because neither of us moved. Even Root stood still, his eyes on the man. And then, not thinking where I was headed, I turned and ran. Root kept up, loping next to me. "You heard me?" he yelled after us. "I know where to find your ass."

I scrambled across the uneven dirt and past some trees, until I had to bend in half and gulp air. I listened for the man, but all I could hear was my own quick breath, or maybe it was his, or the wind. I couldn't tell what was real. The carpet of yellow and brown leaves where I stood looked too bright. They smelled sweet but rotten. When I straightened up, my muscles were ready for more, but I couldn't do it. The loop had started playing in my brain, of the kid on the ground and the look in the man's eyes.

I knew something about getting away. I'd been doing that most of my life, but not like this. No one had tried to stop me when I left the house where I'd lived longer than anywhere else. They had no idea where I was, standing in a park hundreds of miles away, alone in a whole different way. Root whined softly and I put a finger sternly to my lips, as if he'd know what that meant. Quiet, I mouthed. No one was coming to help. I could run through the park all the way to the ocean, but then where would I go? I turned toward the other direction, which led back to the street, and my body took over and I was running again, pretending I was someone who knew what she was doing.

CHAPTER 2

We ran past a group of joggers in black leggings, who nodded at us, then stepped out of the way to give Root room. "No worries," said the last one, over whatever was playing on her headphones. She should be worried, I wanted to say, because she was headed toward the man and that kid. But I was relieved other people were filling up the park. Two gardeners with a ladder walked toward us. I could hear traffic from the street. Maybe I had a chance.

We slowed down when we reached a row of bright green benches surrounded by beds of yellow flowers and trees with big waxy leaves, then stopped at the lake that was supposed to make the park entrance look like a place you'd want to be. Every week they had to unclog the drain and clean out whatever was floating on top, but the water always went back to swampy green. They blamed us. But we were the ones who watched out for it. We made a sign, WE DON'T TRASH YOUR HOUSE, and sometimes people laughed and dropped change.

Ash, Fleet, and Hope sat in a circle near the lake on one of the small dry patches of grass. The lawn was mushy in places and gone in others because we had worn it down, but also because the park people kept turning on the sprinklers, probably so we wouldn't get too comfortable.

"Mad," said Ash. "Where you been?" He was digging in his pack and smiled with one half of his mouth, like the other part was too busy. I was sweating, still breathing hard, but I could have been back from recycling, my pack loaded with change. I could have stayed to clean up the whole shelter. I could have been anywhere. They had no idea. We were all travelers, with business no one else needed to know. Someone always had to go somewhere in a hurry, whether they were running to or from something. You didn't ask because you probably didn't want to know, even if these were the people you were with every day and night. I waved at Ash but didn't stop.

When I reached the street, I snapped on Root's leash and ducked into the music store on the corner. I could spend hours looking through the aisles and no one would bother me or ask if I needed help. No one would complain if I took a handful of the lollipops they kept at the register but didn't buy anything. It was warm and the store played tunes with a deep bass that echoed off the high ceiling and concrete floor into my chest. I didn't have to think in there. The music knocked everything out of my brain. Root always perked up because they kept a little tin bowl of biscuits behind the counter. He never wanted to leave until he got one.

I didn't go to the counter, so he pulled on his leash and I had to push him and squeeze my fingers around his mouth to keep him quiet. He tried to wiggle away, but I clamped down tighter and then slid behind a corner rack while my heart calmed down. Bins of albums and CDs stretched out in front of me. I forced myself to read the names on them and checked the clock every few minutes until I saw that an hour had passed. The man had not walked into the store so I must have lost him. To make sure, I stayed another half hour. A deep steady reggae tune boomed into me. When I got up to leave, Root pulled me to the counter.

"Sit," said the guy behind the register, holding out a biscuit to Root, as if he hadn't been through enough, but he obeyed and planted his backside on top of my foot. He gulped it down without chewing and I pulled him out of the store.

My first week on the street I had found Root tied to a parking meter, scrawny and sad, his ribs looking like delicate sticks. I'd sat down next to him and he whimpered and climbed into my lap. He stayed there, chewing on my fingers until he fell asleep. No one came to get him, so I untied the rope and took him with me. I did have a habit of taking things, but Root was different. It wasn't the same as walking into a store in Los Angeles where there was too much stuff and no one noticed if I lifted chapstick or a pack of batteries I didn't need. I sometimes left my take on top of a trashcan or the free bin at the shelter. It was a private deal I had with myself: I could take things as long as they weren't for me. But Root was clearly my dog. He followed me everywhere, into the bathroom at the park or at the shelter, and he barked if anyone tried to touch him when I wasn't there. His eyes, one blue and one brown, were on me all the time.

Outside the music store, a group of tourists filtered past me, pushing to stay close to the leader who carried a blue flag on a stick. They followed her like noiseless baby ducks. One woman aimed her camera at me, but I turned my back. Someone needed to tell her that nothing was free now. If you stared you should pay, Ash said. Usually I would put up a cup for change, but I wasn't in the mood. Where was I going to sleep? The guy in the park might come looking at the shelter. And I couldn't go back to the park. I'd have to post up somewhere, maybe without Root. If anyone wanted to find me all they had to do was ask about him.

I passed a store with a leftover cemetery scene from Halloween in the window, a ghost lifting its bloody, smiling head out of a grave. It looked like it was staring at me. The used clothes store next door had a mannequin in a Cinderella costume hanging on a zip line. I sat down outside a head shop, the front painted a bright neon rash of stars and planets. I leaned back, Root between my knees. My legs felt like bags of sand. What did I do to deserve this? I avoided trouble most of the time. I stayed away from drama. I didn't fight. So why did I have to see a kid who got wasted and the guy who probably did it?

The last of the tourists straggled out of the park, finished with the museums and gardens and ponds. They didn't want to be left alone, not at the end of the day, with us, and the knots of kids chanting "X, buds, X, buds, X, buds" like it was a prayer. Some took out cash, hunched over so they could hide it, and bought plastic bags of who knows what. You could sell anything and charge them double. They didn't know.

I was too undone to look anyone in the eyes, which might have gotten me a box of food or a sandwich. One time a lady started a fight with her man on the sidewalk right in front of me, telling him how selfish he was for not handing over the rest of his steak dinner. He didn't need it so why didn't he give it to the girl, who was obviously hungry. He stomped off, the box under his arm, and she yelled after him about how he didn't see anything unless it had to do with his own self. But then she went running after him. Who could figure that out?

"There you are," said Ash, coming up next to me. He sat down, put a hand on my back, where it felt like an electric pulse.

"Hold on to Root?" I said.

I passed him the leash and he took it, without asking why. He thought everything was still a big love project the way it was on the street years ago, long before he was here. Just show up and you'd find what you need.

"Only tonight," I said. "I'll hit you up in the morning and get him."

Ash wrapped the leash tightly around his hand. He was a skinny upside-down triangle, with heavy dark blond dreads that ran down his back and a single patch of beard on his chin.

He had one tattoo, what looked like a loop of string, in the crease of his right arm.

He handed me the end of a bottle of Wild Turkey and headed off toward the shelter. It was edging colder, and the sun was dissolving into thin layers of pink and blue on its way behind the trees. I didn't see anyone I knew. They would be at the shelter, bunched up in line, waiting to get a bed, or disappearing back into the park. I headed around the corner to an empty flat where someone had jacked open a window last week. Word got out. We knew, even if we didn't stay there, because you never knew what you were going to find in a squat.

There were already six kids on the cracked concrete steps out front. I held up the bottle of Wild Turkey and sat next to the one guy I'd seen before, Serenity. He sold the same weed as everyone, except he named it after himself. People remembered and they came looking. He smiled and passed me a joint. I tried to turn it down, but he narrowed his eyes in disappointment and I took it, inhaled deeply, and handed him my bottle. My head was spinning because I hadn't eaten anything since breakfast. I leaned back and looked at the bright blue apartment building across the street. It had what looked like real gold trim along the roof and windows that curved out over the sidewalk. A man on the top floor inched a pot onto a table. Steam rose up and started fogging the window. I imagined going over there for dinner, eating whatever was in the pot. I would be sitting across from him and it would be like every other dinner he had. Except for me. I was set to wave if he looked out, but he didn't.

Serenity passed me the end of the joint and I took a hit. He put an arm around my shoulder and led me up the stairs to the front door, which was cracked and looked like it had been glued back together. I let myself unwind the tiniest bit. The front room had a stained couch, a metal lamp bent in half and boxes of what looked like rusted nails. The carpet was rolled to one side. I sat on the couch, put my head back, tried not to think about the guy in the park, and closed my eyes, hopefully signaling that I would be out of contact for a while. I was drifting, buzzed from the weed, when the jamming started, first Serenity on his harmonica, then a kid with a banjo and someone drumming on a plastic bucket with chop sticks that made a hollow, sharp sound. Another kid danced around the room, working his hips, pawing the air with his hands. Someone brought out cups of crusted lentils that the Civil Food people had handed out in the park in the morning and cans of Red Bull from the guy who drove around in a car shaped like a giant soda can. You'd wave at him and he'd toss cans out the window. He didn't care how many times you waved. I sipped the sharp sweet liquid to force down the cold lentils. It was pointless to try to sleep. Every time I closed my eyes, I would see that kid laying in the park, just on the other side of living who knows what kind of life.

CHAPTER 3

Most of the time I could shut out everything else and talk to myself like I was another person. The first time I cut school I looked in the bathroom mirror. "Maddy," I said, taking myself in, "what are we going to do?" And I knew I would go to the beach, hang out, walk by the house I used to live in, which is exactly what happened. But sitting on the couch, still speeding on Red Bull and fear, I could not force the conversation. I made myself stare up at a hole in the ceiling, right above me. With both eyes open it was an egg about to drop, but if I closed one it was a far-away star. Fixing on that kept me from thinking back on what happened. Maybe the kid in the park had gotten up and walked away. How did I know? I hadn't gotten close enough to touch him.

Near morning the room was quiet, but my brain felt like someone was in there moving furniture. I was jumpy and sweaty when I heard a knock on the door. Through the crack I could see Ash and Root, his nose wedged at the bottom of the door. Ash's dreads hung in a wet clump down his back and his eyes were red, but at least he'd gotten a bed last night. They opened the shelter every winter, but there were always too many of us. We lined up if it was cold or rainy, even though we all felt the same way about the rules. If you got a bed, you had to be inside before eight at night, no coming and going, and leave at eight each morning. They said they wanted you looking for work or going to school or attending to your future, which was not sitting around in there doing nothing. So mostly we hung on the street, at the park or the library, as soon as it opened since they had to let you in there.

Root ran at me and jumped up, reaching to lick my face. I hugged him and then told him to get down. Ash followed me into the living room. People were asleep all over the floor and Root roamed the room, smelling everyone, first around the face and then getting more personal.

"Root, off," I whisper screamed when he stuck his nose on the half-naked butt of the guy who'd been dancing the night before. He rolled over and pulled his shirt down over his sagging jeans without opening his eyes. Ash laughed, until I put my hand over his mouth.

"Will you just shut it for a minute?" I said. "Except for him," I pointed at Serenity, curled in a corner next to his pack, "I have no idea who these guys are. How'd you know where I was?"

"He knew," he said, pointing at Root, who was trying to jump on me again. It shouldn't have surprised me because every particle in the universe left notes for him to follow. "I figured you'd be here. Where else were you going to crash?"

He was right. Anyone could know where I was. I looked around at the windows and hallway, thinking which way I'd go if the man from the park showed up.

"He missed you last night," said Ash, patting Root's head. "Barked his ass off at some cop who came by asking about a kid who got carved up in the park. He wanted to know if anyone knew him or saw what happened. And then I remembered how you came booming out of there yesterday."

"I never saw that kid before yesterday," I said.

"Maddy, what the..." Ash's voice trailed off. "You knew him?"

"I didn't *know* him," I said. "But I might have watched him die."

Just saying it out loud, I knew it was true. It made my heart jam again, like my chest was splitting open. It was strangling the air out of me. I started panting and I could barely see Ash or Root.

Ash took my arm and pulled me down the hall into the kitchen. He looked for a cup but couldn't find one, so he scooped his hands under the faucet and brought them to my face. I gulped, half of the water dripping down my chin. My breathing settled, enough to notice the wreck in front of me. Paper plates with crusty noodles and pizza crusts sat on the cracked tile counter. Sacks of trash were pushed up against the sink. The smell of rot and the clutching inside my chest made me gag.

"Hey," said Ash, leading me to a stairwell at the back of the kitchen. "What happened?"

I told him how Root had run off into the bushes where the kid was lying on the ground and we'd walked into the man who was standing there, almost like he was waiting for us. I could tell Ash wasn't sure if I was telling it straight. It's not like I didn't make stuff up, Ash said. I put my hand flat on his chest so he would get it, I was serious. I told him how the man yelled he knew where to find me and how he looked not all there. Maybe Root had watched it all happen, but I'd only seen the body.

"That is so fucked up," said Ash.

"You're sure the guy who maybe killed him didn't just show up at the shelter?" I said.

"He said he wanted to know what happened. Why would some dude who stabbed someone pretend to be a cop and then go out asking about it?"

"I don't know. So he can take care of me, like he did with that kid?"

"That's twisted, even for you."

I knew how the undercover cops dressed and how they watched us on the street. It wasn't a big secret. They would stand on the corner, try to talk to us. How you doing? You've looked better. What happened to your shoes? One used to wear a leather hat and reflector sunglasses so big you could check yourself out. We'd walk by, say hey, and he'd stand there, a statue taking it all in. Then last Christmas he brought a bag of peanut butter sandwiches and new socks and left it on the corner for us. We never saw him after that. I couldn't tell anymore who was a cop or who wasn't. Everything had changed after yesterday.

We walked down the street and Root pulled on his leash, trying to get back to the park. We could hear the creaking of metal gates being rolled up, a bus beeping as it pulled over to let people off. The fog was starting to melt but it still threw the street out of focus. The mural on the corner was a blur of yellow and red roses, with giant letters, LOVE, floating in the middle. Ash picked up a piece of cardboard from a trashcan and stuffed it under his arm. I thought about sitting on the sidewalk with a sign, NEED BUS $, so I could go back to Los Angeles, somewhere so big that no one saw you. I could get myself into beauty school like everyone told me to, and forget about the guy who was after me. I could apologize for going away, for thinking I could figure everything out on my own.

CHAPTER 4

I pulled off my sweatshirt and dropped it on the pavement for Root, who circled a few times and then collapsed on top. The sun was still trying to break through a thin paste of white clouds. We sat in front of the empty sneaker store that used to be full of brightly colored shoes parked in rows like cars at a lot in Los Angeles. The manager would tell us he was going to call the cops if we set up outside and then he'd flick his fists open and closed so we would think about police lights. People used to line up all night and sleep on the street for their big events. Then a guy would toss the first pair of shoes, free, into the crowd in the morning. People shoved and jumped to get them because someone famous had signed his name on the side. Ash said one time a kid who'd caught a pair got shot, but he'd stood up and walked away, cradling the shoes in his arms. A few weeks ago, the store closed and now no one cared if we sat in the doorway. Someone had spray-painted a tree on the window and the words HAPPY CHRISTMAS in bright red, even though it was just past Halloween. It was an invite to draw on the tree, so people had scribbled words, added a ring of black roses and a tiny man with his tongue hanging out. I'd made a picture of Root with his nose up in the air, except no one but me could tell what it was.

Ash handed me a bagel from a sack he'd found outside the grocery store down the street. I broke it in half and Root swallowed his piece fast while I gnawed on mine. People walked by like it was another normal day. The world hadn't jolted to a stop and thrown everyone off the surface and into space. Ash said it would be stupid to go back to Los Angeles. He'd hitched down there once and it was worse. Everyone was all pumped up, about to go over the edge. No one cared what happened to you.

He took his cardboard and laid it down on the pavement while he wrote. HOMELESS ANYTHING HELPS. His signs were always straight up honest. He was the most no bullshit guy around. BUY ME A SLICE. $$ FOR BEER. Not something like KARMA STATION, or showing up with a pan, as in, we get it, panhandle.

Even without a sign, people would still drop coins on the sweatshirt in front of Root. They figured poor dog, he was hungry, which he wasn't. He ate more than we did. Ash said he was going to get a dog, or a kid, so people would give more freely. He was sitting next to me, knees crossed.

"Dough, dough, dough for burrito," he sang out. "I don't smoke crack."

A woman with a bob of curly white hair and a small gray poodle smiled at Root. She leaned down and put a dollar on the sweatshirt.

"See what I mean?" said Ash. "It's better not to be human."

I was still in a daze from the lack of sleep and the weed and my worn-out nerves. I hugged my knees and looked down at Root, sleeping. Dogs could turn it on and off. No why did I do that last night? What will happen if I do the other thing? Who is out to get me? He half barked and kicked his hind legs in his sleep.

"Hey," said Fleet from behind me, grabbing a chunk of my hair and twiddling it in her fingers. Her tattered sweater hung down to her knees. She had pulled her coarse strawberry blond hair into a bun. The gauges in her ears were the size of quarters. Her nails, caked in dirt, had an inch on them. There was a time when I would have minded them in my hair, but now I wasn't that picky. She sat down next to me and put her arm around my back. She smelled of weed, beer, eucalyptus trees, and stale sleeping bag. It was probably the same way I smelled but didn't notice until I got a whiff on someone else. I know people looked at me when I walked into the library or went to the coffee house down the street that let us use the bathroom. I knew they were seeing my knotted hair and beat-up jeans, but they were also following my smell.

"Where is Tiny?" I said.

"With his father," she said. "Custody thing." Then she pulled him out from under her sleeve.

I forced myself to smile. There was a world outside my head and I had to try to live in it.

"Hey, Tiny." I put a finger on the top of his head.

Fleet looked bent. She could drink a handle of anything and still be walking and she'd try whatever was around. I liked her quiet presence, the way she would slide over and check up on me. She would give me her last money, even though she didn't expect me to pay her back. She never expected anything, not after her parents split up and fought over who was going to take her. They left her with friends and someone called Granny, who wasn't, until they lost custody. She couldn't remember what they looked like. The thing was, Fleet could go home if she wanted. Her foster mom kept a room for Fleet even though she kicked her out a few years ago when she'd turned eighteen, saying she was turning off the faucet for her own good. But Fleet still called her Mom and would go over to the other side of the bay and stay a few days, until the two of them started fighting. She said her mom had a nose like a dog that smelled for drugs at the airport and she'd come near and start sniffing. Last summer her mom posted signs around the Haight with a picture of Fleet from years ago in a blue shirt, her hair in neat braids. LOST AND AT RISK, it said, under the picture. Fleet had ripped down all the signs, said she wasn't her real mom but she acted like Fleet was her private property. She could go where she wanted. "And really, lost?" she said. "Am I lost?" She opened her eyes wide, the way she did when she wanted to make a point. "Hello. I'm here. If she fucking wanted to know."

We sat there, our heads together, not talking, when Hope walked up and slammed down next to us. Her spiky black hair looked like it could cut you open. It's not that she didn't have a sweet side. She could turn it on when she needed to and she knew exactly when that was. She said her parents had called her Sweet Pea when she was little, because her name was Penelope, which you couldn't expect anyone to actually use.

Hope knew how to make things happen. She'd talked a crew on the street into giving her scraps of weed they couldn't sell. She set up and was happy for about a week, until they wanted a bigger cut and she said it wasn't worth it, that she'd go into business on her own. Then she'd told the pizza place down the street that she'd deliver for them, no charge, if they'd give her a free pie every night. The manager said she had a job if she cleaned herself up. He wasn't going to hire someone who looked like she slept in the gutter. Hope came away with a super large pizza, but never went in for the job. After that, the manager gave us pies that no one picked up, setting them on the sidewalk and waving. We'd picked up trash in front of his store if he was there to see it, just to let him know we were looking out for him.

Hope talked to everyone. "Where y'all from?" she'd say, like she was from the South, even though she came from Mendocino and went back there every season to trim weed because that's where the real money was. "Oh, Texas. Great state." And she did collect more than the rest of us. Sometimes she'd follow the tourists all the way down the street, jabbering the whole time. She'd tell them about the amusement park that used to be on the street a long time ago and Fish Man, who ate and smoked underwater. Seriously. We were not the first freaks. If they asked directions, like to the famous corner of Haight and Ashbury, the actual headquarters of the hippie movement, she'd volunteer to show them the spot, as if she had been there when the hippies were all over the street, handing out free food, taking acid and listening to the Grateful Dead and whatever else they did. "Turn on, tune in, drop out," she'd say. Then she'd take them to see where the famous musicians lived, houses now fixed up and painted bright as parrots. "Jerry and Janis couldn't afford them now," she'd say and pose for pictures in front, wearing her tie-dyed T-shirt from the free box at the shelter. "Hardly anyone can." That would start the tourists talking about how much had changed, no wonder so many people were living on the street. You couldn't go anywhere in the city without seeing them. Hope would say how it was different for kids here. It was still about free love and peace and everything. She probably believed that. Her parents were old hippies. They lived in a house with no running water or electricity, except what they got from her dad pedaling a bike on a stand. It didn't sound good to me. I hadn't seen my mom in ten years, but I had lived with electricity and if I got settled one day it would not be in a dump with no lights or water.

Fleet, Hope, and I were tight, even if we didn't always think the same. I came from a house full of kids, the ones no one knew what to do with and a few who were sort of related to me. But we were not what you'd call a family, not that my real family was either. I never had anyone like Hope and Fleet. We had been here the longest. Other girls would come and go, but usually it was the three of us. And Ash. We called him an honorary sister, which he ignored. He sat against the wall with his sign, his skateboard between his outstretched legs.

I was still leaning into Fleet, her arm over my shoulder, when a heavy black shoe appeared next to my knee. We knew most of the beat cops and they knew us. But this guy must be new. He had a fresh buzz cut and wore his hat too far forward, sunglasses stuck around the back slab of his neck.

"Ladies," he said, tipping the hat slightly back. "You will have to move along."

Hope saluted him. "Yes, sir," she said.

I elbowed her to stop. I didn't need to make it obvious to whoever was looking for me that I was right here. The guy in the park might have told the cops that I attacked the kid. Who were they going to believe? Besides, this was the usual routine; no one paid attention unless we gave them a reason to. There was a law against sitting or lying around on the sidewalk during the day, but it was a violation of our rights. That's what they told us at the shelter. People who stayed outside had the same rights as people inside. No one could talk down to you because you didn't live in a house.

"You know the rules," he said, sticking his sunglasses back on his eyes. "Gotta share the sidewalk." He reached out a foot and pushed Ash's sign against the wall.

"It's him," Ash whispered to me. "The cop who was at the shelter last night, asking about that kid."

I pretended not to hear him. We stood up and leaned against the wall, starting the game that might last all day. As soon as he left, we'd sit down again or move around the corner and stop in at the library. They left us alone if we went to the park, but we couldn't get anything going there and they knew it. All day we moved from spot to spot, with the cops following. It was a stupid law and we all knew it. Hope once found an office chair in a dumpster and rolled around the sidewalk in it. They couldn't do anything about that. Ash got on his knees and said he wasn't sitting or lying so they couldn't make him move. That worked for a minute before one of the cops called him a clown and said if he was on his knees he'd better be praying not to go to jail. Then he'd taken out his phone and asked us to sing happy birthday to his wife. On the last part Ash screamed out, "I want to do you so much" instead of "Happy birthday to you," but the cop said it was cheaper than roses. "You know how much fresh roses cost?" he said. "You get them, then they die."

We had all been written up before for blocking the sidewalk, meaning that they could bring us in, no questions asked, whenever they wanted. But usually they didn't want to spend the time or money doing that any more than we wanted to go into the station. They knew we'd never pay any fines and so they'd end up tossing out the charges. We all lived the game. But the new cop didn't seem to know how it worked. He looked annoyed after Hope saluted, like she had flipped him off.

"Anyone want to talk to the outreach team?" He looked at each of us. "A ride to the crisis shelter? Sober center?" No one said anything.

"Didn't think so," he said. "I see you again and I'll have to cite you all." He adjusted his hat once more and went off down the street.

"Fuck," I kicked Hope's steel-toed boot. "What are you trying to do?"

"Excuse her," said Ash, leaning down and pulling me up by my arm. "She had a hard night."

We walked down the street to a head shop and settled in close to the building, our feet tucked in so it was clear were not blocking anyone. Ash found a piece of cardboard and started writing. NEED LUNCH. Fleet lowered her face into a torn-up paperback she'd found at the shelter. She was always picking up books. She didn't care what they were about, vampires, building tree houses, world war, whatever someone had dumped at the shelter or in a box on the street. Soon Hope was up and standing at the corner asking a guy with a map if he wanted help. Then she was off with him, toward the corner of Ashbury and Haight, where she would give him the tourist talk and maybe he would buy her a cone at Ben & Jerry's.

"Excuse me, what did I say?" said the new cop, standing next to me again.

Ash stood up and glared at him. "This is America and last time I checked we had rights," he said. The cop turned away and spoke into a small microphone pinned on his shoulder. It crackled when he talked. I heard the word backup and a squad car raced down the street, its lights flashing, like it was some emergency. Where were they when the kid was getting stabbed, all the blood running out? My stomach started to twist up again. Everyone on the street was craning to look at us. Drivers slowed down to see what was up. The man who owned the bookstore across the street stepped out. He sometimes bought us food from the grocery and said we could come in and browse, looking was free. He raised a hand and gestured toward us with two fingers, but it was too late.

Two cops got out of the car. I recognized them both and they nodded at me. They probably had notes from the outreach team. Female, twenty, calls herself Maddy, prior warnings about civil sidewalk, attitude issues, no interest in reunification with family, has turned down Homeward Bound. What else did they know? They didn't say anything to stop the new cop. He wrote down our names and said he was going to cite us as soon as he finished a background check. He went to his car and started pecking at a computer, while the other two waited. Ash went over to talk to them. He sounded like he was arguing, but I couldn't hear what he was saying.

"I'm going to have to take you in," the cop said when he got back. "I want you to walk, and I mean slowly, to the car and put your hands on the hood."

I put my hands on the car and he patted my sides and up and down my legs. I wanted to scream about how they should be looking for a killer instead of hassling someone minding her own business, but I pushed it down. I didn't want to get into it with them. Why would they believe me? We were lucky Hope had moved on because she wouldn't be good with this. With her mouth, she'd cause more trouble. We'd be hearing how there was a reason they called them pigs. Ash was cursing nonstop under his breath, fuckingshitgoddamnwhatthefuck, but he went limp and let them twist his arms back and put plastic cuffs around his wrists. They did the same to me, with Root standing next to me. They could see he wasn't wild, but they put a muzzle around his nose. He shook his head back and forth and tried to pull it off with his front paws. I started telling him it was all going to be okay, but I couldn't even reach down to pet him. He looked at me with his crazy eyes until they grabbed him with a metal stick that had a hook on one end.

"He'll be waiting for you at Animal Control," said one of the cops we knew, sounding like he was apologizing for the new guy. "We'll get you cited and out."

Now there were three squad cars lined up and they loaded each of us in a different one. The new guy put his hand on my head so I had to get in the car butt first. I had never been inside a cop car. It smelled like shoe polish and spray paint, strong and acidic. A gun and a computer were bolted to the dashboard. My mind was going off in a lot of directions, even though I kept telling myself I hadn't done anything wrong. I wasn't going to jail for sitting on the sidewalk, not bothering anyone. But the more I told myself that the more I felt the prickle of fear go through my body.

The cop drove faster than he needed to, then outside the station he put his hand on top of my head again while I climbed out of the car and led me inside. The front door opened into a room lined with wood benches. Fleet and Ash were already there, still in cuffs; Ash nodded at me and wiggled his fingers. I turned around and touched them with my own before I sat down.

Fleet looked glum. Tiny's pink nose was sticking out of her sleeve. They had either missed him or figured it was more trouble to get rid of him. I was too afraid to talk, but I looked around the room. Almost every spot on the walls was covered with black-and-white pictures of faces, a collection of fierce eyes and out of control hair, beards, angry mouths, tattoos. Only one was a woman, her short hair in uneven bunches, staring into the distance. To me, they all looked blank. You couldn't tell anything about what they were thinking. The words in big letters at the top of each photo: WANTED.

"Your mug's going to be right up there," said Ash, smiling.

I rolled my eyes at him and scanned the faces, looking for the man I'd seen in the park. For all I knew the dead kid might be up there too. I could still see his body, the way it was in the dirt and the small bloody slit on his chest. His eyes had been open, but did he feel anything? I hoped I would spot the guy who stabbed him. At least I would not be the only one who knew what he could do. But I didn't recognize anyone on those walls.

I had to pee. And I was starting to think the cops had left us with these freaks so we would realize how lucky we were not to be on the wall. A high school counselor once took me to the police station when I got caught shoplifting. The cops talked about the things that happen in jail, how it didn't take long until you started acting like the people in there. You ended up losing all touch with reality. If you thought you were getting yelled at before, they said, just wait until you are locked up. When you got out you'd have a record that it would take a long time to clear.

Everyone would know where you'd been. I started clacking my knees together to keep from leaking pee onto the bench. I was going to yell for someone to get me a bathroom break when the door opened again, and the new cop came in.

"I wish I didn't have to do this," he said.

He unclipped my cuffs and then Fleet's and Ash's and handed us slips of paper.

"You can pay the fine after you show up in court," he said. "Hall of Justice. It's all up there at the top, everything you need to know."

Ash crumpled the paper, put it in his mouth and swallowed.

The cop shook his head. "That was not smart," he said. "You already have half a dozen citations. Make your court date or you'll get arrested."

Ash nodded his head sideways toward the door and I followed him back onto the street. I turned to look back at the station. Maybe the cops would tear up my ticket if I told them what I'd seen. Wouldn't they at least protect me? Maybe I should have done something so I'd be put in a cell where the guy couldn't get to me. Let myself piss on the floor, right in front of them. That didn't seem bad enough. I went over what I could do. Ash tugged at my arm.

"We've got to go find Root," he said.

The three of us walked in a tight line back to Haight Street. We took up the whole sidewalk. It was ours, as long as we kept moving.

CHAPTER 5

People didn't think I was from Los Angeles because I didn't seem like the type. It's not just that I had a wild bomb of brown hair, skin the color of baby powder, and was flat chested enough to look like a guy until I was sixteen. It was more that I didn't act like most people there, all hey baby, and like, oh my god. I never wanted to be a girl who thought everyone was looking at her. I was set on being invisible. Let anyone try to find me because they wouldn't. The one glamorous thing about me was my name, Madlynne, which my mom pulled out of the air because she liked the way it looked when she wrote it on my birth certificate.

We lived in a house near the beach where the sand worked its way through the windows and doors, into everything. You felt like you were eating it and sleeping on it. Every night my mom wiped a grainy film off my feet before she tucked me into a blanket on the living room couch. She and my dad stayed in the bedroom, when he was in town. I could hear them yelling at each other, his screaming, her answering in a higher pitch. One day he shoved her against the wall in the kitchen and held her there. "You look at me," he told her. "You never listen to a thing I say." He pinned her with his body, his hands turning her face so she had to look at him. "I don't know why you care," she said. "You're never here." I don't know how long they stayed like that because I left and hid myself on the sofa.

My dad drove a truck back and forth across the country, delivering boxes to people. He said they always wanted things faster so he had to stay up all night behind the wheel, slapping his cheek to keep awake. If you fell asleep it was over, he said. When he came back home he'd bring me something, an electric toothbrush, a bright pink princess pillow, a kid-size rocking chair, which he made a show of presenting, *here you go, baby doll.* My mom said he stole it all off the truck so it didn't qualify as a present.

When my dad left for good, my mom tossed it all in the trash. I wanted to tell her not to, it belonged to me, but I just watched. She stuck her foot inside the big metal can and pushed so hard that I could hear things breaking. She hardly ever talked about him after that. I took it in, like it was the next thing that was supposed to happen. I went to kindergarten and then to first grade. My dad disappeared.

"We are starting over," my mom said when we moved into an apartment. It was smaller, but I had my own bed and the heater didn't bang all night like someone trying to break down the door. She wrote up a schedule and stuck it on the refrigerator with a magnet shaped like a thumb.

Get up

Eat breakfast

Go to school

Do homework

Clean kitchen

Wash clothes

She said chores were good for me. She would do what she called the second tier. Dust, wipe down cabinets and tops of tables. We had to keep moving forward until we accomplished everything. Breathing, I said, why wasn't that on there? She told me not to act smart. Then she stayed up late, writing more lists.

"I want to have some order here," she said. "I don't want you to think your dad walked out on you. It had nothing to do with you. It was me he left. And now I'm getting myself together."

I knew she was trying. She'd put herself through college and finished her degree in accounting because that was something practical. Then she'd married my dad and he didn't want her to work. He told her his mother worked every day of her life and it got her nothing, only worn down. That was not what he wanted for his wife. But after he left, my mom got a job on the checkout line at the Safeway near my school. She came home full of complaints. The people in charge, what a joke, didn't know what they were doing. The incompetence flowed down from the top. How was she supposed to ring up specials when they weren't marked? And why did her register keep shutting off? She reported everything to her boss, who told her he was more interested in winners than whiners. "What goes around, you know, goes around again," my mom said to me. Things don't change just because you want them to. How was it that she had a degree in accounting and some idiot was running the department? She hoped the management would get a clue and fire him. She dropped her nametag on the table at night and poured herself a glass of wine. Then we watched our dinner spin in the microwave oven. She tried to keep to the schedule, at least in the beginning.

We slept in twin beds, so she only had to reach over to shake me awake in the morning. I took a bath while my mom made up her face with red lipstick and black eyeliner around her dark blue eyes. It gave her a startled look, but she was naturally pretty so it didn't matter. "Show the world an optimistic face," she said. Then we'd have breakfast, mugs of milky coffee and two waffles each, mine covered with syrup or powdered sugar, hers plain.

I liked school back then. My second-grade teacher assigned me to the highest reading group so I could read chapter books while most of the other kids were still looking at pictures. I'd say I was fine when I was sick so I could get a perfect attendance award. On weekends my mom sometimes let me invite a friend to spend the night. We only had two beds so she'd help us build a tent in the living room out of sheets. Once she slept in there with us and watched *Power Rangers* cartoons in the morning. I think she liked them more than we did.

It was at the end of third grade when she began looking like she was focused on something in the distance I couldn't see. Then all at once, she would remember I was there and she'd be in a terrible mood. Any small thing set her off: I didn't say thank you for dinner or I opened the bathroom door when she was in there. I forgot to fold the clean clothes that were in the dryer. It got harder to figure out what she wanted so I performed extra chores. I'd straighten the throw rug, arrange the bottles of shampoo and soap in a perfect line at the back of the bathtub. But that didn't work. She went into a rage when I forgot to make my bed. "You are impossible!" she yelled. "I don't know why I had you!" I wanted to yell back something worse, but I went in and smoothed the sheets and cover on my bed. I refused to cry. She came in like nothing happened and put her cheek on top of my head. "Sweet girls have sweet dreams," she said.

Then she started forgetting the schedule. I would get up and make my own breakfast and then wake her up so she could walk me to the bus. She didn't like me to go by myself because she had read about people grabbing children off the street. Nowhere was safe. She was obsessed with the case of some boy who lived in Bakersfield and was snatched on his way home from school. His face was on a flier she'd brought home from the Safeway. "Look at those eyes," she said. "Isn't that the saddest thing you've ever seen?" He didn't look sad to me. He looked like a quiet kid about my age, thick bangs, freckles, clear eyes. She never let me go anywhere by myself, so I didn't know why she was so worried.

One day I couldn't get her up even after I started shouting, "Mom!" I shook her shoulder softly, then harder. She rolled over. "If I don't get some sleep, someone will be paying for it," she said, and pulled the covers over her head. I went back to my own bed and back to sleep. When I woke up, it was too late to get the bus on my own. I missed being at school, the little carpet squares, one for each of us to sit on at story time, and the neat arrangement of desks on the other side of the room. One of them had my name taped to it, with a picture of a dog. The teacher had asked what animal we wanted to be and my last name was near the front of the alphabet so I still got my first choice.

I watched TV so I wouldn't think about school and what kids were playing at recess or eating at lunch. My mom got up in the afternoon. Her eyes were swollen, but she had brushed her hair and looked like she might want to go back on the schedule.

"Why are you watching TV now? Don't you have homework?" she said. She didn't know she'd forgotten to take me to school. She sat down next to me and watched cartoons until it started to get dark. When I said I was hungry, she heated up a can of chicken noodle soup and we each ate a bowl. I smashed crackers into mine and she sat there like she'd never seen anyone do that before. Then she went back to bed.

She stayed in bed again the next morning. I wondered if there was someone I should tell, but I didn't know anyone at the Safeway and I didn't know how to call the school by myself. Maybe they'd wonder where I was because I'd never missed school before. But I didn't know the number there. Who would I talk to anyway? And what would I do if my mom got mad at me? I put on my clothes, had breakfast and walked down the street to the bus. I only made it the first block when I got scared and turned back. What if something happened to my mom? Or what if I got snatched? I ran back to the apartment, which I'd left unlocked, and sat on the couch with my polka dot Minnie Mouse backpack. I took out a math workbook and did some problems. Addition and subtraction were so easy I almost didn't need to bother. When I got tired of them I read a chapter book about the Pilgrims that my teacher had given me. I wondered how I would have done, stranded in the freezing weather with hardly anything to eat. I don't know how long it was before I noticed the doorbell was ringing and then someone was knocking. Whoever it was knocked strictly, like they expected an answer. I put my ear to the door the way my mom usually did, so she could hear who was there before she opened it. The knocking got louder. Someone outside said very loud. "Mrs. Donaldo? Madlynne?"

I ran to the bedroom. "Mom, someone is here and it sounds like he might break the door off if you don't get up." She opened her eyes, which were still unfocused. "What?" she said. And then she starting screaming that every path in the world led to the same empty hole and anyone who said otherwise was a fool. Why did people keep bothering? She just wanted to be left alone. Leave her alone, she yelled louder, and then she went quiet. I put my hand on her back, but she didn't look at me. She couldn't hear me, or the guy outside calling to us.

She was still in her clothes from the day before when the front door finally opened. I was thinking that might help. She might look like an ordinary mom taking the day off with her kid. But that is not at all what happened.

CHAPTER 6

The next day Ash made a sign, NEED $ GET DOG OUT OF JAIL. I held it in my arms, leaning against a wall, because we couldn't sit down. The one time Root had been to the animal shelter he came back in a bright blue bandana, completely shaved. They said it was the only way to get rid of the fleas. I wondered what they'd do to him this time. The bandana had disappeared in a few days, fallen off or gotten snatched by one of the punks. I saw a guy on the street wearing the exact same one up around his face, but I didn't say anything. It wasn't worth starting a grudge.

"Is that true? Your dog's in jail?" said a lady yanking a limping Chihuahua.

"The fascists took him while we were being arrested for sitting on the sidewalk right here," said Ash. "Anything you could do, much appreciated."

He could act like he cared, especially for older women. He poured it on for them. This one seemed nice, but pinched, like she measured out every nice thing she ever did. Her dog looked like he was going to croak on the sidewalk in front of us. He was dragging his rear legs and his coat was scraggly. He must have weighed two pounds.

"Who's this?" I said, bending to let him smell my hand and then petting his head. He had his own smile, the way dogs do if you give them a chance.

"Marco," she said. Like the explorer, but it was also her father's name. She didn't have kids and she wanted to keep it in the family. She repeated the name a few times, like I didn't understand what she was saying. "You probably don't know about Marco Polo or the Silk Road."

"Hell, I do," said Ash, looking all animated.

"What is it with you kids?" she said. "Something has broken down and I don't know what to do."

"A donation is good," said Ash.

"We should be out protesting," she said. "Or you should. It's your future we're talking about." She pulled out a twenty. "You don't even know what I'm talking about." She handed it to Ash and then dragged her dog on down the block.

"So, you knew who that explorer was?" I said. Ash had some college. He knew things.

"I could come up with it, if there wasn't so much else going on here." He pointed to his head. "But you have to try to make them happy. You could, Mad. Let's go get Root."

"She didn't seem happy," said Fleet.

We headed for the bus stop, but Fleet wanted to stay with Tiny. It was easier to have a rat on the street than a dog. The rat could eat anything out of the trash. He could sleep in Fleet's sleeve. She never had to worry that he'd be stolen or beaten. Or taken to Animal Control. The cops took away Root, but they had let her keep Tiny, who was crawling through her hands, one to the other.

The wind picked up so we stood up in the doorway of the bar on the corner that served punch in pineapple-shaped bowls. A group of people inside sat around a little table with long straws, like insects. The manager came out and asked us not to block the door, even though it was barely noon and the place was almost empty. At night people filed out regularly, went around the corner to pee on a wall and went back in. No one hassled them.

We jumped on the bus through the back entrance. The driver glanced at us, but let it go. What did he care? We weren't going to bother anyone. People parted to let us through, like they didn't want to be near us or stand in our way either. We sat in the way back and Ash rested his skateboard across both our laps.

"Next stop, dog jail," he said.

"But what am I going to do if we get him? I'm not sure I can come back here after what happened to that kid in the park."

"You should wait before you get all worked up," he said.

How could I wait? My whole life had flipped in one day. All I wanted was to get Root and figure out where to sleep that night. It seemed like every time I set myself up somewhere, everything changed. One place to another, nothing stuck. The bus jolted us when it stopped and started, and swayed in between. I thought I might throw up.

"Jesus," shouted a man in front of us as his cup flipped out of his hand and onto the floor, where it rolled down the aisle spewing coffee.

"Thanks. Thanks a lot," said a woman in a tight black skirt, wearing ear buds and looking at her cell phone that was suddenly flecked with coffee.

"I'm sorry," said the man. He scavenged in his backpack for something to clean up the mess and dropped a newspaper on the pool of coffee.

The woman leaped out of her seat. "You're going to have to pay my cleaning bill and take care of my phone if it's damaged," she said.

"Calm down," he said. "It was just caramel latte. Not battery acid."

"Easy for you to say since you don't have to show up at work this way. You're not even supposed to bring food on the bus," she said. "See the sign up there?"

"I told you I'd take care of it," he said. "I'll give you my contact information. You don't have to act like a bitch."

He stood up to fish in his backpack again, which is when the real trouble began. She was so close that he bumped her with his elbow and she stumbled backward, grabbing onto a railing. The rest of us watched, like it was a show on TV.

"Stop the bus," the woman yelled, and pulled the emergency cord along the window. "I've been assaulted."

The bus jolted to a stop, which sent everyone standing into the next person. The bus driver got up, squared his shoulders and headed toward the back, which was slick with coffee. I could hear his shoes getting sticky with it. Ash and I looked at each other. It was one of those times when we didn't have to talk. We bolted for the back door and off the bus. There was no sense getting mixed up in that scream fest.

"What a total be-otch," said Ash. "It's not like he was all after her or anything." He laughed, throwing his head back. But I was annoyed.

"He was the bitch," I said. "He acted like she was nuts for complaining."

"Complaining? More like making it into a crime scene."

I could feel myself growing angrier with every step. I walked like I was marching.

Ash could take his skateboard and go back to the Haight. I'd pick up Root alone and figure out where to take him. Who needed that?

"You are a cave man," I yelled at him. "Actually, that's too good for you."

He looked at me and I figured he would turn around and go the other direction, skateboard slung over this shoulder. Instead he started laughing again and then he pounded his chest.

"Cave man go with cave woman to get dog," he said and he couldn't stop laughing.

I stared him down, not willing to give up this easily, even to the person who knew me better than just about anyone else, at least in this city.

"Come on, Mad," he said. "Let's get Root before the stupid place closes for the day."

The lobby of the animal shelter was lined with pictures of dogs and cats—a fat orange tabby, a small dog that looked like it was smiling through broken bottom teeth, a beagle in a banana costume—each one with a story about where it was found, and the words underneath, Adopt Available. All of them had been found somewhere. I thought about the cast of faces on the cop station walls, none of them found.

The room smelled like wet fur and herbal shampoo. A woman with glasses on a string around her neck sat at a wooden desk reading a magazine. She didn't look up when we walked in even though a buzzer sounded. Ash pulled me in front of him.

"Yes?" she said, smiling and closing the magazine, something called *BARK*. That gave me courage. She was working in a place that took care of lost animals and spent her time reading about dogs.

"I'm looking for my dog. The cops at Park Station said he would be here."

"What's your name? You have some ID?" she asked.

I turned around to Ash. "I don't have any ID," I said. "What are we supposed to do now? Do you have anything?"

"Police citation, anything will do," said the woman.

I pulled the wrinkled citation out of my pocket and handed it to her. She smoothed it, then started tapping at her computer.

"He's around the corner because we were full up," she said. "He's staying at the adoption center, but if you sign for him and wait a few minutes, a volunteer will take you over to get him. You're Madlynne Donaldo?"

"Yes," I said. Then added, "Ma'am."

"You don't need to Ma'am me," she said. "We are all here for the same reason. It doesn't matter if you live in a fancy house in Pacific Heights or you live on a street." She handed me back the citation. "You've got to have the right resources to care for your dog."

"We do okay," I said.

"Well, I can see they treated him for fleas and they cleaned him up," she said. "He was hungry. He ate two bowls."

I wanted to tell her he would always eat two bowls, even after he'd already had two before that, but I kept quiet. A girl came in and led us to the adoption center. She wore skinny black jeans but managed to wedge a phone into her back pocket. It moved back and forth as we passed through a few long corridors with glass doors along the walls. We could see dogs in big cages behind each of them. That must have been the jail portion. The girl pushed a switch on the wall and a door opened into a whole other part of the building. This one was wide open like a mall, but instead of stores there were big rooms with furniture and rugs. All around, there were dogs, collapsed on a bed or sofa, or curled on a throw rug. A Great Dane lay draped on one bed, one ear up and the other down, even though it looked asleep. Next door a fluffy black puppy playing with a stuffed giraffe stopped and looked hopefully at me. And then I saw Root, standing at attention, his nose pressed against the glass. He knew we were there and he was waiting. I put my hand on the other side of the glass.

"He's got it pretty good in there," said the girl, reaching to open the door. "But I guess he's not into TV. Some of the dogs watch it all day."

The flat screen in his room was tuned to a nature show, a lion relaxing in the sun, watching a herd of antlered animals in the distance. The bed was covered with a zebra pattern blanket. In the corner were stainless steel bowls for food and water. The girl watched me look around and told me about how when the adoption center first opened it offered to let homeless people come stay with the animals, just to keep them company.

"To get the dogs used to people and give people a place to sleep," she said. "But the homeless groups said it was insulting, it wasn't a real solution, and refused to sign on with the program. Go figure. I can hardly afford my rent. I'd stay here in a minute."

"I'd be down," said Ash. "Tell your boss."

"I will, but I'm no one here," said the girl. "I just fill in when I'm not overloaded at school. I'm getting a degree in public affairs, which I'll finish next year if I can ever get my classes. It is taking forever. Or maybe I'll try to get into vet school."

Root jumped up and put his paws up on my waist, trying to lick me. He was whining like I'd been away for a month. I hugged him and put my nose on his head.

"He thinks he's a biped," said the girl. "He's a sweet guy. Better than most of my boyfriends." Then she looked over at Ash. "Sorry," she said.

"He's not my boyfriend," I said. "Actually, neither of them is."

The girl laughed. "Come on back here if you ever want to

volunteer. It's a good way to build a résumé and you'd get to spend time with all the dogs and take them on walks."

She clipped a leash on Root's collar and handed the other end to me. He pranced like a puppy back to the lobby and pulled to get back outside. Now that we had him, we'd have to walk back to the park. No bus driver was going to let us on with Root, even though he looked cleaner than we did.

We threaded through the downtown business area, past people waiting in line for the bus and rushing into crosswalks in a hurry to get home. The fog was blowing in and it was starting to get cold. The tall buildings blocked what was left of the sun and set up a wind tunnel that whipped my hair around my head. A steel crane turned in the wind on the top of a building across the street. I walked faster, hoping it wasn't going to flip over. Ash crossed his arms across his chest to keep in the warmth. But Root seemed to get friskier, sniffing in all directions. His tongue lolled out to one side.

"Be right back," said Ash, when we reached the Tenderloin, a corner of downtown where we started not to stand out so much. The streets were lined with worn-out hotels, liquor stores, smoke shops, and diners. I'd been there a few times, mostly to a church that served free dinners. People were already sitting outside, waiting in a line that went around the block. A lady in a puffy coat sat with two little girls, one of them on her lap playing with a doll. The other one was next to her, trying to draw in the dust on the pavement. I smiled at her when we passed, but she didn't look at me. The lady probably told her not to talk to strangers. That's what my mom would have done.

I kept walking. Three older guys sat next to a planter passing a bottle of vodka. One of them, a dried bloody knot on his forehead, waved and held it out to me. I raised my hand and shook my head. Down the block a guy in a leopard print dress and a stiff wig combed into a flip was sprawled on the sidewalk. Where was Ash? If I'd known he was going to disappear I could have waited for dinner at the church, with that lady and her kids. I passed a red neon peep show sign blinking in the window. XXX SPECIAL GIRLS. Maybe Ash had gone to take a leak in one of the bathrooms that looked like storage sheds. They gave us tokens at the shelter, but then warned us about using them. People got robbed in there. Or they fell asleep. And if you stayed in too long, a water spigot opened on the ceiling and sprayed you.

I hurried, keeping my eyes down. "Don't talk to strangers," I said to Root. A few blocks later Ash showed up back at my side, holding out a green apple for me. "Did some shopping," he said, crunching into his own. "And this is for Root." He offered a small hard roll to Root, who snapped it from his fingers and started chewing. We stopped until he swallowed it and had licked the crumbs off the sidewalk.

"Don't lift stuff," I said to Ash. "We don't need to get busted again. I don't."

"What makes you think I lifted those?" he said. "Okay, so I liberated a few things. Like you should be talking. The jerk at that market on Eddy charges twice what he should anyway.

Next person who pays makes up for it. It's a cosmic game, with no one keeping score."

I finished my apple and fed the core to Root. We were going to miss dinner at the shelter and it was too late to check in for the night. I'd be relieved to have Ash in the park or wherever we ended up. Root was a good watchdog when he needed to be, but after everything that had happened, I didn't want to be alone.

I held onto Ash's arm and Root pulled us along. It was dark when we reached Haight Street and I was hungry in a way that made me want to punch someone. "Here comes dinner," said Ash, watching a middle-aged couple walking toward us, holding two square pizza boxes. We stopped right as they walked by and tried to make eye contact. That was always the first thing you had to do. They were holding hands, which they dropped apart when they got to us. The woman walked all the way to one side and the guy on the other.

"Excuse me," said Ash. "Want to help us out with some doggie bags? We even got a real dog here."

They clasped hands again after they passed, but neither one slowed down. "Can't we walk down the street without getting harassed?" said the guy, turning to look back at us.

"Sorry, Mom and Dad. What did I do?" Ash yelled after them. "I promise I'll take a shower if you let me come home. I'll clean my room."

Then he tapped the back pocket of his jeans. "Hey," he said, "I forgot we have money." He clawed out the folded up twenty we'd gotten for Root, then put it back quickly when we got to the pizza place and saw some guys set up outside. They usually hung out in a park that was halfway downtown, but they'd tagged their name on the sidewalk, ES EF, just in case you forgot they were here. You couldn't get by them without paying somehow.

One of them held an open pizza box on his lap and the others were gathered around him. A brown and white speckled dog growled at Root as we got close. He had a choke chain around his neck so I wasn't worried, but Root moved closer to me.

"Bastard, down!" said the guy with the box and tightened his hold on the dog. It was about Root's size but looked like pure pit. "Down," he yelled and slapped the dog hard across the neck. It kept growling, but rolled on its back, paws up. "Bastard," he said, and put his face down near the dog's ear. "You listen when I tell you something." We inched past and Ash went inside to order our own pie. I stood with my back turned, pretending I didn't notice them. On the way out, warm box in his arms, Ash stopped, and the group surrounded him. One of them had a shaved head and tattoo that looked like a ring of thorns around his neck. Another had a chain belt, with small hanging links tucked into his front and back pockets. He wore a black knit cap and an olive-green jacket, like he was a military officer. Ash opened the box and handed the military guy half the pie, folded the lid shut and started moving down the street. That was what it cost. They took whatever they wanted, half of anything we had, and then they let us alone. Root pulled to keep up with Ash.

"Fucking ES EF," said Ash, sliding down onto the ground, starting into a slice of pizza. I was taking a bite when they showed up next to us.

"That's how you share?" said the one who'd already grabbed half our pie.

Ash looked up, his mouth too stuffed to talk. I could feel Root's body going tense and his growl growing louder. The guy kicked the empty pizza box so hard that it flipped up into the air and landed in the street. He wheeled around and slammed his foot into Ash's gut. I could hear the air rush out of Ash's body as he doubled up. He reached down toward his feet, like a boot knife was going to solve our problems. The guy with the thorn tattoo laughed as they took off down the street.

Ash was gasping, but already up on his feet. I put an arm around his waist and he shrugged me away, embarrassed. We waited to make sure they weren't circling back and then walked toward the park. We passed two guys in headlamps going through trash cans at the corner, picking out cans and bottles they could recycle. One jumped out of the way as a skateboarder flew by. A few people were tucked in doorways, in any position a body could fit. No one wanted to crash like that. After it got dark, people came and picked you over. They took your pack, your shoes, your coat if you were too out of it to notice. You woke up and everything was gone. It wasn't that where we stayed was so great, but at least it was ours. You have to choose, Ash said. We made peace with ES EF, we knew the rules, we paid, so they left us alone most of the time.

CHAPTER 7

Hope was all but swallowed by her lumped-up sleeping bag, snuggled against a twisted trunk at the top of 40 Hill, where we stayed. Ash had staked it out, strung up empty beer bottles on the biggest tree, along every branch he could reach. On windy days, they clanked and jangled. You could hear them down at the lake, but you couldn't see us. We'd worn a trail on the flat-tened leaves, through the bushes and up to the center of a small windblown circle of trees. All of them listed to one side, blown by the constant wind off the ocean, like they'd been groping for something and then stopped before they got it. We slept below, in the spongy mattress of leaves and dirt. I took down the sleeping bag that I'd hung on a branch, along with a coat I'd found at the shelter. Hope had slung a plastic bag of her things nearby. I didn't want to know what was in there. She hoarded. I kept bugging her not to tie food up in our trees, to put it in a cart we'd parked down the hill so the raccoons wouldn't bother us. They would do anything for food, climb into a backpack at night, even with Root there. He would sit up, growl, and then lie back down. He knew his own food was buried in a plastic tub, safe.

I never got up in the night to pee because I didn't want to see the raccoons. They knew I was scared so they'd attack me first. Animals could tell. One night on the way to our spot we surprised them raiding a trash pile. They looked up at us, chunks of bread in their miniature hands, like they were at a restaurant and we were bothering them. Ash threw a small rock but they just stared at us and then started eating again. I didn't want them showing up outside my sleeping bag in the middle of the night, picking at me with their tiny nails and pinpoint eyes.

I had a fear of the raccoons that Ash said was a sign I was losing it. He didn't mean anything by that because he didn't know about my mom. Still, I got quiet. He might have been right, which is what scared me. How did I know I wasn't born with something that was going to take over my brain? It was there in my mom, making her someone I didn't know. There could be grains of it inside me, spreading, waiting to take hold.

I had trouble getting myself to sleep, even before I'd seen the kid die. At night, something was always rustling nearby, or creeping. Leaves crackled. There were coyotes and gophers and the cats that used to live inside until someone dumped them in the park, where they grew wild. They all probably knew about one another, communicated in some weird way, while we were sleeping. How much of the world happened like that? I couldn't forget about the howling and huffing unless I was wasted. I listened for all of it or waited to feel fog slipping from the air onto me.

We'd given up stringing a tarp because the cops cited us for that too. It meant we were camping. Flop on the ground in a bag and you could still say you were hanging out. Ash got a clock from the Goodwill and set it for 3:55 in the morning, when we would stand up, wrapped in our sleeping bags, and stumble out to the street. The cops came by our end of the park at four and cited anyone who looked asleep. Most mornings we could climb back into our bags for a few hours before the park rangers came though on their bikes, headlamps clamped on their foreheads. They went out of their way to climb up the hill. They weren't going to give us tickets, but they weren't going to let us stay.

"There's granola in the cart," Hope said, sitting up. "Some guy from Australia bought me a big bag after I showed him Jerry Garcia's house. I ate all the cookies. Shoot me."

"It's okay," I said. "We had pizza."

"At least you got Root back."

"Yeah," I said. "He was staying in a dog hotel down there. He probably didn't want to come home."

Hope motioned around the soggy nest of leaves and mud. "We figured you weren't making it inside tonight," she said.

Fleet was still asleep, scrunched up in a blanket, Tiny under one arm.

"Root and Tiny are both here. I think we need to celebrate," said Hope.

"I got nuggets," Ash said, "but I dropped the fucking light back on the street."

He told Hope how ES EF had pushed us around for a few slices. Now he couldn't go back to get his lighter. They were probably gone for the night, but he wasn't going to risk it.

Fleet sat up, put Tiny in her lap, and reached for a book of matches at the bottom of her bag.

"Emergency supplies," she said, tossing it to Ash.

He took out a joint, wet a finger in his mouth and smoothed the paper. There was a sharp smell of sulfur as he lit the match and then a small glow near his face when he drew in his first breath, deep, taking his time. He exhaled slowly and then took another hit.

"Hello?" said Hope, reaching over for her turn.

"Hang on, you'll get yours," he said, holding it up, out of her reach.

Hope stood and grabbed the joint. She turned her back to him and he crossed his arms over his chest and smiled the way he did when he was lit. Hope nudged Fleet, who took her turn and handed it to me. I knew it might make me paranoid, but one hit could be enough to fall asleep when a guy was out there looking for me. The fog was settling on the trees, making its way through the sleeping bag around my shoulders. I put on my extra coat and another pair of socks but I was still shivering. In Los Angeles, the fog sealed in the heat and sat on top of your skin. Here it pushed and pulled you in every direction and worked its way inside.

Ash took a kazoo from his pack and started screeching on

it. Hope slapped his hand and it flew over the tree branch into the dark.

"Fucker," said Ash and then he couldn't stop laughing.

"You should play that thing when you get hassled. It's scary," said Hope.

She and Fleet lay down and looked up through the fog at what fuzzed patches of stars they could see. Root was digging in the dirt furiously. I leaned against the tree, staring out to see if someone was out there, about to make a move on me. The light from the joint went around in a triangle from Ash to Fleet and Hope. Who knows why we all found one another. It happened, one of those things that you don't expect or maybe even deserve.

"Hey, the moon is half full," said Hope.

"I think it's half empty," said Ash.

"That's because you're a fucking pessimist," said Hope.

"I am an optimistic pessimist," said Ash.

"Proving that you are an idiot, even with all your college classes."

"I'm bypassing you next time," said Ash.

Hope laughed and grabbed the joint in the bossy way she had. Root let out one high-pitched bark.

"Root, kick it down," I said. He sneezed and shook his entire body, ready to play. "Hey, settle," I said, and scratched behind his ear. He had been cooped up in that dog hotel room, no exercise, and so he was all wound up. But I had no intention of letting him go off in the dark. He wouldn't know what to do if he saw a coyote. I put my arms around his neck. Just thinking about leaving the ring of trees made me shiver more. I tried to change the subject in my brain by looking up at Ash, but it was too late; my mind was racing, fueled by the weed and the long day. I squiggled into my bag, pulled it up to my neck, and hauled Root down next to me. The wind rattled the bottles and leaves above me. Beats in the distance sounded like soft footsteps. Or maybe it was fog condensing on the trees and dripping on the ground nearby. Root relaxed against my side. He would let me know if someone came near us.

Ash's clock went off at 3:55 like a school bell. All I wanted was to stay in the warm pocket I'd made in my bag, but Ash grabbed the end and practically poured me on the ground. I knew he was trying to help, especially after the day before. Neither of us wanted to go back to the cop station. I shook Fleet and Hope and soon we walked across the street while the cops went by, poking into the bushes with their batons, shouting, "Good morning. No camping."

We sat at the bus stop where the plastic seats tipped if you moved so no one would try to sleep there. Ash leaned back on his and slipped off, landing on the pavement, and then kept doing it like he was on a ride. Hope told him not to ask her for help when he broke his neck. As soon as the McDonald's across the street opened we begged a breakfast sausage sandwich from the morning counter girl, who always gave Ash anything he asked for, for free, including the code that unlocked the bathroom door. I could see why. He looked right into her, which made me want to push him away from the counter. But when he got the sandwich, he broke it into fours and handed the pieces to us.

It held us for a few hours, until we could get breakfast at the shelter. One guy was always first, standing at the door, silent, looking down. He must've stayed nearby, but I never saw him at night. We hung behind him and I draped my arm around Fleet, who had Tiny on her arm. We could smell eggs and overcooked toast.

"I may shower," I said.

"Yeah, do us all a service," she said.

"Eff you," I said. "You and Tiny are an atomic smell bomb."

She tightened her grip on my arm. "No problem," she said.

I tied up Root to one of the long tables in the dining room. I told him to lie down and be quiet, he was lucky not to be outside, alone. "You better be here when I get back," I said as he flopped on the floor. The worn linoleum floor held the smells of everything we ate in there. I knew how the mop crew pushed around the food film.

When we got to the front of the line, a small thin woman plopped a spoonful of scrambled eggs on my plate.

"Toast?" she said.

"What?"

"Do you want toast, dear?" she said softly. She lived in the neighborhood and I'd seen her before, serving meals at the shelter. Maybe I'd do the same thing if I lived in a house here, and then I'd go home thinking about the people who drank until they caved over, the kids and drifters who passed through outside.

I was far away. "Uh, yes," I said. No one had called me dear, not like that, for years, not since the child welfare lady showed up at my mom's house. I grabbed a banana and sat down next to Ash, whose plate was piled with eggs. He always managed to get doubles and triples of everything.

After breakfast, Fleet went with Root out front so I took my time in the shower. A volunteer handed me a hygiene bag with mini bottles of donated shampoo, soap, and a toothbrush so small it would have suited Tiny. I squeezed all the shampoo into my hand and then slapped it on my hair. It smelled like cucumbers and lemon. The soap was strawberry shortcake. I wanted to stay in the shower forever, covered with fruit smells, and live in the warm spray, where nothing could get me. I watched the water drip off my arms until it turned cold. It's what they did to get us out of there. Otherwise, who wouldn't stay in there all day?

I stepped out, towel around my body, and looked in the steamed-up mirror and squeaked off a corner so I could get a look at what the rest of the world was seeing. The reflection wasn't as bad as I expected. My hair was snarled up on the sides, but my skin was clear. I could see why people said I had a heart shaped face. Despite the bad sleep and the nerves that made me feel like I had the chills half the time, I still looked like me. I was pale, but I was always pale. I was still in there, somewhere.

"Nice daggers," said a woman behind me, pointing at my toenails, which were clean but did look like weapons. She was covered by the same square of too-small towel. "You should do something about them. Ingrown toenails are the worst, and that's what you'll get and then you'll end up at the General Hospital. I know what I'm talking about. If you don't start out with an infection, you'll get one there."

Don't pay any attention, I told myself. You never knew when someone might go off on you. I combed my fingers through my hair, brushed my teeth with the tiny toothbrush, rubbed my gums to get the blood circulating.

Ash was waiting outside the bathroom. Usually he'd make some comment about how clean I was, a new woman ready to get dirty. But instead he grabbed my arm and pulled me into a corner.

"That kid's dad," Ash said. "He's here. The one in the park. They made an announcement while you were gone. He wants to know if any of us knew his kid."

Ash pointed at a man, who stood with his back to the door. His shoulders rounded forward, a baseball cap in one hand. He wore perfectly creased jeans and a plaid wool button-down over a T-shirt that said SHANE in big letters. Underneath the lettering was a picture of the face I'd last seen lying in the dirt, except he looked tan and hopeful on the T-shirt. I could not take a normal breath.

"I don't see how I have anything to tell him," I said. "I didn't know his kid."

"Maybe he can help set you up," said Ash. "He looks like he can afford it."

I wanted to kick Ash as he pushed me toward the man, who looked serious and so unhappy I couldn't turn away. What was I supposed to do?

"Dave Golden," he said, and held out his hand. "Shane's father. Your friend said you were there in the park with him. That day."

I let him take my hand and he held onto it tightly. I tried to pull it back, but he wasn't going to give up. Ash had talked to him, told him I was here? I wondered if he'd offered Ash anything for finding me. He was tall and fleshy. But his eyes were a blue so light they looked transparent. Did the kid in the park have eyes like that? I couldn't remember.

"I wasn't exactly with him," I said. "But I did see him, at the end. Ash told you that?"

"Can we go someplace and talk?" he said. "My car is outside."

I must have looked scared because he added, "Your friend can come with you. I just want to talk. Someplace outside the neighborhood, if you don't mind. I'll take you back here whenever you say."

"I'd have to bring him," I said pointing to Root, who was in the doorway with Fleet.

Dave looked at Root and I could tell he was thinking it over. Root pushed his front into a downward dog position, yawned and wagged his tail. I wanted to yell at him. He was supposed to be taking my side, looking out for me.

When we got outside, Dave stuck out his hand slowly, like he thought Root might bite it. "I don't really know what to do with dogs," he said. "But okay. He's got a leash?"

I snapped it on like Dave was my dad, but I was burning inside. I was the one who should be worried. I didn't know this guy. Someone had almost killed me for being in the wrong place, for happening to see his son, who I didn't know. Dave guided us to his car, a blue sedan parked at a meter around the corner. I stood back when he opened the passenger door, but Ash jumped in. I climbed in back with Root because there was no way I was going to sit next to the guy and talk to him. Maybe he would stay quiet. I kept my fingers on the door handle while we drove down Haight Street and headed across town.

"I'm taking us to a coffee house in North Beach where Shane and I met the one time I was out here," he said. "I hope that's okay. Unless there's somewhere else you'd rather go. I don't know many places."

"Yeah," said Ash. "I haven't been over to North Beach in a long time."

I stayed silent in the back, one arm around Root, looking out the window as we threaded our way through traffic, then down a steep winding brick street. Someone had planted purple flowers in perfect rows along the road.

"Lombard Street," said Ash. "Windiest street in the world."

I kicked the back of his seat and he looked back at me. "What?" he said. "It isn't the windiest?"

"I read that a film crew once sent someone riding down here on a piano," said Dave. "I read a lot about your city. Or I did, when Shane first came here."

He pulled part of the way into a parking space and Ash got out to direct him. Ash motioned him forward and back and then flashed a thumbs-up. Dave got out and opened my car door so there was nothing I could do but join them. I left my window open for Root and followed behind as they walked down the street and into a cafe that had a giant neon coffee cup in the window.

Dave went to the counter and came back with a sandwich held together by toothpicks. Ash picked it up and started wolfing. I sat with hands in my lap, looking down. Dave had a cup of coffee, black with no sugar, and watched Ash, like he'd never seen anyone eat that fast.

"So," he said, putting his baseball cap on the table. When he leaned forward I could see the kid's eyes on his shirt. What would he think, if he knew I was eating with his dad? He might have hated the guy. Something drove that kid out here from wherever he lived.

We stared awkwardly at each other, waiting to see who would speak first. "So," Dave said again.

"You said your friend was with Shane right at the end." His voice cracked. "Sorry. Sometimes when I say his name out loud . . ." He took a few breaths and then his shoulders shook.

"Maddy, tell him," said Ash.

I gave Ash a mean look. This was easy for him. Free food. He didn't have to go over it all in his head again, see the kid lying there, worry about some maniac coming after him.

"Anything you know would help me," said Dave. "I am still, both my wife and I are, in shock. You can imagine."

"I didn't know him," I said. "My dog ran into the bushes. I

thought he'd found food. He smells something a mile away and takes off."

I stopped myself. I knew he wasn't there to hear about Root eating and getting into everyone else's business. But what did he want me to do?

"A lot of you kids have dogs, don't you?" said Dave. "But I don't think Shane did. At least the police didn't think so. He might have had a chance against the guy who attacked him if he'd had some protection from a dog."

"Root is scared of most things, including other dogs," I said. "But he looks like he is going to jump on your throat. I swear he makes himself look bigger when he needs to."

I was doing it again, going on about Root. But if it hadn't been for him I'd never have gone into those bushes. I was not looking for Shane. That is what I was trying to say.

"Did you see Shane before he, before it happened?" said Dave. "I'm not going to repeat anything to the police. I just need to know."

"No." I had nothing else to say. He rubbed his eyes again and started talking about how Shane had disappeared from home, a town I'd never heard of, all the way up north of New York. He had left before, to stay with friends or his older brother, but he'd always come back. In high school Shane got in trouble, but he wasn't a bad kid. Not in his heart. He got sent to the principal's office so many times they kept what they called the Shane Chair, so he could sit and wait there for his parents to pick him up. One time he'd been suspended for riding his skateboard down the front stairs, something that wouldn't even have meant detention at my school.

"It was always something small. Or it seemed small," said Dave. "But I ran a hardware store in town. I was head of the volunteer fire department. I brought Shane in there from the time he was born. They all knew him."

I looked down and didn't say anything. I should have ordered a sandwich, at least to take back for Root.

Dave said he used to think Shane was smarter than most other kids so maybe he was bored in school. Shane floated through, didn't pay attention. By the time he was in middle school, he had a pack of scruffy friends and smoked a lot of pot. Dave couldn't figure out why someone like Shane, with brains to spare, would waste his time with what looked to the outside world like kids headed for jail. They didn't bring him up like that.

"I don't mean that the way it sounds," he said.

"It's okay," said Ash. "Better a pothead than a corporate dick. And I didn't mean that the way it sounds either."

Dave laughed. "Shane would have liked you."

Dave did not have a clue about Shane. That was clear. I didn't either, but Dave had no idea what his kid was thinking.

One weekend Shane and his friends had jumped on a boxcar and went almost all the way to Canada, riding with a group of vagabonds. Dave couldn't figure out why his son would do something that careless, not to mention thoughtless. He never considered how his parents would agonize. The counselor at school told them that normal teenage behavior looked so much like mental illness that sometimes it was hard to tell the difference. She thought Shane was what she called oppositional, but, basically, he was fine, he'd come around. But after the train episode, Shane seemed more restless. He wouldn't talk to Dave or his mom. They'd wait up until he got home every night. When he didn't come home, they didn't sleep. When he did come home, he didn't talk to them. When he disappeared the last time, they thought he'd be back. They never guessed he would go all the way across the country or live outside.

"I wish I could describe how I felt," Dave said. "Guilty and angry at the same time, but mostly worried. It was like the ground opened up and swallowed my insides. I was sick. We both were."

"I didn't know Shane," I said. "I didn't know what he was into or what he was thinking."

"I want you to know what it's like for your parents, if they don't hear from you," said Dave. "Do they know you're here?"

Ash and I didn't say anything.

"I just need to know where he was, how he lived when he was here," said Dave, his hands clasped, in the middle of the table, like he was in church. "Please."

Ash was staring down at the table, rubbing his beard stubble. Maybe Dave was thinking that this was what Shane must have looked like. Clothes so dirty they were stiff, smelling like every place he'd slept. Even I could smell Ash, but maybe that was because I'd had the chance to get clean. Everyone else always seemed worse after I'd had a shower.

"Like I told you, I didn't know Shane," I said.

"Just please let me know what you saw when you went in after your dog," said Dave. "I'm sorry. This must be hard for you. If you want, I can help you call your parents later."

Why did he think he could fix things for us? Or that we had anything in common with his kid? He should have been the one to see Shane out there, dying. Why should I get stuck with that forever? Then I found myself talking, mostly because I was angry in a way I couldn't stop and I wanted to hurt Dave, a firefighter who couldn't stop anything. I told him how I found the guy standing near the body that I now knew was Shane. I told him how I ran and wasn't sure what I'd just seen.

"Was Shane awake?" said Dave. "Did he say anything?"

I told him that Shane looked like he was gone. I thought about how easily I'd said it at school. "My dad died before I was born." But I didn't know exactly what had been going on with Shane. I'd seen fights on the street. Someone was always getting loaded into the box, lights flashing. In Los Angeles once I saw a car smash into a guy on a bike. I could still call up the sound his body made when it hit the metal, a loud plunk, no screaming. He'd tumbled over the front of his bike and gotten up by himself. Blood ran down his head, but he kept saying to leave him alone, he was okay. But I'd never seen anyone actually die.

"Did he seem to be suffering?" Dave said. "I need to know that. I need to. Please." His voice was collapsing.

"I can't say," I said. "I don't know."

"I'm sorry," he said. "It's just that you might have been the last person to see him alive. Maybe you saw him when he passed, and that makes you connected to him in some way. At least that's the way I see it."

"There's not anything else I know," I said. "He didn't say anything to me. He wasn't talking."

"Did you tell anyone? The police?"

"Like they were going to do anything," I said, "besides hassle me every single day."

"But maybe there's something I can do," Dave said. "Shane's mother wants to meet you too. She has so many questions."

"I don't think so," I said.

"Listen, just meet with us once more," said Dave. "I can't tell her I found you and then let it go. She won't forgive me."

"You know where to find us," I said.

Root was sitting up on the seat when we got back to the car, his nose out the window. I gave him a biscuit I'd taken from the cafe, marked homemade organic. The city stepped all over itself for dogs. Dave reached in and petted Root's head like he wasn't sure if Root would take off his fingers.

"You could probably teach him some tricks," he said. "He seems smart."

What was it with this guy, thinking I needed his advice? If he really wanted to be useful, he could fork over some money for a hotel so I could stop worrying about getting knifed. Maybe Ash would ask on the way back. There was no way I was going to. I'd had enough.

"This must be the place," said Dave, pulling his car over at a bus stop on Haight Street. He opened my door and stood awkwardly next to me. I wondered if people would look at us and think he was my dad, obviously here from out of town, his fancy jeans held up by a wide belt. I could see the comb marks in his gray hair, slicked back with gel so thick it glistened in the sun.

"Take this phone at least, so I'll know how to reach you," he said.

I kept my hands in my pockets. A new phone would last about a day on the street, before someone grabbed it. Or maybe I could sell it.

"I got it for Shane," he said. "He lost about one a week. Please take it. Or how will I get in touch with you?"

I reached for Root. Shane had a phone and his dad and mom still couldn't find him. I didn't have a phone or anyone looking for me, except a guy who maybe wanted to kill me.

"I'm around," I said.

"Well, okay then," he said. "So long."

He looked so sad that I almost told him he could hang out for a while. I could feel it coming through his pores, a heaviness that was going to take over everything it touched. But what was he going to do here? I was torn, watching him standing near his car with that stupid belt and his dead kid on his T-shirt, looking at me. He wanted too much.

"Yeah," I said. "Bye." It was all I could offer him then.

CHAPTER 8

Ash gave me a hard time that night. I should have taken the phone, at least gotten money from Dave. I didn't say anything because I just wanted to have him next to me. He smoked and then was out, but I lay awake, turning over whether I should trust Dave. Why was he different from anyone who acted sweet to get what he wanted? I couldn't help it, going back to the day when Valerie Nelson opened the door at her house and showed me around. "Make yourself at home," she said, smiling, but someone paid her to say that. She told me to call her Miss V, put her arm around me and led me down the hall to a room with three cribs and one small bed pushed against the wall. Usually she took in sick babies, she said, but her house was empty the day they moved my mother to the hospital, so she had space for me. She said it was a relief for a change to get a kid who could talk.

"Don't get me wrong, Miss Maddy," she said. "Each one of us is special and we all have needs. But a person gets tired going all day, no one to talk to."

In a corner of the room was an oxygen tank sitting on a doll-size wheelchair. The bed had a pale pink bedspread and soft pink sheets pulled tight, waiting for someone. A big stuffed panda lay against the pillow. Miss V cooked macaroni and cheese from scratch, smooth and buttery. She poured me chocolate milk and sat with me at the table while she ate a salad. What was my favorite subject in school, she wanted to know. And what about my friends? Did I need clothes washed? I didn't say anything, but I kept eating. Her nails, long and red, had a sparkling star painted on each end. She clicked them on the table and looked at me, trying to make it all seem normal.

I let her tuck me into bed and put the stuffed panda under the blanket, right next to me. She said we would talk about visiting my mom the next day, which just reminded me that I was in a strange bed, by myself. I was used to my mom being in the other bed where I could see her if I opened my eyes. A day before I didn't know Miss V, but there I was in a bed in her house while she fussed in the kitchen. I could hear dishes clinking, water running. I tried to force myself to sleep but I started shaking, even though I wasn't cold. I couldn't stop no matter what I tried to think about. Miss V came into the bedroom the next morning and said she'd never had someone squeeze the panda so hard, even asleep. She was so nice it made me cry and I hardly ever cried. That was still true. It's not that I didn't feel like crying, curled close to the warmth of Ash's body. It's just that it took so much to get the tears outside on my face. Usually they were backed up in my throat or in my head.

Miss V drove me to school the next day, where everything was the same. The sticker of the dog, happy and smiling, was still on my desk. No one knew about my mom or even asked questions. I went to recess, sat in the lunchroom, walked around like I was supposed to be there. When Miss V picked me up she said she was going to take me to see my mom. She might seem different, Miss V said, because of the medicine they were giving her. Her brain was not functioning right and they were trying to figure it out. It was like having a car that slipped into the wrong gear. It went too fast, without warning, and other times couldn't start up. No one could tell when it would happen. Did I understand? My mom had been broken-down when they took her to the hospital, but she was getting good care now, so I shouldn't be scared. Medical science had made advances that could help her. Miss V put her hand under my chin.

"You're too young to have to understand this, but somehow I think you do," she said.

"How long will she stay in the hospital?" I asked.

Miss V said she didn't know, but she would try to make sure I got to visit whenever I could. At the hospital, she parked and walked with me down a concrete path that cut through a bright green lawn. When we got inside she told me to sit down. She went up to a desk at the front of the room and said she had Miss Maddy Donaldo to see Mrs. Donaldo. I flushed bright pink when she announced my name like that. I didn't want anyone seeing me at the hospital visiting my mom who had something wrong with her brain. No one else had a mom who couldn't get out of bed. No one else had a babysitter they didn't know hauling them around to see a sick mom. Of course, no one from school would even be there, but that didn't occur to me then.

When I went in to see her, my mom looked at me part of the time, but she was like Miss V said, a broken-down car. She didn't see me at all. I asked her when she was coming home, but she didn't seem to hear. Miss V squeezed my hand and didn't say anything until it was time to leave. She said to give my mom a hug, so I wrapped my arms around her. She had lost the sweet tangy smell of the perfume she used to spray up in the air and walk through. She put her cheek on the top of my head but her arms hung limply at her side. It was weird to hug someone who didn't at least put a little effort into it. Ash called that a dead man's hug. He didn't know I had a mom who hugged like that.

"I'm sorry, Miss Maddy," Miss V said when we got back to the car. "You shouldn't have to see your mother like that."

"Like what?" I squeezed myself against the car door.

"It's her depression, is what the doctor told me. She's had a psychotic episode. There are people who say don't tell kids the truth, but I think we should. Kids can catch on faster than adults, in my experience."

"My mom is . . ." I couldn't think what to say. My mom was what? I reached over and pinched Miss V on the thigh as hard as I could. For the first time, I could feel that mean small center of myself. She didn't know me, so why was she trying to tell me about my mother?

She grabbed my hand and I pulled it away. "She is not psycho," I said.

"Of course not," said Miss V. "She has an illness and they are taking good care of her."

I stayed with Miss V another week. I made up things to say about school, but I was not going to tell her about my mom. She'd ask me what my mom cooked for dinner or what we did before bed and I acted like I hadn't heard. When I was younger, my dad brought me a miniature metal safe with a slot for change. I forgot the combination lock, but I kept the safe on a shelf, full of pennies and scraps of paper. It was what I did at Miss V's, hide everything inside.

The next week someone from the child agency came and took me to stay with my cousins Karen and Chip. They were not even close cousins, but they took in foster kids. I'd only met them once, but Miss V said I had to move in with them because they were family, which was the best place for children. I wanted to stay with her. I'd gotten used to the bedroom, the way she let me stay up late and watch TV game shows with her, then put out three cereals in the morning so I could choose which one I wanted. But she said her house was the place you go for short stays when you were in the midst of an emergency. She held out the panda, creased in the middle from where I'd gripped it, and said I could take it. I shook my head no, I didn't want to. She said I was going to start a new part of my life and it would come with opportunities. She was right about that. I went to a different school the next week. I didn't have time to return my library books to the other one and no one asked me about them. It was like I stole them without trying.

I didn't tell anyone, even Ash, about how I got taken away from my mom and then from Miss V. He and Fleet and Hope, they all had their own problems. Ash had a mom somewhere in Arizona, but he never talked about her except when he picked up a package at the post office around the corner. He usually divvied up the food with us, candy bars, peanut butter, little boxes of Cheerios. She must have thought he was on a backpacking trip somewhere. He said that was like her. She saw what she wanted, which was not a kid like him who would not sit still or listen. She would have been happier with a robot programmed to act right.

"Look who's got it going on," Ash would say, opening a box from her, picking the money out of the bottom, always five $10 bills. It meant no signs, no sitting on the sidewalk trying to cadge change. He had enough to stay buzzed or do whatever he wanted all week. Last year he used it to buy a book for a business class at the community college on the other side of town. He went for a while, then said it was a waste, that he already knew how business works. Why shouldn't he use the one thing he was truly good at to raise some cash? So he lifted a pack of Sharpies from the craft store on the street and there he was, in business, making signs. He sat on the sidewalk next to his own sign, NAME IT, in big red letters. It didn't draw as many people as the guy who hauled an old typewriter out on the street and wrote poems, rhyming or free form, your pick.

Ash made him a free sign, POETRY FOR RENT, because you couldn't own poetry, the guy said, even though he charged by the line for what he pecked out on the typewriter. Ash stuck it out for a while, then he got another package from his mom and he quit. There were probably signs of his sitting in houses around the country, asking for money, beer, free hugs.

The last time I saw my mom she barely looked at me. She was out of the hospital, living in a boarding house that didn't allow kids. We met at the county office, in a room filled with plastic chairs, tables, and toys that looked like kids had thrown them off a tall building. They were smashed every way, trains without wheels, torn picture books, puzzles with only a few pieces. I was ten, too old for any of them anyway. I sat with a woman from the agency who put one hand on my arm and managed to turn the pages of her magazine with the other. There was a picture on the cover of a smiling woman with two little kids on her lap. Everything would work out if I could step into that.

My mom was there and not there. She saw the outside of me and that's what I saw of her. Her hair had grown past her shoulders and it sat in one wavy gray pouf. She had never been very interested in food, always on the edge of too skinny, but now she was flabby. Her stomach pushed up against her shirt and her upper arms jiggled when she moved them. She'd reached for the end of my shirt and fingered it slowly the whole time I was there. No hug. No how is school? How is your new life? What's up with Karen and Chip? I'll get you out of there soon as I can. There was a hard pit in my stomach. I couldn't look at her anymore. I decided right then that I was going to get out. I was not going to wait at my cousins' house and go off like my mom. If my mom didn't go to bed and think about me, I wasn't going to think about her.

I turned over and pushed Root, spooned so tight next to me that my arm was numb. He sighed, moved a few inches and went back to sleep.

CHAPTER 9

The weather turned wet and windy, one storm after another rolling in from the ocean. It was impossible to sleep in your bag, rain plinking on you and gradually working its way inside. The ground never had a chance to dry so we slept at the shelter when we could. I kept going over it, how the guy who killed Shane could show up there while I was eating a plate of spaghetti and attack me from behind. I tried to face the door, especially at dinner, in case he tried to slip in. When the lights went off, I climbed in a bunk and turned sideways so I could watch for him.

After the rain broke we went back to 40 Hill, but the leaves had melted into a slurry. Some of the bottles were smashed or hung down loose against the branches. Fleet found a guitar someone left near the lake and she played it nonstop. She said she'd taken lessons when she was little, but I couldn't tell. She sounded like she was playing with her eyes closed. She punched me when I put my fingers in my ears, which made Root sit up like he was going to lunge at her. I would have thought the sound of her playing would set him off, but he didn't mind that. He minded it when she pounded my arm.

"There are a lot of noises dogs don't even hear," she said.

"He knows when I'm in danger." I hugged his head. "He's protecting my ears, which is more than your little man there would do."

Tiny was in a cage Fleet had made, a cardboard box covered in a plastic bag she'd dotted with air holes. She had twisted a paper clip into a collar, but she worried it might strangle him, so he wore it like a loose necklace. Fucking rat jewelry.

One afternoon we stood outside the smoke shop watching Fleet pound on the guitar, with Tiny on her shoulder. A man holding hands with two little boys dropped five dollars and snapped a picture of his kids petting Tiny. Fleet bowed.

Fleet was still playing when a lady from the shelter walked up and waved us all over. I thought she was there to tell us to keep it down, the cops were around the corner. But instead she pointed at the sky, where a black line of clouds squatted over the ocean, waiting to open overhead like an immense faucet. We needed to get inside before the storm broke. An atmospheric river, she said. It sounded like a mood that would wind itself up tight and then explode.

The shelter beds were already full, but the city had set up an emergency center where we could stay. She said she'd help us sign up for it and give us free bus tokens. We looked at each other and didn't have to say anything. There was no way we were doing that. It would be crowded with zombies. Get us together, all twisted in different ways, and you never knew what would happen. A river of rain, we would take our chances. Last year a guy called the Shepherd came in to the emergency center with a long wood pole covered in scraps of fur. Root kept barking at him, but he was there, same as us, to keep dry. "Sorry, man," said Ash. "He has a lot to say but he doesn't mean anything." The guy ignored us. We took pads and blankets and slept as far away from him as we could. In the middle of the night he started smashing people with his pole and screaming how everyone was trying to steal from him. Wasn't someone going to help him? The cops came, which made it worse. The guy quieted down while they were there, but then he started up again, with Root barking across the room. No one got any peace. There was no way I was going back there, no matter how bad the storm got.

By late afternoon the sky went fast from soft gray to black. The first rain fell softly, kicking up the dust from the pavement, then laid it down like thick gravy. We sat in the doorway of the smoke shop until dinner. The food line was twice as long as the night before, mostly because of the storm, but also because it was roast chicken and biscuits, which always got swarmed. Fleet, Hope, Ash, and I got our plates, shoveled in the food, and left. It was raining hard by then, big slapping drops. When the smoke shop closed at midnight, Fleet and Hope decided to try to get back into the shelter. Hope grabbed Fleet's arm and pulled her up. Fleet reached in her pocket and brought out a handful of wet bills.

"All that work and, shit, this," she said. "I was thinking we could find a room somewhere, but this would be like dropping a turd."

"I'll take it." Ash said and held out his hand.

She shoved it back in her pocket and walked away, holding Tiny in a fold of her sweater. "The path less chosen," Ash said.

"What?" I was wrapped in two sweatshirts and still cold.

"Robert Frost. I'd still be at City College except for all the self-righteous assholes."

Ash got in a funk sometimes, like everyone had turned against him. He went somewhere inside himself. He needed it all to make sense. I got that. There were times I wanted to put my arms around him, but I needed him too much for that. It would come with too much drama. Or a kid. Hope got knocked up three years ago, and went up north to have her kid, who lived with her parents. She called him my boy and my angel and carried a picture of him in her backpack, but she never went to see him, like it was enough to know he was in the world somewhere. I didn't want any of that.

The wind blasted wet trash down the sidewalk. A pair of plastic chopsticks clinked into the gutter. The doorway of the smoke shop was not going to keep us dry, even with Root stationed in front of us to block some of the rain. I felt bad using him like a shield. I had squeezed him into a sweatshirt, but he was shaking through it.

We headed toward the Panhandle, a stretch of the park a few blocks away. I used to think the place got its name from the people who hung out on Haight Street grubbing for change, but they'd actually named it because of the shape, the handle of a pan attached to Golden Gate Park. Ash laughed at how I thought someone would name a park after panhandlers. He said it's because I always thought everything had its beginning with me. I could say the same about him. He always took everything in a personal way, but then tried to pretend he didn't care.

....

The Panhandle was empty when we got there. Even the ES EF crew was gone, chased off by the rain. They usually kept a guy at one end, watching, pretending to look at his phone. No one chopped down a bike or sold anything without him taking a cut. Sooner or later, he would come for you if you tried to do business on your own. He could sit in the middle of a pile of wheels, gears, and handlebars and the cops didn't care. They walked by him and didn't say anything.

The wind roared through the eucalyptus trees. The tall narrow ones at either end of the Panhandle swayed and creaked. The grass was soaked, but the biggest tree was as thick as a building, the branches overhead almost a roof. We stood underneath while Ash opened his poncho and put it around me. Root leaned against my legs. I could smell the mint and honey of eucalyptus and feel the scratch of the bark through my sweatshirts. Standing against Ash made me feel safer. I wasn't as cold. The only problem was going to be standing up all night. It was too wet to lie down.

"Maybe we could take turns," said Ash. "I'll hold you up while you take a nap and then you can hold me up."

"Maybe we should tell ghost stories," I said. I remembered nights at Karen and Chip's when everyone in the girls' room put blankets over their heads and I made up stories about slashers and no one could sleep. Ash said no thanks, the night was bad enough already.

Up above us there was a loud crack and more creaking. I pushed myself tighter to Ash, hoping that would anchor me down. It was practically a hurricane on top of us. The tree tilted, then snapped back in place. There was another loud bang. I looked up at a branch above us, which was thrashing back and forth, scattering leaves.

"You think it'll hold?" I said.

"It's not going anywhere," he said.

We stood clutching each other. I was trying to talk myself down and think about being under the blanket at Karen and Chip's or at the beach on a calm sunny day. I closed my eyes and concentrated, but the wind distracted me. I was still trying to push it out of my mind when I heard an explosion above us. Ash pushed me against the tree trunk and we both watched as the branch, bigger around than the two of us together, hurtled down. I could feel the edges scrape against me as it came to rest a few feet away. Root barked what sounded like a shrill scream and took off across the Panhandle.

"Root!" I yelled, and started off after him, but Ash grabbed my arm.

"He won't go far," Ash said. "You can't go get him now."

The rain was coming at us sideways. I couldn't see Root anymore. Inside, I was yelling at myself. Maddy, he is a dog, he knows how to take care of himself. But I wasn't listening. He had already caused me so much trouble and now he was trying to get me killed. I was furious at him. The people at the animal shelter were right. How could I take care of him? I told myself I'd be better off letting him go. Maybe he'd find someone who wouldn't let him go out in a storm. That's probably where he was headed. My mind was skipping away. It was stupid to be out here, to think there was something special that was going to make us survive. This was it. Root knew.

"Hey, let's go," said Ash, his arm around my shoulders. "Now."

I couldn't resist him, since we were sashed together by his poncho. We hobbled and ran through puddles and crossed the dark empty street, back toward Haight Street, a two-headed drenched monster. Outside the shelter we banged on a metal side door with our fists.

A man in a black windbreaker, walkie-talkie attached to his hip, opened the door and shined a flashlight at us. It didn't take him long to see that we were soaked and miserable so he let us in, threw us two of the small, rough towels and said we could sleep in the hallway outside the kitchen.

"If anyone asks, I didn't let you in," he said. "We're full. Can't take another body. Just be quiet in there. Lights are down and so are the phones."

Ash took off the poncho and we dried ourselves as much as we could. I sat down against the wall, shivering, and put my head on his shoulder. All I could think about was Root running off into the rain. Where would he go? Maybe he'd find his way back to the Panhandle. What would he do when he realized we weren't there? When dogs warmed up to someone, didn't they fall apart if that person left, or were we easy to replace? They only needed food, a dry bed and suddenly that was home. I was seized up thinking about that while Ash dozed off and then rearranged himself so he had his head in my lap. In the dim light coming in from the kitchen window, I could see people lined up for breakfast. The electricity was still off, which meant cold cereal and powdered milk, canned fruit cocktail. It also meant that everyone would be allowed to stay inside a few hours longer. It wasn't like we could get to business outside.

Ash and I found Fleet and Hope and tried to stand in line with them, but we moved to the back when someone started complaining about cutting. There was no point starting in with him, not after being up all night. Everyone was keyed up. Whatever we'd stashed behind at the park was soaked and probably trashed. There was not going to be anyone on the street. Tourists would stay away. No money was coming anyone's way. The heavy rain was over but there was still a steady cold sprinkle that would keep us wet all day.

"I can't eat when Root's out there, who knows where," I said, pushing away a bowl of Corn Flakes.

"I'll eat it for you," said Ash.

I handed him my bowl and opened the side door where we'd entered. A lady with a drenched blanket wrapped around her shoulders and head was standing outside stamping her feet. I couldn't tell if she was waiting to get in or just waiting. She looked at me, lit a cigarette, and inhaled deeply.

Jax was alone on the corner in his wheelchair, halfway through a tall beer, another tucked in the pocket of his coat. He lived in a room above the liquor store but usually sat in front with his buddies, drinking until he sagged over in his chair and then someone would call the paramedics. He'd come back a few days later shaved and cleaned up and start all over again.

"We almost got washed away this time," he said, his voice coming from somewhere out of his long gray beard and matted hair. I hoped he wasn't going to start in about the end of the world, how everything was leading to it.

He finished his beer, put the bottle down and used his good foot to push himself over to where I was. The other sat in the footrest, curved inward. He'd told us that after the war he'd been a carpenter, making decent money, until he fell off a roof and broke his spine. If people thought it was the military that put him in the chair, let them, he said. The military had caused plenty of grief.

"You made it through," he said. "Where's your friend?" I didn't know if he was talking about Root or Ash, who liked to hang out with him. "I am going to get a sign. END OF THE WORLD AS WE KNOW IT."

I told him how Root had run away from me in the Panhandle. "Have you seen him?" I said.

"I saw a dog earlier on the street," he said, reaching for the beer in his pocket and adjusting his bad leg. "Oh, hell, no I didn't. But I wish I had. You look like you need good news."

CHAPTER 10

The Panhandle was a lake, tiny blades of grass poking up through the water. In the daylight, the fallen branch seemed bigger. The place where it had cracked was raw and bright. It looked painful, a broken leg, sticks of exposed bone and flesh.

I could see Root wasn't there, but it didn't stop me. I called him and my voice was a shriek. I searched behind every tree, but there was only a guy sleeping on a piece of mushy cardboard. He looked freezing, soaked ass to ankles, but at least he'd covered his feet in plastic bags. I kept thinking Root might be hiding, pretending this was a game and waiting for me to throw a ball. He was a dog, with instincts, so he would find his way to me. That's what I was telling myself. I had heard how dogs could get lost on the other side of the country and make it home, through their sense of smell. If that was true, I'd have to wait by the tree or by our sleeping spot until he appeared. Unless he was in trouble somewhere. I pictured him hurt, lying in the bushes, whimpering, waiting for me to find him, not knowing that I didn't have instincts. I should have brought food for him.

I squatted against the tree. People in the neighborhood started showing up with their dogs, tiptoeing through the water and mud and leaving quickly. No one wanted to stay slushing around in there. A woman walked by with two big Dobermans in matching red raincoats. One of them picked up his leg and squirted near my feet, like I was part of the tree. My boots were still wet from the night before, so it didn't matter. The arcing stream of piss mostly missed me.

"Oh, god, I'm sorry," said the woman, her raincoat a lighter shade of red. "He always pees on this tree. He thinks it's his tree."

"It's okay," I said.

"But I feel bad," she said, putting her hand in her back pocket and holding out a $10 bill. "Why don't you take this and go get some dry shoes when the Goodwill opens."

"What I really need is to find my dog," I wanted to yell at her, but I took the cash and stuck it in my jeans. "Have you seen a black-and-white pit mix, weird eyes, running around anywhere?"

"Where'd you lose him? "

"Here," I said patting the trunk. "At your dog's tree, when that branch cracked off. He ran and now I don't know where he is. It's like he disappeared."

"It takes them so long to clean this stuff up," she said, looking at the branch. "This is a hazard. Someone could trip and fall. They'd be liable. Half the time I'm scared to come here."

"Do you have a cell I could use to call the shelter downtown and see if they have him?" I said. "He's kind of a regular there. It wouldn't take long. A sec."

"I don't know," said the woman. "I'm weirdly picky about my phone. With everyone. But keep the money. I'm sorry about your shoes."

I stood up and faced her and she stepped back and clapped her hand over her pocket, which must have been where she kept her phone, just in case she got attacked by a homeless girl, wet, the kind of person who'd be hanging out in the rain waiting for a dog to pee on her shoes.

"They usually do turn up," she said. "You'd be surprised. Maybe someone is keeping him for you. It's what I would do if I found a dog out here all alone."

I wanted to tell her that some of us here knew how to take care of our own selves. I'd have felt worse for Root if he was living with this lady, stuffed into a raincoat that made him look like a toy fire truck.

"What if I find him? Where do I reach you?" she said.

"Here," I said. "His name's Root."

"Does he have tags?" she said, a Doberman on either side like guardian statues. "Or a microchip? That would make him easier to trace."

"See you," I said, and turned back toward the street.

Ash, Fleet, and Hope were sitting outside the smoke shop, passing around a glass pipe.

"There she is," said Hope, who got even more talkative when she was high. "Where you been?"

I waved away the pipe. It was not going to help right then. "Trying to find Root," I said.

"Well, hey to you too, girl," said Hope. "Come sit. I got something to make you feel better." She reached in her pocket and took out a half bottle of whiskey. "I was thinking we could get warm and then divide up and find Root, if he hasn't moved in with someone else. I mean, wouldn't you, if you found a really good place? I am a living hunk of ice right now."

I took the bottle and the first sip almost made my throat close up going down and then burned every inch of the way to my stomach. In there, it kept burning. I remembered that I hadn't eaten breakfast and gulped down another huge mouthful, waiting while it followed the same fevered path. My throat was numb and so was my head. I rested it on a parking meter and closed my eyes while the warmth spread around my body. My brain felt smoothed out, the tight squiggles loosened up. Root was out there somewhere waiting for me. I was sure of that now.

Hope had her mouth around the pipe but she snorted, choking out a curl of smoke. "You're looking kind of nuts," she said.

"Like you're the one to call me out," I said and turned back toward the Panhandle. If I had to stay there all day, another night, I'd do it. I'd stay all week. Root had probably spent the night in the cold, alone. I had to be where he could find me. I was feeling halfway between queasy and hungry when I heard a scream from across the street.

"Maddy!" I looked up to Dave's blue sedan across the street. "I have your dog!"

Root sat in the front seat, looking fine, at least from the neck up. I touched the rolled-up window where his nose was making a wet splotch. He wiggled his body, trying to get to me, but it hit me that he looked happy sitting there. He'd found a new home. At least he was dry. Hope was right. Why would he want to jump out of the car and come with me? Dave had probably bribed him with steak and let him stay in front of a heater all night.

"Get in," said Dave, unlocking the door. Any doubt I had about Root's loyalty disappeared as soon as I opened it. He leapt on me and started licking my face and whining, his tail whapping against the seat. I bent down and hugged him.

"You look miserable," said Dave, patting the seat next to him. "Come on in and warm up."

"I gotta get going," I said, but climbed into his car. The car's heater was pumped up and I relaxed into the seat, Root against my side. I was feeling lightheaded with relief and then just lightheaded. When I started heaving, Dave took a plastic bag out of the glove compartment and handed it to me before I made a mess all over his car.

"You need to rest," he said, but he didn't look rested either. He had deep gray circles under his eyes. "Let me take you up to our cabin. It's just over the bridge. My wife's up there already, waiting for us."

"Us?" I said.

"I told her I was going to bring your dog back here. I thought he'd find you if I couldn't," he said. "He was on the street last night, shaking in the rain."

He probably was thinking that I was reckless, like his kid. All I had was a dog and I nearly lost him and then I came and puked in his car. I remembered the bedroom at Miss V's house and how it was set up for kids who might show up there any time. She planned for it. Maybe Dave had a room like that in his cabin, if he really had a cabin and wasn't going to knock me out and put me in the trunk. My mom was right: people were out there, ready to take you if you didn't stay alert, all the time. I knew it was ridiculous to think that. Dave could have done that before if he wanted, when he'd taken us to North Beach. But there was something he wanted from me.

"Come for the day," he said. "I'll bring you back whenever you say. We just want to talk. And you look like you need to rest and get into dry clothes."

I told him I'd go, but only if he drove down Haight so I could tell Ash and everyone. When we got close I shouted hey to them from the car and said I was going to visit Dave and his wife. "Look at you," said Ash. He jumped up and down, his fist raised. Then he waved at Dave like they were old friends. I could see he wanted Dave to invite him along. "Let's just go," I said. Sometimes it seemed that Ash was trying to scrape my nerves raw. Dave wanted something from me, not from Ash.

"Later," I yelled to him.

"See you, dude," he said. I waved my fingers, half friendly, half fuck you, I'm not your dude, and we drove away, across town toward the Golden Gate Bridge.

Dave didn't say much and I was too dizzy to talk. Root turned around a few times on the seat, then lay down with a loud tired sigh before closing his eyes. Thick fog closed in so tight on the bridge that Dave had to slow down and turn on his headlights. "A lot of nothingness here," he said. He leaned forward, as if that would help him see through the haze. I couldn't make out the rusty orange of the bridge or the water below. Unable to see where we were, I was dizzier. I was thinking how he might turn in the wrong direction and flip us over the railing, but we drove into the clear as suddenly as we'd entered the fog. Dave sat back, squared his shoulders, and turned on the radio to some soft rock station.

"My father hated the Beatles," he said. "Long hair and all that. I always thought they sang exactly what I was thinking but magnified to the extreme."

He looked at me and back at the road. "I get it," he said. "Shane didn't like the Beatles either. Too much melody. He listened to rap music, which sounded like a lot of swearing and noise to me. But how could anyone not like the Beatles?"

He turned up the radio and started singing along. "When I find myself in times of trouble . . ." He knew all the words. The song got to him every time, he said. He bopped his head back and forth and then wiped at the edges of his eyes.

I tried to imagine what he must have looked like when he was young. I thought about the picture of Shane that had been on his shirt, similar, but square-jawed and handsome in a chiseled way. They must have had the same eyes, like blue crystals. This was going to be a long night if every little thing made him cry, if he couldn't listen to the stupid car radio without having a breakdown.

"Actually," I said, "I like the Beatles."

Dave laughed. "I didn't mean to say that all of you," and he stopped, searching for the right word. All of us what? Runaways? Punks? I almost filled it in for him. "I don't mean that kids coming up now didn't like them. I don't know what they like."

....

CHAPTER 11

Karen used to let us watch *Little House on the Prairie* if one of us wasn't in trouble. On TV, the cabin's roof had a high peak on one side and sloped down like a skateboard ramp on the other. That's what I was expecting to see when Dave pulled off the road onto a steep gravel driveway, but his cabin was not a one-room house with a wood stove. And it was not small like the apartment where I'd lived with my mom. We walked into one long front room that smelled of fresh cut wood and lemons, as if someone had just finished nailing it together and polishing it. There were windows along three of the walls that looked out onto a lake that Dave said was a finger of the ocean stretching for miles. He said it was a giant hotel for birds passing through on their way to South America. They came every year at the same time and left at the same time. If one stayed behind, there was a good reason. It was sick or there was a temperature-changing storm brewing. Birds, he said, were easier to figure out than people.

The guy knew a lot, for someone who lived in a small town in New York. I couldn't decide whether it must have been cool to have a dad whose brain was an encyclopedia. Maybe Shane was embarrassed. I didn't know anything about what was in my dad's mind. My mom said he didn't care about anyone except himself. How did I know if that was true? I had almost no memory of him. I had one picture of the three of us, which I'd left in my room at Karen and Chip's. They probably threw it out after I took off. Someone new would have moved into the room, another kid who would find my initials on the bottom of the dresser, if she stayed that long. In the picture, my dad had an arm around me and my mom, who was staring into the distance. My dad had a slight smile that he probably faked for whoever was taking the picture. I was wearing ladybug rain boots, which must have meant we had gone to the beach and they'd let me run in the water. I thought I remembered that, but maybe I made it up because of the picture.

Dave went into the part of the room that was a kitchen and put down a bowl of water for Root. He said he didn't have any dog food, but he could go get some. I told him Root usually ate what I did, or anything he found. He wasn't picky. I stopped myself from telling him how Root had poisoned himself on weed brownies and rotten food he found on the street. Dave opened a can of tuna fish and put some slices of apple on top, all of which was gone about a second after he put it down.

"It's what we gave him last night and he liked it then too," he said. "And you? What can I get you?"

"I'm fine," I said. "I don't need anything."

"Why don't you let us help you?" Dave said. "When did you eat last?"

I told him I hadn't eaten in a while so he started going around the cabinets, saying how his wife did most of the cooking when they were at home, but that he'd learned a few tricks. The guys at the firehouse took turns cooking. Beef stew, grilled steak, things like that. "It's how I got this," he said, patting his stomach. I sat on a tan couch that was low to the ground. There were two matching chairs and a coffee table colored the same as the light shiny floor. There wasn't a single piece of paper anywhere, just furniture, a shelf with a row of tall white candles and a giant photograph behind the couch of a waterfall under a full moon. Somehow, though, the room didn't feel empty, just empty of what went on before. No one lived there, or anyone could. Even the waterfall in the photograph looked stopped in time.

"Don't get any ideas that we live anything like this," said Dave, watching me as I looked around the room. "Our house in New York is a mess. And not a fancy mess. Shane's brother saw this place on the internet. The owners are selling it and they didn't want it sitting empty. When they heard why we were coming, they let us rent it for almost nothing. I don't like charity, but sometimes you have to take it."

He must have realized how that sounded, so he got quiet. Now I was his charity case.

"The owners call it minimalist," said Dave, coming over to pet Root. "They said they only stick to what's necessary. No clutter. Said it makes it easier for them to concentrate on what's truly important. Experiences, instead of possessions."

"I don't get it," I said.

"Then it's working on you," he said. "The minimalism."

"I'm not so distracted by stuff that I need it all taken away, is what I mean," I said.

"Of course," said Dave. "These people have so much money they used it to get rid of all their stuff."

"That is stupid beyond belief," I said.

Dave laughed. "Agreed," he said. "At home we layer our things. Old papers over older papers, over winter clothes and shoes no one has worn in ten years. And Shane's things, his hockey sticks and skateboards, of course. We never got rid of anything in his room even after he left. Marva never wanted to. She was still washing his clothes once a week, then putting them back in the drawer. In case."

I took in a sharp breath. I thought about what his room must look like, imagining it like the one that the boys shared at Karen and Chip's, with blue walls and plaid bedspreads, every inch of wall space full of music and sports posters. Probably no graffiti. Dave would not allow that. Karen and Chip didn't either, but that didn't stop the boys from tagging the walls. Someone had to know you were there.

"I hope this is okay," said Dave, putting a bowl of chili on the white counter along with a plate of orange sections and crackers. "It looks a little pre-fab."

Root followed me over to the counter and sat looking up at

me hopefully, waiting to lick the can, which he always got to do. He wasn't thinking about what he was going to do after that.

"It's some organic brand," said Dave, offering me a chair. "All they had in the cabinet. I prefer the regular kind. But the owners, they use organic sugar and tea. They even have organic bath soap. I guess in case they eat any of it while they are taking their two-minute shower with the water-saver showerhead. It delivers a drip a minute."

I looked at him while I ate the chili, not as good as what we got at the corner store, which we ate cold, from the can.

"I'm not making it sound too homey, I know," he said. "But I think you'll like it here."

I put my spoon down and looked up at him. "I'm getting ahead of myself," he said. "I just wanted you to talk to us and get a rest. I promised my wife I'd try and get to know you more. That's all. Why don't you finish up and I'll get Marva and then we'll take a walk. Look at the marsh, get some fresh air?"

He left me at the counter, and I held out my bowl for Root to lick clean. Squares of sunlight gleamed on the floor. My stomach had settled down from queasy to rumbling and I felt drowsy. I needed to block everything out. I had made it through the storm. I had Root. We'd survived. I moved over to the minimalist couch, my wet, smudged up boots hanging over the edge, an arm across my face. Maybe I could get used to this, a place where no one left a trace of what went before.

"I think she's sleeping," said Marva. I could see her walking into the room on her tiptoes.

"No," I said and jerked my feet off the end of the couch.

Marva was tiny, at least next to Dave, with his thickened middle and wide face. I could fit one hand around both of her wrists. She was wearing a pair of tight jeans that made her look, sideways, only a few inches thick. I wasn't that big myself, but I'd been born larger than Marva. She smiled, the lines on each side of her mouth turning into crevices, and stuck out her hand. When I didn't respond she swept me into a hug. I stood there and took it, and let her cradle my head into her bony shoulder.

"Want to take a walk?" Dave said.

Root was already waiting at the door, his tail flapping like he'd known these people forever. One night with them and he was ready to move in. I'd rescued him, fed him all those months, and he could just forget about it all. Shit, Root, I was thinking and only half laughing to myself while we tramped in a line down the driveway. My boots sunk into the gravel that crackled at every step. Dave and Marva walked ahead, like they weren't fighting the sludge the way I was. Root wove in and out of the redwood trees that lined the road, his nose down, noticing, as always, what I couldn't. The air smelled wet and sweet. Drops of water fell on my head from the branches stretching up to a sky that was dotted with silver clouds.

Dave turned onto the main road at the end of the driveway, Marva behind him, with me at the end. I called Root, who ran up beside me and stuck his muzzle against my leg. We walked for what seemed like an hour, in silence except for the peaked cries of birds and shrieking seagulls that hovered above us like little helicopters.

"I brought the lens so it will take me a minute to figure out if that is a heron or an egret," said Dave. He stopped and pointed across the water to a tall gray-white bird that looked like it was dancing in slow motion. "Great blue heron, I'd say. Look at how he uses his neck to force down the fish he just caught."

The bird had a bulge in its throat that was moving slowly down its freakish neck. I thought how weird it must be to be able to move one muscle, control one shivering piece of your throat or your stomach. Or your heart.

"I've started going on these bird walks early every morning I've been here. That's when they're all out here on the lagoon," said Dave, reaching into his pocket for a small pair of binoculars. "Terns, coots, loons, kingfishers. They are all out there. Magnificent, huh?"

He looked at me and gestured back to the bird. "See if you can tell if he has anything hanging out of his mouth. If he's got another fish we'll stay and watch."

"I don't think he's got anything new, at least nothing I can see," I said. The bird was standing still, only its throat slowly working and inching down whatever was in there.

"Marva's not that interested," he said, "so I usually come out here alone. I started back home, which isn't too far from Sapsucker Woods. They have more kinds of bird sounds there than anywhere else in the world. I was amazed to find out I could learn to recognize each call, like I'm listening in on their conversations. They use a certain tone of voice when they are threatened or if they're happy."

"I'm interested, just not obsessed," said Marva. "I don't need any hobbies right now. I need to focus on why Shane ended up in that park." She turned and looked at the bird for the first time.

"I am focused, Marva," Dave said sharply. "I just need to get away sometimes. I can't do it all the time. I can't think about him every second I'm awake."

"It's all I do, think about Shane," said Marva, looking at me, like I was supposed to explain it to Dave.

The bird stood still, but the wind ruffled the flyaway feathers on its wings, which were pouched out like it was deciding whether to take off. The water churned on the lagoon, the top layer white as diamonds moving toward the shore.

"He sees something," said Dave. He pointed the binoculars at the bird. "I think he's going after it."

The bird flapped its wings, then stabbed its face into the water and emerged with a silvery fish whipping around in its beak. The fish disappeared slowly down the bird's throat, one minute swimming, the next being punched down into darkness.

"Oh my god, that was great," said Dave. He handed me the binoculars. "I bet you've never seen anything like this."

"That's okay," I said. "I can see without them."

"Not the point. Look through these and it makes you feel like you are right there with him. Or her. I'm not sure which gender yet."

He held them up to my eyes. All I could see was an enlarged blur of shapes.

"Fiddle with the little wheels here," said Dave. "Adjust them and you'll see what I mean."

I took them and twisted the lenses. The bird came into focus slowly. It was not the holy moment Dave experienced, but I could see the beady yellow eyes and the thorny black feather standing up on its head, like a hat it had found at the Goodwill. I felt myself sliding into its world. After a minute, it squished itself up into a solid block and stood gazing into the wind. Dave took the binoculars back and kept looking at the bird even though it wasn't doing anything.

"I've watched herons before," he said. "But I've never been lucky enough to see one this clearly while it's fishing. I guess I had to come all this way to see one this close."

"Let's turn back," said Marva. "It's cold. Maddy, you must be freezing."

I could see she was using me to get Dave home. She'd had enough bird time. She might have had enough of Dave. She looked like she was bored and annoyed and just holding it all in. Maybe Shane got his nervous system from her. I thought about what I'd be doing if I had stayed in San Francisco. It would almost be time to line up for dinner at the shelter. We'd probably all be staying there tonight, if only to take a shower and dry off for real.

I walked behind Dave and Marva again on the way back to the cabin. Root loped along beside me, panting. I put my hand on his head and squeezed a handful of his fur, glad that at least he was there with me. Dave put his arm around Marva's shoulders and she pulled away, but let his arm stay. He stopped and put his arms around her, holding her so tight that her tiny bones disappeared behind her puffy coat. As puny as she was, she gripped him back. This time I could hear him crying, loud enough for both. She let him go and rubbed his back as I caught up to them.

We walked together up the driveway, but I felt like an outsider. Dave didn't try to wipe off the tears dribbling down his cheeks. Marva's were dry, but I couldn't tell what she was thinking. Had my dad ever cried? Did my mom ever put her arms around him like that? She talked more about people she barely knew than about him. She'd told me about the other clerks at Safeway, how one woman had nightmares about a baby she gave up for adoption at fifteen and another who took money out of the cash drawer every Friday. "You can't judge people because you just never know why they do what they do," she'd said, in one of the moments she'd made sense.

Dave and Marva belonged in a different world. They must have lived together forever. I could tell Marva had been pretty, even though she looked sunken now. Maybe Dave had been a football player and she was a cheerleader and they thought they would have a perfect life, with two kids who looked as great as they did. Instead they had a geeky kid named Marcus and a kid named Shane who was not at all what they expected. You never know. My mother was right.

"Sorry," said Dave. "It hits me when I'm thinking about something else. I'll be back in the world and then there it comes, what happened to Shane."

I didn't know what to say, so I kept walking alongside him, squirming inside. Root ran ahead after a squirrel and stood startled when it ran up a tree. He barked, as if that was going to bring it down.

"Shane would have liked the woods here," said Marva. "I wish we could have brought him."

"He hated looking at birds," said Dave. "Or maybe he hated the way I looked at birds."

Root was already at the door, waiting. When Dave opened it, he rushed to the water bowl and began lapping so loud that no one had to talk, then he shook his head hard enough to fling water onto the shiny refrigerator, where it dripped to the white floor. Marva sat on the sofa, which looked even plainer after the bird show over at the lagoon. Dave started arranging logs in the fireplace and soon an orange glow was bouncing off the oversized windows. Root lay down on the stone hearth, as close as he could go to the fire without climbing inside, and sighed loudly. He alternated his gaze between me and Dave, raised one eyebrow and then the other, not sure who he belonged to.

"Don't get too comfortable," I said, sitting down next to him, but I knew I was talking to myself.

"You want to call your parents?" Dave said.

"Is that what I'm here for?"

"I'm sorry," said Dave. "I don't know anything about you. I assume your parents are worried about you. You don't think about something like that when you're young. I know Shane wasn't thinking about us. It's just . . ." He paused and took his time arranging another log on the fire so that all the wood stood in a teepee shape. "Well, I thought about Shane all the time. Was he lying out on the sidewalk? I saw that in your neighborhood. You have to step right over bodies. You forget how every single one of them is someone's kid. Or used to be. I guess folks over there are used to it. I read how they have a memorial service every year for all the people who died on the street."

He went on like that, tinkering with the fire and talking about the people he'd seen on Haight, like he was talking about the birds on the lagoon. I didn't tell him that he might have stepped over any of us. He could have walked by me. One day I had a bad cold and was sleeping, curled up against a wall near the smoke shop, when a lady who worked in there poked me in the back, just the tip of her shoe at first and then tap, tap, tap like she was nudging a ball. I nearly turned around and grabbed her foot just to hear the scream. "You can't lie there all day," she'd said, but she could see I was wiped out. "Just make sure you clean up after yourself." I'd told her I would, of course, and then I'd left as soon as she turned around. I didn't need her making me feel worse.

"I want you to call your parents, Maddy," said Dave. "I want them to know where you are."

"My parents are not wondering where I am. I can tell you that," I said, my hand resting on Root's head.

"I think you'd be surprised that, wherever they are, they are worried. They are worried all the time."

"First of all, I don't know my dad," I said. "He's dead." Dave didn't change his expression. He kept looking at me like he might start crying again. Marva sat on the couch and massaged her birdlike hands so hard I thought she was going to break some bones.

"And what about your mother? Where were you before you ended up"—and then he corrected himself because Shane had clearly ended up, but I was still going—"before you came to the park? Where did you live?"

It was what the counselors asked when they visited the shelter or came to talk to us on the street. The cops sometimes said it too, after they hassled us. Where did you come from? What were you escaping? Who beat you or molested you or threatened you or never spoke to you or told you every day you were someone you weren't, so that finally you had to leave? What is it you need? If we get you what you need will you go home?

"It wasn't that way," I said.

"What way?" said Marva.

"What you were thinking," I said. "No one was beating me up."

"I didn't think that," said Dave. "You seem to be such a bright young woman. How did you come to live in the park?"

Dave looked at me the way my mother used to, like if I didn't play along with whatever game was in her head that she would get unhinged. But I was not going to tell him how my mother had gotten sick, which was what Miss V said, that the chemicals in her brain were so mixed up that she went psychotic. And how I had gone to live with my cousins, who might as well have lived on another planet, but who didn't hit me. Their list of punishments was taped on the refrigerator where everyone could see. Go look it up, see what you have coming, Karen would tell us. She went to Walmart every week and bought enough food and clothes for us all. There was cable TV in the living room. We got an allowance.

"Your parents?" said Dave.

I didn't tell him that Karen and Chip were like air. You need it but you don't feel it around you.

"Maybe we could help you get a job," said Marva. "Or you could go to college if you wanted. You could still think about that. You have time."

"Honey," said Dave, watching me try not to roll my eyes too obviously at Marva. "We're just trying to understand, right?"

"I just don't want you to give up," said Marva.

Dave was giving me this look I couldn't stand. The worst thing would be to have us both crying. I was starting to see that the guy could do that to me. My throat was tight, a sore spot of pressure building up in the middle. So I started talking, about how I liked staying in San Francisco. I couldn't wait to get back there. What I didn't say was how everything had changed, that I felt like I needed to watch in every direction or I would end up like Shane.

"I didn't know Shane, if that's what you're after," I finally said.

"But did you know some of the same kids?" said Dave. "Did you ever run into him?"

"I never saw him," I said. "I mean, before."

"I just figured you would know how he lived when he got there, what it was like for him," said Dave.

I wanted to tell him that Shane was probably like everyone else. He got by any way he could. Maybe he was strung out or played music on the street or was on a waiting list for some program. Who knows what he'd had to do? The fire logs had collapsed into embers, still giving off so much heat I thought Root's fur would melt. He was panting loud but didn't move away.

"You must be tired," said Dave. "How about I make up the couch for you?"

"I'd like to go back, like you said I could." I stood and put on my coat.

Dave put his hands on my shoulders. "Please," he said. "Please stay."

I wanted to yell at him to leave me alone, I had enough to think about. No wonder Shane wanted to get away, with his dad on his ass all the time. But I sat on the minimalist couch, which Marva had covered with white sheets.

"You'll stay?" said Dave. "Just tonight?"

Marva handed me a fluffy white towel nearly as big as the couch. "Bathroom down the hall has a nice walk-in steam shower, so make yourself at home. There is more food in the cabinet if you're hungry. We didn't even give you a proper dinner. Sometimes when it's just the two of us, we forget to eat. Well, I do."

I took the towel and stood by the fire. Marva stepped toward me, hoping for a hug, but that was not going to happen. She waved instead. I nodded and got into bed. I knew I should have showered, especially since the white sheets were going to have the outline of my body. I was full of fire smoke and sour body odor, but I was too tired to make the effort. Root jumped up on the couch and burrowed by my feet.

The door to Dave and Marva's room was shut when I woke up. The sun was still low, but I couldn't tell how early it was. I found an apple and the rest of the chili in the refrigerator, which I split with Root. The bathroom felt bigger than the room all the girls shared at Chip and Karen's, a tiled white cave with a skylight full of tree branches and fluffy clouds. The steam shower had too many knobs and pipes so I settled for a quick bath in the giant white tub, where I left a ring of dirt. Then I put my clothes back on and took the ocean blue ceramic soap dish, the only spot of color in the room, and stuffed it into my backpack. I thought about leaving a note, but what would I say? I couldn't give them what they wanted. I didn't know who Shane was or how he lived. It was better if they didn't see me leaving. I clipped on Root's leash, shut the door behind me and walked down the driveway, turning away from the lagoon at the end, back toward the city.

CHAPTER 12

Karen always said that everything starts with a plan. A genius without one was going to live in a van. An idiot with a plan could get somewhere. I guess she didn't follow her own advice. Living in the San Fernando Valley with two rooms full of problem kids did not sound like a good plan. She and Chip had their own two boys, who were in high school when I arrived, and their house was in a commotion all the time. They couldn't keep track of who went where. The foster kids moved in and left. You never knew why. Sometimes there were four of us and other times it was just me. I was the only one who stayed for so many years, until the state said I was grown up and had to find something else to do.

Some days when I cut school, I took the bus all the way down the 405 to the beach, near the house where my parents used to live. I'd wander around and eat hot dogs or pizza that people left on the tables or lift candy from the mini mart. That's when I got good at stuffing what I wanted into my pockets. I knew how to turn and do it so the cameras didn't see me. I'd get home and stash mascara, lip gloss, or a bag of M&M's under my bed. It made me happy to know it was there, a small secret no one could take from me. Karen would ask how school was and I'd say fine. She'd ask what happened and I'd say nothing and that was it. She and Chip collected money for keeping me and they gave me food and five dollars a month to keep in my plastic wallet, but they had no clue about me.

Karen left us alone as long as we weren't fighting. She said we needed to be team players. She gave us T-shirts that said TEAM BANDER, over a row of smiley faces, and said we had to wear them on Sundays, to show respect for ourselves and others. We were not born civilized, but we could learn. That didn't work, but what did she know? When she wasn't home we sometimes snuck change from her purse, tried on her clothes, and dared one another to pee in the little sink off her bedroom. The boys watched porno on her computer until it froze, a big picture of naked boobs on the screen. "Someone is not going to be having dinner, I'm telling you what," she said, when she saw that. That was Team Bander.

Then I graduated high school, which surprised Karen and Chip. They'd gone to meetings when the vice principal called to say how many days I'd cut, but then they forgot about it. Other kids caused more trouble at school. And I did the homework even when I didn't turn it in. I filled in workbooks and math sheets for other kids in the house. Sometimes they paid me, but it didn't matter. I liked writing down the right answer, one small problem after another, solved.

Chip and Karen signed me up for a county program that was supposed to teach me how to live on my own, but I'd basically been doing that, even if they didn't notice. I was eighteen, done with being in Los Angeles. Karen wanted me to work at a hair salon and learn a skill so I could support myself, and probably so I could take care of her hair that looked like a dried-up palm tree. But I was not a hair salon kind of person. I couldn't tell what would make anyone look better.

"Missy thinks she knows it all," she said.

She didn't expect I'd stuff clothes in my school backpack and buy a bus ticket north. I never called or wrote a letter to tell her where I was. My life with her was over and there was nothing she could do. I sat awake all night on the bus, afraid to close my eyes while it climbed past the foothills, through the huge dirt fields of the valley and back over to the coast. I had heard about San Francisco, how you can just live your life, because everyone isn't watching you all the time.

When I got off the bus, it was breakfast time and I thought how Karen would be setting out bowls on the kitchen table. She'd call me the way she always did, her voice deeper and heavier if I didn't answer. She'd figure out I'd left, but what was she going to do? I should have taken more money from her drawer. I looked at a big map on the wall and read it out loud to myself.

"Where you headed?" said a guy with a deep sunburn, carrying a worn pack and guitar case. I didn't need to answer because he talked enough for both of us. He said he was from

Houston and was on his way to Oakland. Everyone was ending up there. I could join if I wanted, he said, gesturing to two other guys sitting in a corner, with paper cups out and a sign saying they needed money for bus tickets. I said I just got to town and I was staying, at least for now.

"Okay," he said, "but take a grape for the road." He handed me one purple grape and I popped it in my mouth. I studied the map to show I knew what I was doing and then walked out of the station. I had no idea where to go.

I passed office buildings and a huge tower that reflected the sun so sharply I had to turn my face away. I ended up at Fisherman's Wharf, a place I'd seen on the map, on a street lined with restaurants and pots of boiling crab. I got enough to eat by swatting away the seagulls for what was left on outdoor tables. The first night I stayed in a small park at the end of the street, but I could see it wasn't going to work. I was too cold to sleep, and people were up all night, one group in a tent and another in a car that blasted music every time someone opened the door. The next day I wandered, watching jugglers and dancers and someone who painted himself gold and pretended to be a statue. Crowds gathered and then paid, but that wasn't going to help me. I didn't have an act.

I spent all of my money on a hostel that was above a souvenir shop. They said they'd pay me to clean the bathroom and sweep up outside, but it wasn't enough to stay there so I was out after a week. But by then I'd learned I was at the wrong park. Golden Gate Park was all the way over on the other side of the city.

When I got there after hours of walking, it was like people were waiting for me. This is where you set up, this is where you sleep, where you'll get hassled. If you are hungry here, people said, then you're doing something wrong.

....

Up ahead the Golden Gate Bridge looked like it had been pasted in the sky. I had seen it from the top of a hill in the park and I'd driven over it with Dave. But I'd never been next to the giant spiked columns and curved ropes that hooked onto the road and kept it from falling into the water. Ash said walking across it would be creepy, that all he would be able to think about was how it was the most famous place to jump. People came there from all over the world to do it. They parked their cars or bikes nearby and then went over the railing when no one was watching. Ash thought he would look down and get the urge, but I wanted to see what it felt like to be over the bay, hanging between two places, suspended away from everything else in my life.

Root and I walked under a line of trees. The fog was bunched up, away over the ocean and I started to get warm. Root's tongue was hanging out. I had forgotten to bring water for either of us. Birds circled overhead and the longer I listened the more I could tell the difference in their voices, chirps and hard cries. It wasn't any kind of song that went together, more like a punk chorus. Dave had made me think about them. Terns, coots, and whatever else had been out there, the gangly bird that had invented a new way of swallowing. I thought what I would tell Ash, how I was sort of kidnapped by Dave the birdman and his birdlike wife and their house of nothingness. Fleet's rat would probably be bird food out here. Tiny wouldn't have a chance. The only one who would make it was Hope, who could lead bird watching tours.

The sun burned off strings of fog as they tried to settle on the bridge. I could feel the rush of wind from cars passing by me. Root trotted along, leaning forward, but I needed to stop. I had exactly fifty cents in my pocket and there was nowhere to set up with a sign, even if I'd had cardboard to write on. SAN FRANCISCO. GET ME HOME. I had nothing to contribute for gas or anything else if someone even stopped to pick me up. Why would they? I had seen myself in the mirror at Dave and Marva's, torn jeans, a flap of one shoe hanging loose. And there was Root, looking kind of crazy.

Ash said all you had to do was stand on the road and look like you wanted to go somewhere. Make a face that says slow down, pick me up. Point your thumb and wave at any driver who even half pays attention. If he were here, we would already be in a car instead of thinking up every reason to stay invisible. I put my pack as far from the road as I could and tied Root's leash to one of the straps. He sat and watched while I waved a thumb at cars and projected my open mind. If Dave pulled up in his sedan, I'd run toward the sign for Mill Valley. Dave wouldn't follow me because it would be obvious I didn't want to get in his car. "Okay, Maddy," I said. "Missy." I hummed and then stopped when I realized it was one of Fleet's stupid songs. It seemed like a long time passed but no one stopped. A few drivers met my eyes. A guy in a red convertible sports car waved but didn't slow down. I tried not to think like my mom, that everyone out there was ready to snatch me.

I was going to untie Root and start walking again, maybe after a stop in the Mill Valley, whatever that was, when a lady who could barely see over the steering wheel of her dented white car stopped in front of us. The back bumper was crammed with stickers—BE KIND, SAVE THE BEES, LIFE IS GOOD—and close to dragging on the ground. She rolled down the window and waved at me. "Get in front," she said, "but put your friend in the back seat."

The door clanged when I opened it and again when I managed to pull it shut. She reached over and attached an elastic cord to the handle. "Sometimes it flies open," she said. "I keep saying I'm going to get it fixed." There was a pile of newspapers and an empty cup from Starbucks on the seat and the woman tossed them in the back like confetti. Root settled where one of the sections of paper landed. "Belt," said the woman, and I snapped on the stiff canvas across my chest. "Him too," she said. "You know, dogs are like projectiles if you have an accident. I don't want him slamming himself into the dashboard here if something happens."

I turned so she couldn't see my expression and then slipped into the back seat to stretch the belt around Root. He looked like a freak, the belt squishing his chest fur and shoving him onto one haunch, but he didn't complain. He had been around long enough to know when he needed to step up and act like a street dog that would rip off someone's head or suck up and be quiet.

"So where are you going?" asked the woman.

I told her we needed to get to the other side of the bridge. From there we could walk. But she said she had time to kill before she went to meet her friends for lunch, like she did every Sunday. Haight would be fine, she said. She used to like it there when she lived in the city, before she had children. Sometimes she wished she hadn't moved to Marin County because it was too out of touch with reality. People there didn't know the first thing about community. They donated to a million causes and then closed their blinds so they didn't have to talk to the person next door. She didn't like the way the whole country was going. She kept talking all the way across the bridge. She wagged her head when she spoke, which made her small stained-glass butterfly earrings flutter from side to side. I stopped listening and watched the fog on the ocean. A foghorn bleated from out in the bay. I thought how it must feel to be at the exact center of the bridge when the mist moved onto it, be able to look down at the water with nothing above or below me.

"You never did tell me about yourself," the woman said when I got out of her car on Haight. I shrugged and thanked her. She didn't want to know. She probably closed her own blinds at her own house, over the bridge, in that valley. Root and I walked a few blocks, looking for Ash, Fleet, and Hope.

The wind pushed me down the street, which was quiet except for a bar with TVs hanging from the ceiling, all tuned to a football game. I leaned in a big open window next to the sidewalk and took a glass of water off of a table. Four guys in shorts and backward baseball caps were watching the screen and they didn't notice. I held the glass down for Root, who lapped most of it, and put it back. I looked for chicken wings or chips, any kind of food, but they were just drinking. One of them, in a bright yellow sweatshirt, reached behind for his glass and finished off the water. He wiped a sleeve across his mouth and I thought he was going to turn around and see us, but he kept his eyes on the TV. A second later he shot out of his chair and jumped into the arms of the guy next to him, wrapped his legs around his waist and smacked him with his cap. "Yeah, buddy," he screamed.

No one was at our sleeping spot, but Ash's extra coat was high up in a tree and a few of Hope's tie-dyed T-shirts were strung around another limb like dying flowers. The rusty shopping cart sat in a stand of trees down the hill, piled with bags of sliced bread, Ash's torn up red sneakers, Fleet's rumpled paperbacks.

I dug up the plastic tub of Root's food, which smelled moldy even though it was sealed. He didn't seem to mind and finished it as soon as I dumped it on the mushy leaves.

The dinner line had already started at the shelter. From down the block it was hard to tell anyone apart, the overflowing packs, knotted hair, dirtied up jackets and sweatshirts. When I got closer I could make out Fleet, strawberry hair tied up on her head, Tiny in a box under her arm.

"Hey," she said, like I hadn't been gone. "What's up?"

I stood there, no expression, and she put down the box and pulled me in for a hug. I gave it back to her.

"Hey yourself, sister," I said. "I didn't think I'd ever get back."

"But here you are."

"Where is everyone?"

Ash was with some kids from the high school who lived around the corner. Sometimes they gave him their lunches, names printed out on the brown paper bags, because they knew they could count on him if they wanted anything. And Hope had hooked up with a guy who worked on a weed farm up north.

"So who is this guy?" I asked her.

"Pizza John." Fleet laughed and I could see she was high. She'd probably smoked with Hope's friend, whoever he was.

"So she went up there with him?"

"The harvest ended last month," said Fleet. "He's trimming in some warehouse in the East Bay. He goes wherever there's a crop. He says they used to pay him good money, until weed went all legal. Now there's too much of it, which I don't personally notice."

I put an arm around her and she smiled. I held on to her but I hoped she was not going to tell me any more about Pizza John. I was still thinking about being in the cabin with Dave and Marva.

We inched our way toward the dining room and Fleet pointed him out, standing up near the front of the line with Hope. He was tall, with a ponytail peeking out under an oversized straw hat.

"I'm not going off with him to trim weed," I said.

"I knew you'd be that way," she said.

"I'm not any way." I took my arm off her shoulder and picked up a plate. A server spooned spaghetti onto it. Another added the mixed vegetables. I sat at one of the long tables with Fleet and three guys with skateboards. I started telling Fleet about Dave and Marva. The skateboarders leaned in to listen and I tried to ignore them.

Fleet kept interrupting to ask questions. She liked the part about the birds, except when I said that they would have eaten Tiny. She said I should have stayed longer, taken the chance to sleep and eat all I wanted. They sounded nice. Besides, Dave and Marva had to have bucks, she said. She was surprised to hear that I hadn't lifted anything. I didn't tell her about the blue soap dish, which was still in my backpack. It had been a while since I'd taken something so pointless.

"Watch him," she said, pushing Tiny's box across the table. "I'm going for seconds."

Tiny had bunched himself into a ball in a corner of the box. I dropped a piece of corn from my plate by his twitching nose and he reached for it and started chewing. I put what was left of my dinner on the floor for Root.

"I wish someone would take care of me like that," said one of the skateboarders, and laughed. He was wearing a black knit cap with eyes painted on it.

"I bet," I said. Ash's least favorite crew was the skaters, even though he had a board too and could flip down any hill. He said you couldn't trust them. They would share food one minute, then be all cranked up and in your face later. They could go either way and you couldn't tell when it would happen.

Fleet came back with her plate refilled. She had to be wasted to eat like that.

"I knew a chick in Santa Cruz who had a rat," said one of the skaters, his elbows reaching halfway across the table. "She let him sleep in bed with her, but one night he ate one of her fingers. Chewed it right off."

I gave Fleet a look that said, "Just pretend this idiot doesn't exist," and she pretty much did. She dove into her food. I took my plate and dropped it in the compost bin. One side of the room had colored cans, each with its own set of cartoon drawings of what to put in there. If you dumped your paper into the landfill bin someone serving dinner would call out, "Compost! Compost!" like someone was being killed.

"Maddy Donaldo?" One of the volunteers stood near the door and looked around, one hand shading his eyes from the overhead light.

I went to sit back down with Fleet, who was still shoveling in food. She poked me and looked over at him. I was hoping she wasn't going to say anything. I'd signed in, so they knew

I was here. Dave and Marva must have discovered I was gone and had stolen something from their house. I was about to get arrested for taking a soap dish.

"Maddy? Donaldo?" he called again, as if I was in first grade and didn't know how to raise my hand.

What was I supposed to do? Ash wasn't there, I was stuck in a shelter with skaters who watched rats chew people to death, and now the police were after me. I could picture Chip, how he sawed his fingers back and forth in the air whenever I complained. "Getting out the world's smallest violin," he said. It felt like everyone was looking at me.

I raised my hand halfway, since it was obvious I was there.

"I have someone who wants to talk to you," the volunteer said.

I followed him into the hallway between the dining room and dormitory where I could see two cops. One had his arms behind him. The other was the one who'd cited me for blocking the sidewalk. Of course, I hadn't paid the fine. None of us had.

"Ms. Donaldo?" he said. His buzz cut was standing straight up, rooster style, on the top of his head. I couldn't tell if he recognized me. "We have a pending investigation on a homicide in the park, and we were hoping you could help us. We heard that you might have seen what happened."

What was it with everyone wanting my help? I'd been minding my own business, with no one noticing. Now I was the one everyone needed to find.

"I didn't see anything actually happen," I said. "All I saw was the kid, the one who died."

"We need you to look at some pictures," he said. "See if you recognize anyone. If you don't want to do it for us, do it for Shane Golden's parents."

I'd been thinking about the stupid soap dish while Dave and Marva were ratting my story to the cops. The cop said he would send a car for me in the morning, if that made things easier. I told him I'd rather walk. Having a squad car roll up outside with everyone watching was not what I wanted. He nodded and told me to have someone call if I changed my mind. He handed me his card with his number on it. OFFICER WILLIAM PATZ, it said. I tucked it in the back pocket of my jeans.

"Okay," he said in a voice louder than it needed to be. "So we'll see you tomorrow?"

I didn't know if I could make myself go. What else had Dave and Marva told the cops? Seeing a killer was not something they could arrest you for. They couldn't make me talk to them.

I slept on the top bunk that night, above Fleet, who tucked Tiny's cage under the bed. Root had to stay tied to the side of the bunk, but he didn't make any noise about it. Usually I tried to take the bottom spot so he could jump up beside me, but I wanted to be harder to find. I tried to remember what the guy who killed Shane even looked like. I could see Shane lying on the ground, the way his eyes were open but not looking at anything. I held onto the scratchy blanket and listened to the snoring and coughing and sleep-talking. One girl moaned in her sleep, shaking off a bad dream.

In the morning, I was first in the bathroom, which was a mess of used toilet tissue and small wet towels on the floor. I splashed my face with water. Someone had stuck a sign on the bottom of the mirror. KEEP ME CLEAN. THANKS, YOUR SINK.

It made me think about Ash, who would write something like that. I wondered why he didn't show up at the shelter last night. Maybe he was in the park or posted up on a stoop. In the mirror, I looked like the same person as yesterday. I slapped my cheek. "Be here now," I said, which I had picked up from an acting class that met last winter at the shelter. The teacher had trooped over from a nearby Catholic college to work with us. It was supposed to build confidence, he said. He stood in the middle giving directions. Find a character. Look into your neighbor's eyes. Reach deep. "Be here now! Be here now!" Ash and I had gone for a few of the classes, partly because he passed around homemade cookies at the end and then let us stay there until dinner. But I liked pretending to be someone else, even if was just for an hour. The teacher said I was a natural, that I must have acted before.

When I opened the metal side door of the shelter I saw the squad car parked out front. The cop reached across and opened the passenger side door, like he'd been expecting me. Root climbed in, then jumped into the back seat.

"Good morning, Maddy," he said.

I hesitated, but got in. I probably had no choice and I didn't want to have my arms snapped into cuffs and twisted behind me again.

"You want a doughnut?" he said, after I closed the door. I purposely didn't look at him. "Kidding," he said. "I just thought, you know, everyone expects the cop to have doughnuts."

"I like doughnuts," I said.

"We could get some then," he said. "Why not?"

He pulled a U-turn and drove around the corner to Donut World, a rundown shop that blasted the smell of sugary frying dough onto the sidewalk. I was not in the mood, but I got out of the car anyway and walked into the shop in front of him.

"Two creams, two jellies, two plain," he said to the clerk.

Back in the car he picked out a jelly donut and took an enormous bite. Purple jelly stuck to his fingers, which he licked one by one. The bird on his badge looked like it was sitting on flames and trying to escape. He picked up the box and held it out to me. I took a plain one and nibbled it around the edges.

"Okay, then. Headquarters," he said.

I broke a chunk off my donut and gave it to Root, sitting patiently in the back seat.

"I'm not sure that's good for his digestion," said the cop. "Just make sure he doesn't crap on the seat. Can I ask you something?"

I looked over at him. He had a speck of jelly on his lower lip.

I knew he was going to ask about my parents, about how much they worried, how I should let them know where I was.

"Why didn't you tell us about the kid you'd seen when we cited you on the street?"

I didn't say anything. Could I get in trouble for staying quiet? Why didn't he tell me last night that he knew who I was? He was playing games and I could too.

"Well, you're here now," he said. "Do the right thing. I always tell people that, especially young people. It helps, in the end. It's a shame they don't teach that to kids anymore. Just do the right thing."

We walked into the station, to the same room where they had held us for hanging out on the sidewalk. The same angry, vacant faces stared down at me from the walls. Root stood still beside me like he felt the seriousness of the place. I sat on one of the long benches until a door opened and Patz called out my name.

"Let's get started," he said, and led me and Root into a small room with a table and no windows.

The black cloth of his shirt was tight across his bulb of a belly. He asked me if I had seen a line-up before. I said I had seen them on TV, where people sit in a room and look through a window, but the guys inside can't see you. It was how I used to feel at Karen and Chip's house. I watched everyone in the house, but no one really saw me.

"That's TV," Patz said. "In here we're going to show you some photos in a book. That's how we do it. You tell us if you recognize anyone. But first we have to set up the equipment. You understand all this will be recorded?"

I nodded, but I wasn't sure what he was talking about. If I was going to look at a book of pictures, they could have brought them to me at the shelter instead of giving me the cop car escort. Another cop came in with a camera and a microphone that he set up on a little stand in front of me. Patz put a black plastic binder on the table. He opened it to a page filled with photos of faces and then announced his name, the day and time, and that he was talking to Madlynne Donaldo. He asked me to spell my name and to state my home address. I didn't say anything. He knew where I lived.

"Take your time and look at these men," he said. "Really look at each one. And then tell me if you recognize any of them."

I forced myself to look down at the rows of faces, which were covered with a sheet of plastic. My eyes skidded over them. They all looked like they could kill someone, if they found you alone somewhere. They didn't need a reason. A small space heater spewed warm air at my feet, but I was cold. My whole body shivered once, hard. I stared across the page left to right, like I was reading, and I came back to one at the end of a middle row. He had patchy gray-and-black hair brushed back from his face, a few days of gray beard on his chin, and eyes so dark they looked like they went on forever. I knew I should not have eaten the doughnut because I could feel it coming up in my throat.

"Look carefully at all of them," said Patz. "Even if one jumps out at you."

I took a deep breath and was quivering, but wasn't sure if he could tell. I could have lied. It would have been easy to say I didn't know any of them and then I could leave, walk back to the shelter and find Fleet and Hope. But I put my finger on top of the man's plastic-shielded face. I skimmed the other pictures again. Some of the men looked in the camera, but most stared away to the side. The man from the park had an empty look. Nothing before and nothing after. Until that moment, I couldn't have described his features, but it turned out I had memorized them.

"That's him." I had a finger on the picture.

"Ms. Donaldo is indicating a positive on number eight," said Patz.

He turned to me and put an arm around the back of my chair and switched off the microphone. "Good going," he said. "That's it. You did the right thing."

"That's it, as in now I leave and the guy comes after me?" I said. "Won't he know I'm the one who turned him in?"

"We will be putting out a bulletin," said Patz. "We think we know where he is. He's not exactly a stranger to us, if you know what I mean, but neither was Shane. Neither of them was up to any good."

"What does that mean? Am I a stranger?"

"That depends," he said. "We see the same people every day. Not much is new to us. Your guy there was involved in some things, unfortunate things, but there is only so much we can do."

He shifted and his chair creaked. "We can find you a place to go," he said. "We can put you at the top of the waiting list and set you up with a caseworker, a bed, counseling. You can even keep your dog with you. You want to know why I walk the beat, instead of staying in here all the time? It's so I can talk to kids like you. One day you'll look back on this and hardly remember you were here. I've seen hundreds of kids pass through here and sometimes one will come back years later and you know what? The same thing happens every time. They thank us. They goddamn thank us."

"I'm not trying to go somewhere else," I said.

"Shane's parents told me they'd like to help you get off the street," he said.

"They talked to you about me?" I said, even though I knew. "They practically kidnapped me two nights ago."

"They're here at the station now," he said. "Most kids don't get offers like that. Think about it."

"Can I ask you one thing?" I said and didn't wait for him to answer. "Did that guy in the picture know Shane? Was there a reason he was in Shane's face? Or was it just a freak thing? They think I know something, but I don't. I mean, if they did know each other and they had some fight, then you should be out there talking to Shane's parents."

"Now you're thinking like a detective," he said, crossing his arms over his chest and half-smiling at me.

"Can I get out of here?" I said. Root was sitting by my side. He had gotten too comfortable at the station, probably because the cops kept dropping dog biscuits on the floor for him. He should've been the one identifying the creep in the picture because, after all, he was the only one who'd seen what happened. I came after it was too late.

"You're free," Patz said. "No one's keeping you here. But we'll need you when it's time to testify in court."

I didn't stop to think about what he meant by that. I picked up my pack and Root's leash and went to the door. Marva was sitting on the bench where I'd waited, her twig legs crossed, her eyes fixed on me as I made my way to the exit. Dave was next to her, his hands bunched in his lap. I wished that I felt like being nice to them, but seeing them there made me angry in a whole new way. I wanted to tell them to leave me alone. Why was I responsible for something I didn't try to see?

"Hi, Maddy," Marva said in a soft voice. I should not have paid attention to her, but of course I couldn't have known what she was going to unleash.

CHAPTER 13

Root knew when someone was keyed up and about to explode. It was like he could smell whatever was going on inside and seeped out onto your skin. He started licking Marva's arm and tried to climb over the back seat into in her lap.

"All I wanted was to see him," she said, like she was talking to Root. "Dave came out here once, but I stayed home. I was the worrier, like that was going to keep bad things from happening, so we both thought it would be better if he went alone. Plus, someone had to be in the store. It wasn't going to run itself."

She cradled Root's head and he stared at her. I had stomped out of the police station, but she'd called after me, her voice growing louder, as if I'd stolen something and she was going to turn me in. I'd turned around and followed her to the car.

The thing is, she said, she hated the store. She always had. She'd wanted to live right in Albany. She liked seeing people on the street, knowing they were headed somewhere important. But Dave insisted on staying in the country, near where he grew up. He never liked change. The hardware store, with its front window full of saws, power tools, and light fixtures, was always the same. The wood floor was so old and soft she felt like she was going to fall through. She didn't mind doing the bookkeeping two days a week; she was good at it, even though the small back office had started to feel like prison. It was so stuffy it was hard to breathe in there.

"Honey," Dave said, "I'm not sure Maddy wants to hear about all this."

Marva went on. She'd been at home the day they got a call from a police officer in San Francisco, she said. Dave had left early for work. The officer wanted to know if Shane Golden lived there. "Shane?" she'd said over and over, as if it was a question she didn't understand.

"What kind of mother doesn't know where her son is?" she said.

She must have said she was Shane's mother or the officer wouldn't have told her anything else. "I have some bad news," he'd said. "Shane had been," and she lowered her voice so I could hardly hear her say it, "the victim of a homicide." She said she'd started screaming at him, "Why are you telling me this?" She didn't get it. Who would call and say something like that? She didn't remember her neighbor coming over, but she must have been there, Marva said, because she found herself wrapped in a blanket, sitting on the couch, when Dave came home.

He had handled the details, calm and ordered, in the way he always was. It was what made him so good in the fire department, where everyone looked up to him. Stay focused, he always told them. Respond, assess, and then go forward. Don't rush in without all the information. He was the one who'd arranged for them to go to San Francisco.

"The worst thing was I never knew where Shane slept," Marva said. "You want to know that, where they put their head down at night. Then when I went to bed I could have pictured that. It would have helped. I should have been here with him. I thought I'd go later, but I didn't. You always think you have time."

She was the one who wanted to rearrange furniture, get new rugs every spring, cook new dishes from recipes she found in magazines. But ever since Shane had left she kept his room like he left it, the pictures on his wall, mostly cartoons he'd sketched of tiny armies of men facing off, a stockpile of catapults and bows and arrows behind them. She wished she'd asked him more questions when he was there because when she started examining the miniature cartoon faces after he left, she could tell each one was different. From a distance, they looked the same. Maybe he was telling a story, not just doodling.

The last time he'd called he almost sounded liked he missed her, but maybe she had imagined that. "Where are you staying?" she'd asked. He didn't answer. She had offered to wire him money and was half glad when he refused because Dave had said that only enabled him, and she should let him go and find his own path, as if she had any choice. He'd gotten off the phone as quickly as he could. "Bye, Ma," he'd said. "Some guys and I, we're going for food."

"The guys?" she said, turning to me again. "Do you know them? Who was he talking about?" But she didn't wait for me to answer.

"I thought he'd come back for Thanksgiving because we're always together then, no matter what," she said. "But clearly that didn't happen." She looked at me, pleading. "Why didn't I trace his phone? We could have pinpointed where he was. There is technology for that. At least we'd know where he was."

"We should have moved," she said to Dave, who was hunched in the driver's seat. Root had made it over the seat and was sandwiched between them. "There would have been more for him in a city. We could have lived out here." Her voice got louder. Dave reached over Root and put an arm around her. She slid away and turned completely around in her seat. "Ma," she said. "Just like when he was little. He called me Ma."

Marva grabbed at my hand. Maybe she thought that would help. I let her hold it as if it was some stuffed animal she could squeeze. It wasn't my hand anymore.

"Maddy, I don't expect you to understand, but I can't take it if he thought we didn't care. That could be the last thought he had. I need to know what was in his head. You have to tell me what he was doing here."

Marva was gripping my hand so tight she must have been able to feel my racing pulse. Root was licking her again. I pulled my hand away and dragged him into the back seat.

"I don't know what Shane was doing in the park," I said.

I opened the car door and shoved Root out onto the

pavement. My arms felt stiff from holding onto him so tight and my throat was achy.

"Please," cried Marva.

"I don't have anything to tell you," I said. And then, "I'll think about it." I had to say something to make her stop, even if it wasn't true.

CHAPTER 14

Hope and Fleet were sitting outside the smoke shop with the skateboarders from the shelter. Fleet had one of Ash's signs, with its blocky writing. $ FOR FOOD. She held it up as a two-story red tour bus passed, burping out a trail of dark smoke.

"This is for Ash," she said. "Double decker pussies." He thought we should be on the tourist maps, along with the head shops and poster stores and famous hippie corners. Make it official. Fleet put the sign down on the sidewalk, on top of a pile of his others.

"What's up with those?" I asked her.

"It's not like he's going to need them." She laughed. "In Wyoming."

Fleet put an arm around me. "Ash gave himself up," she said. "I thought at least he'd resist."

There was no legal way they could have made him go, not halfway across the country with some guy he'd never seen, she said, but he did. He looked shocked at first, then mad, swearing and having a fit, and then he gave up.

"The guy said it was a wilderness camp," said Fleet. "My mom said she was going to send me to one of those if I got kicked out of one more school. She kept putting me in these weird places where there were only four kids in a class or the teacher wanted me to talk about my relationship to math problems. I spent a lot of time in a chair in the hall, by myself, which was okay because they let me read. There was one where we tutored one another all day. I thought I was going to die in there. A wilderness camp might have been better."

I sat on the sidewalk and put my arms around Root. The top of his head still smelled smoky from the fireplace at Dave and Marva's.

"Maddy?" said Fleet, watching me press my face into Root's neck fur. "It's not like Ash is in jail. He can take care of himself there."

The skateboarders were looking through Ash's signs. One took a few and tied them on top of his pack. I felt knocked in the stomach. Why did he agree to go to Wyoming? What was he going to do in the wilderness?

Tourists passed, stepping over my pack and around Root, who was flopped beside me, still except for his tail waving around on the sidewalk. Every few minutes one of them dumped a few quarters into a dirty tweed cap Fleet had put on the pavement next to Tiny's cage. She pulled a book out of her pack.

"Go ahead," said a man wearing a Golden Gate Bridge T-shirt, his arm around a little girl with a blond ponytail. "You give it to them." He pushed her forward and she dropped a dollar in Fleet's cap. "Can she take a look?"

"She can hold him if she wants." Fleet put Tiny's cage on her lap.

"We just want to look," he said, and aimed his phone at her. "And get a picture for Mom."

"What an asshat," she said as he walked away. "Afraid of Tiny, in a cage."

"Let's get going," I said. Two bike cops were down the street headed toward us, scanning the sidewalk. I stood up, but Fleet didn't move. She said they had me trained. I said there was no way I was ending up at the cop station again. Then I told her about seeing those photos and pointing out the guy who killed Shane. Fleet wanted to know how I could be so sure it was the right guy. Maybe I didn't remember and the cops were pushing me into something, she said. They did that. They twisted what you said so they could arrest someone. That was their job so they had to make it happen. It didn't matter to them if they got the right person.

"My whole body knew it was him," I said.

"The police lie a lot, is all I'm saying," said Fleet.

"Everyone lies a lot." I took the book out of her lap and she snatched it back. I told her I didn't want to think about the cops anymore so I was going to the library. She said she and Tiny were staying put, she still had business.

Hope was on the next block in front of the biggest head shop, talking to a couple wearing baseball hats. The skateboarders trailed behind. One stomped on the edge of his board, flipped it in the air and caught it. Hope waved at him, like these were her tourists, stop the show. He gave her the finger, tossed his board into the street and took off, holding onto the back end of a delivery truck. Hope said hey when I walked by, then went on with her talk, telling the couple that she knew the owner of the head shop, he gave great deals to everyone she sent there. They looked at the front window filled with bongs, scented tobaccos, rolling papers, weed crushers, and souvenirs, but it didn't seem like they were going in. One took out a few bills and thanked Hope. She walked with me to the next corner, where a guy had set up with a guitar and a small amp, a shepherd mix curled next to him. The notes were sharp but sweet. Hope sat on the sidewalk across from him and didn't seem to notice when I left.

I tied up Root in a small concrete yard outside the library. There was already a bowl of water there and a pug mix with an underbite that was breathing like an overheated engine. I felt better about leaving Root with company, but he froze, looked stricken, like how could you do this to me, you are a traitor, but I walked up the stairs and didn't turn around again to look at him. It didn't matter. I could hear him thinking. Inside, the fluorescent lights almost blinded me at first. When my eyes adjusted, I could see the room was full, the way it got when it was cold out. Jax, sitting in his chair in the back, waved at me. I went past the front shelf of new books, past history, fantasy, and science to a couch next to the computers where I could crash and pretend to wait for a turn, and sank into the plastic hide of the couch, which whooshed underneath me.

A guy in a torn up khaki jumpsuit sank down next to me. He stretched out, but I pretended he wasn't there until he started patting the couch like he was giving it a shine. I turned to face the opposite direction and stared up at a mural on the ceiling, blue summer sky dotted with fluffy clouds, like that was going to relax people in this room. I thought about Ash hiking in a valley of orange poppies or whatever wildflowers grew in Wyoming. I was in a library so I could look it up, an idea that suddenly seemed hilarious. The guy on the couch started laughing with me.

I slid as far from him as I could. It must have satisfied him because he left me alone and dozed off with his head on his pack, which sounded like it was full of empty cans. I retied my boots and ran my fingers through my hair. Maybe I would go on the computer and look up wilderness camps in Wyoming, try to figure out which one Ash was in. How many could there be in a state where most people were cowboys? I could picture it from my elementary school textbook, a state shaped like a lunch box. But I couldn't remember whether it was filled with pictures of tiny bales of hay, lumps of coal, or only horses and cows. I used to like looking at the products each state produced. California had oranges and vegetables and little cameras that stood for the movies. I should have paid more attention to the other states.

I wondered if Ash was getting used to the camp. They were giving him food and a bed, even if it was in the middle of nowhere. He would be talking to everyone, like he always did. He might stay there. Fleet was right about Ash. He could take care of himself, but part of me hoped that he hated the camp, that he was yelling and swearing so much they'd throw him out.

The man next to me shuddered and fell off the couch with a thud that sounded like someone had dropped an armful of books. I couldn't tell if he was deep asleep or sick. A woman who worked in the children's section bent down and tapped his arm. His eyes fluttered open and closed.

"You need water?" She took out her phone and said she was calling for help. "Last time you wanted water."

"I don't need help," he said, and kicked her leg.

I grabbed my pack, ready to run, but instead stood next to her, as if I could save anyone. She kept looking at him, but didn't say anything. There was a red spot on her shin where he'd kicked her. We stayed there awkwardly until I heard sirens in the distance. Two cops ran up the stairs.

"Archie," said one of them, helping him to stand. "What's going on?"

The woman from the library described what had happened, how he'd passed out and fallen off the couch. She didn't say that he'd kicked her.

"We'll get him checked out," the cop said.

"But then he'll be right back here," she said. "What good is that going to do? He needs help."

"We have to take him in," the cop said. "even though it costs more than I'll ever make in this lifetime."

The two cops guided him to the door, Archie tripping to his knees every few steps.

"At least you're here," I said to Root outside, as I untied him. We went by the bookstore to get him a biscuit and then the music store for another one. Fleet was hanging in the doorway, Tiny hiding in the neckline of her sweatshirt.

"Mad," she said, and reached for me. My chest started to relax. We both started talking at once.

"Don't tell me how stupid I am. I know," she said.

"Me too," I said. "I'm a total idiot in a lot of ways. But you first."

She pulled out her money, which was wet, the bills stuck together.

"I made this whole stack and it was in my pocket," she said. "And then I sat on the fucking wet sidewalk again. Why don't I ever know from anything?"

I laughed. "I knew you'd do that," she said, and stomped off toward the Panhandle. "Fuck you, Mad."

I ran after her and caught her arm.

"Wait," I said. "We're coming."

We sat on the grass and I helped Fleet spread out the money. The edges were crisped up, but the centers looked like they were dissolving into pulp. I went back over the bills and patted each one. Even the bank wasn't going to take them this wet. The only thing to do was lay down next to them, give the sun a chance to do its work. We flopped, Fleet on her stomach, me on my back.

"This is going to take forever," she said, closing her eyes.

Sometimes it seems like she was wrecked by the smallest things. I couldn't tell her that I'd been at the library, about to look up Ash's camp and that a guy next to me almost died. He was probably being dumped back on the street already. I wondered if he had a family that ever went looking for him or if all he had was the woman at the library.

"Maybe you should teach reading, since you do it all the time," I said. Fleet sighed, eyes still shut. I put my head against her shoulder.

Root growled and Fleet and I sat up, but not fast enough. Two guys from ES EF ran in circles around us, grabbing the money. Root chased them and barked. He thought it was a game. One of them threw a dollar bill at Root, like that would stop him.

"Root get back here," I called, and he sat down next to me. I knew what they could do, so I put on his leash and held on to his neck. The guy straightened the bills into a neat package and tipped it at us, thank you very fucking much, before walking off. He was so sure he had us he didn't have to run. Fleet looked like she might jump on him. She had tears at the corner of her eyes. Now I couldn't tell her what happened in the library. I was going to, but I couldn't come up with the words when all she wanted was for me to take care of her. Of course, I couldn't do that.

CHAPTER 15

Ash stood in the shelter door, backlit by the hazy morning sky. He had been gone two weeks and he was tanner and his dreads were covered in back with a red beanie. We had finished breakfast and I was feeding Root bread that someone left on the table. I had imagined Ash with a shaved head, wearing military clothes. I had told myself stories about where he was, at a camp with a big fire pit in the middle. He would make breakfast with the other kids and then they would go hiking, a different trail every day. Maybe they went in a sweat lodge and talked about everything they had done wrong. I felt better after I imagined these scenes, like he was not lost to me, even though part of me wanted that. He had gone off and I wanted him to know I didn't care.

He opened his arms when he saw us and then he was down on his knees, hugging Root and me. Root licked his hands and Ash held me tight around the waist. He smelled of patchouli and sweat. I pounded a hand on his back, harder than I needed to.

"Let's get out of here," he said into my ear.

We sat down at the end of Haight, outside the music store. Root settled between my knees and I held onto Ash. He knew I was going to ask him why he went to Wyoming, because he started telling me about the day his mother had come to get him.

"I had my own kidnapping," I reminded him and pushed him in the ribs. He'd acted like I was lucky to go with Dave and Marva.

"My mother showed up here," he said. "No warning."

She had walked down Haight in her khakis and button-up sweater, followed by a man in cowboy boots. His mother didn't even greet him. She left that to the guy she was with, who grabbed Ash by the shoulders so he couldn't move.

"He called me son and said something about how things were going to get worse and then much better."

Ash didn't look him in the eyes, but the guy kept talking. Maybe the guy was planning to hypnotize him. Ash had heard about that. It was like being awake and asleep at the same time. You couldn't move or resist. He told Ash they were going, that it was not negotiable if he wanted to have any relationship with his mother, and Ash, who usually didn't take shit from anyone, got his pack and followed him even though he was twenty-two and no one could make him do anything. He refused to talk to his mother, though, who sat in the front seat of the car, a black pick-up with giant wheels, while they drove to the airport. On the drive, she turned around and handed him a folder from a place in the mountains that said it was a therapeutic wilderness camp.

"It had these stories of kids who sat on the couch getting stoned and playing video games or cutting school and being so drugged out of their minds they ended up at the camp, where they all learned their lessons and came out perfect," said Ash, sitting wedged up next to me, but looking straight ahead, a hand on Root's head. "I opened the window on the freeway and threw out the folder."

The rest of the drive he'd thought about how the guy driving the truck would have to put him in restraints or knock him out to get him on the plane. But when they got to the airport, his mother said she loved him but didn't much like him. She knew he didn't want to be in Arizona, but he had to be in a place where he could be productive. He could not stay on the street.

Then the guy opened Ash's door and Ash went with him, because what was he supposed to do? He couldn't stay there with his mother. She drove off, leaving him on the sidewalk with the guy. He said Ash could consider the trip a vacation, with rest, food, righteous people. And restorative nature. He could always come back to San Francisco. Ash thought again about bolting, but also how he had never been to Wyoming. It would be a mind trip. Maybe he would hike all the way back, have that to talk about. He might walk through the mountains, fish and hunt and eat wild berries, until he got back to the coast. Or he could get on a train and see every state on the way.

"Life is not endless, despite what you think," the guy said on the plane. "There's a limit. The next time you're picked up, the cops will keep you in jail."

"What did he mean?" said Ash. "Was he talking about how I was wasting my life and that smoking weed was making it harder for me to think straight? That's what my mother said. Or maybe he was saying my mother wasn't always going to be around, that next time no one would be there for me. He had me confused, which is probably what he wanted."

Ash said they landed at what looked like a toy airport. I'd only flown one time when my mom took me to Las Vegas. "At least you'll get a taste of the world," she said. When the plane lifted, I'd seen houses set in rows that stretched forever in a neat pattern, even though from the ground Los Angeles seemed like a place where you could get trampled or separated from everything you knew.

Ash climbed down from the plane onto a blacktop surrounded by nothing. It wasn't Arizona, where the desert was like a city. Everything he could see, including the mountains, was in the distance. The air was full of dust. He said he never realized how much he considered the mist that poured over San Francisco as the juice of life. I snorted.

"I know it sounds stupid," he said. "But when you go away you see it differently. I thought I was going to dry up and turn into dust."

"Then maybe some of you would have ended up back here and you'd be there every time someone breathed. You would get in our lungs." He put his hand over my mouth and his fingers tasted slightly sweet and salty.

"I was trying not to let the guy totally freak me out," said Ash. "He had me trapped."

Ash gripped me tighter and I let him stay like that. He said the guy drove and they didn't talk. By that time it had been so long since Ash spoke that he didn't know if he could. He wanted to ask questions, but he didn't want to make it look like he was okay with being swiped off the street by his own mother. He thought about opening the door and jumping out, but what was that going to do? He would tumble into the dirt by the road. He'd have broken arms and legs but he'd still be in Wyoming.

After an hour, they got to the camp. It didn't have horses or cows or most other animals he'd expected. There were only chickens and a big orange rooster, all walking around wherever they wanted. The kids stayed in round blue tents. Ash was assigned to one with two other guys. He put his stuff down on the only empty cot, next to folded sheets and a blanket with strings hanging off the end. Someone had combed the dirt floor into a neat swirled pattern. He lay down and looked up at the tent ceiling. The sound of his roommates' boots crunching outside woke him up. They didn't look happy to see that someone was occupying the free cot and he was not thrilled to see them either.

"So you're a hippie," said the first one to walk in. He had a slow southern accent. "I'm John Robert. The other kid nodded. "Sebastian," he said.

John Robert was from Tennessee, which is why he had two first names. Sebastian was from Connecticut. The only thing they had in common was getting kicked out of the house. John Robert was high every day, but his parents were more freaked that he always wore black clothes and thick black eyeliner. He couldn't figure out why they cared so much. In the end, he'd been happy to get away from them, even if it meant living in a tent and looking like everyone else in the world. Sebastian had stolen his grandmother's car when she was in the hospital and crashed it into a street pole. His parents didn't know that he'd been smoking A-bombs. It wasn't like he was addicted, he said. He could stop when he needed to.

Ash told them about Golden Gate Park. They'd never heard of it, but they both said they'd come when they left Wyoming. The three of them were like freaks from different worlds, but he sort of liked them, he said. He even lied and said he had a middle name when John Robert had said, "Yeah, Ash. And what else?"

"Ash Ralph?" I said. "Really?"

"I knew I shouldn't tell you," he said. "It was really my grandfather's name. He died five years ago of a lung disease he got from his construction job and he was the only half decent person in my family. He used to carry around an oxygen tank to breathe. Everyone else, they breathed normal, and acted like shit. I wish I had his name."

His new roommates showed him around the camp, which took about five minutes. Learning the rules took longer. They gave him a heavy coat, jeans, and work boots. He had to be in morning meeting at six every day, held in the only building, to go over the day's events. He had to help build the fire, cook, feed the chickens, and clean, which included the pointless task of raking the dirt in the tent. The only freedom he had was deciding which pattern to carve, a circle, tight square lines, zigzags. It all got ruined the second someone walked in so he didn't see why they bothered. The rooster was the worst, he said. It looked peaceful until he tried to gather eggs from the hens and then it tried to attack him. It charged at his knees and squawked. He'd gotten peck marks all over his legs.

After a few days Ash couldn't follow the rules, which reminded him of being in school. They were constantly on him for that. Even his eighth grade teacher had said he was hopeless with directions. He tried staying up all night so he wouldn't miss morning meeting, but then he fell asleep during the day and got written up for that. Then he had to bring it up in group therapy, where the twelve guys at the camp talked about taking responsibility and making amends. He had a personal goal of never talking during the group, which he usually messed up. He couldn't help that he liked to talk.

Most days they hiked for hours, climbed straight uphill and then had a view of the valley full of ponds and grass in every tint of green. He'd closed his eyes and tried to remember being in the park, or even back in Arizona. Each time it was harder. For a few seconds, everything from his life before seemed to fall away.

"I almost wished I could be the kind of person who lives in a place like that. But surprise," he said, and he pinched my waist, "I'm not."

The idea, the counselor said, was that when they were in nature, sober, they would be open to beauty, that much closer to finding purpose in the world. Ash didn't bother to tell him that he was already sober. He wasn't an addict and the weed and Wild Turkey were long out of his body. Sorry if he lived in the park and was not going to school, but those weren't crimes. His only crime was not being what his mother wanted.

It was growing colder every night, the snow on the mountains inching its way down to the valley. In the morning, the dirt outside was crusted with ice. Ash didn't want to stay around to find out what would happen when the canvas on the tent froze solid. And he wasn't sure how staying in Wyoming was putting him closer to his purpose, if he had one. John Robert and Sebastian talked about how they were making what the camp called future contracts. Sebastian was thinking about studying behavioral psychology in college. John Robert said he might learn car repair or astronomy. Maybe he would get shot into space, see Mars.

At the end of the week, Ash told his counselor he wanted to go back to San Francisco. The counselor tried to talk him into staying for the solo journey, a night alone on the mountain, but Ash said he was already on a solo journey.

"Most of the reason," Ash said, pressed closer to me, "was you."

"I want to see Mars," I said. I gathered his dreads into a single tail.

"I'd go to Mars with you, but then you'd want to leave and we'd be fucked," he said.

He stood and offered an arm to hoist me up, pack on one arm, Root's leash on the other. There was a new awkwardness as we walked to the corner store. Nothing had changed and everything had changed. I hadn't told him about going with the cops to identify the guy who killed Shane.

"I've got funds," Ash said, pulling out some bills from his front pocket. "They gave these to me when I left, like they were paying for the time I spent there. At least I can buy."

He disappeared into the store. I stayed outside with Root because they didn't allow animals. Except cockroaches and mice, which you could usually see if you stayed there long enough. They had posted signs on all their windows, CLEAN UP CACA, with a little picture of a dog squatting, a red line through its butt. NO LOITERING. I stood in the doorway and watched Ash at the counter, across from a guy named Sammy who sometimes came outside and smoked with us. He had been a bodybuilder and had bulging arms that hung away from his body when he walked.

"Missed you," he said, slapping Ash's shoulder. "Where you been? Behind bars?"

"Away with my family, which was worse," said Ash. "But you can relax. I'm back."

"Nice to know you have people," said Sammy. "Because you know what, buddy? I wondered."

He rang up a bottle of Hennessey and a large bag of potato chips. In between slugs of whiskey and handfuls of chips, I told Ash about Dave and Marva's cabin and the police line-up. I was hoping the guy I'd picked out was in jail, but I wasn't sure. No one had told me. He could be on the street, waiting. I'd thought about asking one of the beat cops on the street, but why would I want to start talking to them?

"I could have stayed in Wyoming and you could have gone off and lived in a cabin in Marin?" he said. "That's crazy."

Ash took out a joint, twisted up the end and lit it. He inhaled hard, a screwball smile breaking out as he passed it to me. I told him no, I couldn't take it right then, not with the Hennessey. I had to be conscious.

"More for me," he said, holding the joint between his thumb and first finger, his pinky out straight. Fleet and Hope showed up, along with a group of guys from Santa Cruz. Three small dogs, tied together with rope, toggled behind them. One guy leaned down and took the joint from Ash and then started pumping an accordion that was tied around his neck. The others sat next to us along the wall and the dogs settled in a pile, as far from Root as they could. It didn't take long for a small crowd to gather. The accordion wailed on until Sammy came out with a push broom under his arm.

"How am I supposed to do business with you out here?" he yelled.

The crowd ignored him. People were watching and some danced around to the music. Sammy started sweeping with his broom like he was going to wipe us all off the sidewalk. We knew how he could act so I pulled Ash up and motioned to Fleet and Hope to get moving. When I looked back the guy was still playing his accordion. One of his buddies had set out CDs for sale. Sammy was still yelling.

"You see, nothing changes," said Ash.

But something was different. For starters, Ash had his arm around me and I let him. He was half blasted, but I was comfortable holding onto him on the way toward the park. Fleet and Hope tagged behind. We all stopped at the lake to talk to some kids who had just come from Colorado for a concert, which was not for two weeks. Hope, the tour guide, told them when to show up for dinner at the shelter, and how early they had to be there if they wanted to stay overnight. She went on about how to get on the waiting list if they didn't have space. I stared at her in an accusing way. They were band groupies, hauling army backpacks, long blades hooked to their belts. You couldn't tell what was up with them. They were twitchy, then mellow. And we'd have to listen to them argue about which songs they wanted to hear at the concert, like they were going to kill one another over that.

"Fuck it," I whispered to Ash. "Let's go."

We left Fleet and Hope, who had settled into the Colorado circle, passing a tall bottle of beer and a pipe. They didn't notice we'd gone. We threaded past two other groups on the lawn near the pond and one guy passed out on his back. His face was red from sleeping in the sun and whatever else he'd been doing. He half smiled, deep in a dream that probably was better than the littered grass where he was sprawled. I looked at his chest to see if it was moving. How else would I know if he was dead? He didn't look that different from Shane, except his eyes were closed. Maybe people died with their eyes open, a last second when they knew what was happening.

"You think he's breathing?" I said to Ash.

Ash tapped the guy's foot. He shifted his legs and stopped smiling but didn't open his eyes. "He's fine. Are you worrying about everyone now? How about giving me some of that?"

"I keep thinking about Shane," I said. "What did he do that was so different from that guy, who you're right, is obviously not dead? Let's get out of here."

The shopping cart was parked at our sleeping spot, half full of recycled bottles, so Ash rattled it off outside the ring of trees. He asked if I wanted anything and opened his hand, which held the end of a joint and a small white pill. I shook my head.

"I don't need it either," he said, reaching for me. "There isn't anything I need that's not here."

The leaves crinkled under our bodies. Ash smoothed my hair and looked me in the eyes for a long time and then he kissed me. I ran my hands over the muscles on his shoulders, rubbed lightly along the back of his neck. We both kept our eyes open until we were too close and couldn't see anything. His face was a blur. And then his hands were all over me. I helped him peel off my jacket, shirt, and pants and then he was inside of me. The carpet of leaves felt spongy and thick at first until we moved and I could feel tree roots stabbing me in the back. I winced and arched away.

"Is this the time I'm supposed to say I was thinking about this the whole time I was in that nature camp?" he said, lying on top of me. "Because I did think about this. The whole time."

"You're still a jerk," I said.

"Almost the whole time," he said.

"Uh, hey," said Hope.

I jumped up and held my clothes in front, like blocking the view would make it seem like nothing had happened.

"You got anything left or you bogarting as usual?"

Ash reached for his pants and slowly stepped into them. He didn't try to hide himself, acted like it was normal to be there, his small clamshell ass in Hope's face. He took out a joint and passed it to her. I was in my clothes by the time it got to me and I handed it over to Fleet, who was fussing with Tiny's cage, which was dented on one side. She reached inside and put him inside the sleeve of her sweater, where he dug in his pearly sliver of nails. I attached Root's leash to my ankle and sat next to her, passing up on the joint. I had enough to think about, trying to take apart whatever had just happened. I tipped my head back and could see fog starting to filter through the tree branches above us.

CHAPTER 16

I was lying on the dirt where we'd all passed out when I felt a slap on the bottom of my foot. A cop shined a long metal flashlight into my eyes and I reached for my shoes. Ash had forgotten to set the clock.

"Move on. No camping. You have ten seconds to get going."

He began counting out loud. "One. Two." He smacked Ash's foot with the back of his hand. "Three." He moved on to Fleet and Hope. We hadn't bothered to get into sleeping bags so we stood and staggered away from the trees. "Four. Five." Hope started saying that we were hanging out, not camping, it was a public park and we had a right to be there, but Ash grabbed for her arm and she stopped. There was no point bullshitting him, except to wait for Fleet, who was still curled on her side, "Six," he yelled. Tiny cuddled in her arm. The cop poked the bottom of her foot again, but she didn't budge. "Seven!"

"Better tell your friend to get up." The cop rested his hands on his belt, near where his gun was holstered tight to his body. "Her ten seconds is almost over."

I knelt down in the leaves next to Fleet and shook her shoulder, but she didn't move so I touched her cheek, halfway between a pat and a slap. Her face was warm. I waited for her to tell me to get off her, give her a second, and I would say she couldn't have that because the cop was about to cite us. Tiny backed up and hunched himself into a ball.

"Ash, help me get her up," I said.

"You kids got dogs, now you got rats," said the cop. His knees cracked as he bent down toward Fleet. He put his knuckles on her shoulder and pressed, like he was knocking.

"She's really out," he said, and reached for his radio. "10-52, east end."

He aimed the flashlight at Fleet's face and felt for her pulse. Tiny stayed on her arm, until the cop smacked him with the flashlight and he scrambled into the leaves. He dragged his right side where the cop had hit him. I tried to grab him, but he skittered away and it was too dark to see where he'd gone. I was still trying to make out where he was when an ambulance drove up on the grass, a spotlight aimed at Fleet. Two men, one carrying a small suitcase, ran to her. He took out a stethoscope, rolled her onto her back and cocked his head while he listened to her chest. He pried open one of her eyes with his fingers.

"She's breathing, but it's shallow," he said. Then he turned to the three of us. "What did she ingest?"

"Nothing," said Ash.

"Nothing isn't going to put her out like this," he said. "If you care about your friend, and I don't know the answer to that, you'll tell us what she's on."

"She's not like that," I said, loud. "She didn't take anything besides what we all had." Of course, she could have gotten anything in the park, but Fleet usually knew where her stuff came from. She didn't buy from people in the park who would pass off anything, angel dust, X, doses cut with chalk or talcum. On the surface she could be friendly, huff whatever was offered, hang with anyone new at the shelter, but in the back of her mind she worried that they would turn on her. That's why she had Tiny. Rats are smarter than dogs, she said. They had extra intuition. She'd said she was going to appoint him as official taster, give him food we found and throw out anything he refused to eat. He would know if something was wrong.

Despite the siren and the lights, Fleet still didn't move. I thought about Shane, who'd spent his last minutes with me. Fleet didn't know I was there with her either, but her eyes were closed, not staring up at the black sky. You'd think the medics would know enough not to leave her on her back, where she could suck whatever she heaved up into her lungs.

The man with the stethoscope reached for Fleet's arm. "I'm going to give you something you're not going to like," he said, and tapped her wrist again hard.

"This will send her into withdrawal," he said to us, loading up a syringe. "But it saves lives. We'll take her in as soon as she's stabilized."

"She doesn't shoot up or anything," said Ash, "so whatever you're giving her, she doesn't need it."

The cop told Ash to stand back and he picked up Fleet's backpack and started taking out everything: her clothes, little wads of paper with food for Tiny, a few books, a plastic envelope that held what she called her important papers. He dropped them on the grass. There was a single dollar bill, more scraps of paper, a two-inch pencil stub.

"Anyone know her next of kin?" he said, shining his flashlight on the small pile he'd scattered. "Even her full name?"

"She has a mom in the East Bay, I think," said Ash.

"You have a phone number?" said the cop.

Ash shook his head. I wasn't sure what her last name was. Whatever, it didn't matter. Fleet had told me about her foster mom. She worked for the city, as a clerk. I couldn't remember which city. But I'd seen a picture of her once, sitting at a desk with a cigarette in her hand, her stubby legs crossed. I could probably find the spot where that picture was hidden in her backpack. But she and her mom were not talking right now. She'd told Fleet she wanted to give it a rest, live her life and Fleet could do as she pleased. And don't expect any money or come calling for a place to stay. Fleet had gone to so many schools and she was tired of people who wanted to fix her. At least she told the truth, Fleet said.

"We are her next of kin," I said.

"Yeah, I'm sure you are," said the cop.

The medics, one at her feet, the other at her shoulders, lifted her onto a stretcher and rolled it over to the ambulance. Fleet didn't move, even when they stuck another needle in her arm and held up a bag of clear liquid that began slowly dripping into her body.

"She's going to General," said the cop. "Since you're her kin, you might want to follow."

I tried to convince Hope to take Root but she said she was going to look for Tiny and then she had work to do. I reminded her that Root was usually good for work, that tourists gave more money if you had a dog. But she said she was too tired to drag him around the street all day. She didn't know how to take care of anyone.

We tied up Root outside the hospital and I twisted a note around his collar. WAITING. I DON'T BITE. It was all I could do, but I thought about how I'd found him, alone, tied to a pole on the street. What if someone took him? I had to tell myself not to think about that. I was at the hospital, someone's next of kin. But I had no idea what I was supposed to do. It hadn't occurred to me, not seriously, that Fleet was going to die, until I walked into the hospital. The waiting room was smaller than I expected, especially for a hospital the size of a city. We had followed the signs, turning left and right and edging around sides of buildings, past offices where they took care of one single part of your body, kidneys or lungs or ears, until we found the door marked EMERGENCY.

I'd been in a hospital before to see my mother, but not in the emergency section. We had to take off our backpacks and put them through an x-ray machine. Then a security guard opened them up and sifted through our junk. He took the pocketknife Ash kept in his boot and told him he'd have to check it.

"No weapons," he said, pointing to a sign written in about twelve languages. In case you didn't get it, there was a picture of a gun with a line through it. Same with a bottle and a flaming cigarette. Another had a cartoon of a tiny baby lying in one huge hand, with the words SAFE SURRENDER SITE. Did it mean you could have your baby there and leave, or maybe dump off a kid that you didn't want? It bothered me that someone could drive up and leave a baby. They probably had a room where all the babies waited in cribs, screaming, expecting that someone would come and get them.

More signs said the room was only for patients and family, that we were being videotaped, that anyone could get care even if they didn't have money. No cell phones. No littering. Rows of small black metal chairs sat around the edges of the room and there was a TV bolted to the ceiling blaring a local news show. Most of the light in the room came from three giant vending machines.

We got in line behind a man with a blue paper mask on his face, leaning heavily on a woman who looked like she was his mother. They had the same coffee-colored skin and creases around their eyes, except his were almost closed with pain. He coughed and she adjusted his mask and then patted his hair. A tall man with one crutch got in line after us. He kept shifting the crutch from side to side and groaning.

A nurse came out from behind the desk and took the arm of the man with the mask, guiding him toward a set of doors that automatically opened as she approached.

"We'll get you registered inside," she said. He looked confused, but then he nodded. The woman who was with him gripped his hand and I could tell she must be his wife and not his mother.

"Next," called the woman behind the desk.

Ash explained that we were trying to find out about Fleet, that we were family. The woman tilted her head to one side, like she was going to say something about how stupid did we think she was. But instead she asked us to sign in on a clipboard and said that a doctor would come and talk to us when they were finished with Fleet. My whole body had felt like a balled-up fist and when she said Fleet's name I relaxed a little. It meant she was alive. The woman at the desk typed the information Ash gave her into a computer.

"You're her brother?" she said.

"Step," he said. "That's why we have different last names."

"And you?" she said, looking at me.

"We're married," Ash said.

"Okay," said the woman. "You need to sign too."

I stared at Ash's back while he talked to her. It felt like I'd known him my whole life, but there was no way I'd ever call him my husband, even though it's what Hope said so guys would leave her alone. Pizza John was her husband and he was only around for a week. I thought back to what happened with Ash last night. My husband, at least in the hospital. It still didn't sound right. Family. That's what he'd told the woman.

"Maybe you should sit down," she said, looking at me.

The bright lights, the sharp smell of disinfectant, hospital food, were making me dizzy and off-center. I put my head back against the wall. I was supposed to be thinking about Fleet, but I was trapped in the whirring sensations around me. I couldn't think straight. Everyone in the waiting room was hoping someone would fix what was wrong, but I knew that might not happen. This was a place where everything changed.

"She'll be okay," Ash said, but when he turned around he could see I was holding onto the wall. I made my way over to a row of chairs. Ash sat next to me, but he was not trying to calm me down. My head was about to explode, blow up into a million pieces and settle in with all the diseases and germs and broken people in the room. I couldn't calm Ash down either, even if we were supposedly married.

I was panic breathing, but I closed my eyes until it slowed down. Ash put his hand on my leg. I snuck a look at him and he seemed far away. He could at least be telling me that Fleet was going to make it. But neither of us said anything. Ash eventually turned so he could watch the TV. I tried to force myself to sleep, but it didn't work. I don't know how long we sat there. The swinging doors finally opened and a young doctor with moles all over his face announced that he was looking for Fleet's family.

"Over here." I waved.

He pulled up a chair and crossed his legs. He said they had seen ten other cases of black tar heroin the past week and he figured that's what hit Fleet. But then he'd gotten the results of her urine test.

"She was lucky we got her fast," he said. "She probably swallowed some combo, a pill laced with synthetic opiate. We'll see how she does, watch her for more seizures."

"How did she get that?" I said. "We were with her." Which was mostly true, except when I was off rolling in the leaves with Ash.

"It's in pills, you name it, and we're seeing it cut into heroin. Someone sold it to her, or she found it," the doctor said. "She tested positive for one of the benzos. And Fentanyl. I expect you know what I'm talking about."

"She wouldn't eat a pill," I said. Ash was quiet, his hand still sitting on my leg.

"We'll have to watch her closely for a while, but we are cautiously optimistic," said the doctor. "There were no track marks that we could see. But you tell me what she was doing."

"Can we go see her?" I said. It couldn't be good that he used two words that didn't go together. Cautiously optimistic. It was something people did when they wanted to throw you off. Even I knew that.

"She's unconscious right now," he said. "It will be a few hours before we know anything more. And the blood work will take a few days. I'll let her know you came by. You are?"

"Ash and Maddy," said Ash. "Her step-brother. And his wife. My wife. Tell Fleet we're out here waiting," said Ash.

"You kids live in the park?" said the doctor, who wasn't far past being a kid himself.

"We do okay," said Ash.

"Your friend didn't look okay," he said. "But I'm not going to lecture you." He sat in a chair next to Ash. "Well, yes, I am. I see people in here all the time who are addicted or they got fired or thrown out of the house and it's too hard to climb back and start again. To tell you the truth, I have no idea what to tell them. But you kids, when I see an OD like this one, it bothers me in a whole different way." He took a deep breath. "I hope I won't see you in here again."

"Message received," said Ash.

"We need to watch her and reevaluate her neurological status when the drugs wear off," said the doctor. "That will give us more information."

"We'll stay," I said.

"Can you fill in some blanks on the forms?" the doctor said. He took a paper from his pocket, unfolded and smoothed it. "You know the name of her parents or guardians?"

Ash and I looked at each other and said nothing. What were we supposed to do? I didn't know how to reach her foster mom. If I did, would Fleet want to talk to her? Was she going to say, "Hey, I got poisoned, but don't worry. Like you ever did."?

I was relieved that Ash didn't try to make up their names.

"Her age?" the doctor said. "I assumed she lived in the park where the ambulance crew found her? You have a last known address?"

"She's twenty-one," said Ash. "She stayed in the park." He corrected himself. "Stays."

The doctor said he'd come back when he had something to report. He said the woman at the desk could get us water, that she also had a flier with some resources, if we wanted that. Ash put his arm around me and it seemed like he was shivering.

"What?" I said. He looked away.

"I should be here, not Fleet," he said.

"You knew all this time what was going on with her?" I said, and pushed his arm away.

Ash said it wasn't like that, he'd gotten one dose from the Colorado guys. One fucking pill. They'd said it was a downer. Fleet wanted it, so he'd handed it over. He was talking in a soft voice because people in the waiting room were looking over at us. How was he supposed to know? He'd take it back if he could. He'd swallow it himself.

I couldn't look at him, but I put my hand on his arm. Fleet was lying in the hospital and Ash was sitting next to me, alive. It didn't make sense. I turned away and looked at the TV news. A woman shot dead in Hayward, a bus crash on the 101, a hit and run in the financial district. The news lady, wearing a red suit coat, sat at a desk in front of photos of the murder scene and then the accident. A million terrible things were happening right now and Fleet in the hospital, unconscious, was just one of them.

I told Ash I was going to check on Root, mostly because I had to get away from him. Root was asleep, like nothing had happened, but he jumped up when he saw me. I had my head against his neck when Ash ran out to say that Fleet was awake. She knew her name and what year it was. The doctor said she needed to stay in the hospital, but she was going to be alright. I tried not to laugh when Ash told me, because she was never going to be alright. She started off whacked. But the test showed she didn't have brain damage. I yanked Root into my lap and kissed him on the head. Ash handed me a bottle of water and the flier "Homeless Connections," which the woman at the desk had given him. I tossed it on the pavement where Root had been tied up and we left to go back to the park.

....

Fleet was back two days later, looking bleached but alive. She was all one color, yellowish white skin, light brown eyes, strawberry hair, which together made it look like she'd disappeared. We brought her a sack of clothes from the free basket at the shelter. Black striped leggings, a red filmy shirt and a purple hoodie that said Star Power on the back. We figured the clown costume would make her feel better, especially when we had to tell her about Tiny. Hope had discovered him under the shopping cart at the bottom of the hill and put him in a plastic grocery bag. Fleet reacted better than we thought. Maybe she was too tired to throw a fit. We found a shoebox in the dumpster and buried him near our spot. Fleet wrote a note and dropped it into the box before we patted it down into the ground. It was the first funeral I'd been to. I had a knot in my throat that dissolved and then I was crying. I'd seen Shane and that didn't do it to me, but I didn't see him buried. Ash played his guitar for a few minutes afterward and then it was over.

"You cry less than any girl I ever met," he told me later, when we were wrapped in a pair of sleeping bags not far from Tiny's grave.

I turned away and kept my elbows at my sides so he couldn't get near. I told him how stupid it was to think that girls cry more than anyone else. I hardly ever cried, but I got ripped up harder inside because of it. He said he was sorry and I told him it was okay. I made him promise he would be there if the guy who killed Shane got out of jail. I didn't want to be alone if that happened.

CHAPTER 17

"Look who's here," Ash said.

We were sitting in a tree near our sleeping spot, legs wrapped around the lowest branch. He jumped down and kept his hands by his sides, let the cop see he didn't have anything on him he was trying to hide, which was pointless. They all knew what he had.

I slid down next to him and faced Officer Patz. Small tufts of bark clung to my jeans. None of us had paid the fine for blocking the sidewalk, so he could take us in and keep us locked up until we had a hearing. In my head, I was rehearsing what to say. It wasn't a crime to sit down in public. I wasn't bothering anyone. We weren't camping. We weren't lying down.

"Maddy," said Patz, "we've arrested the man you identified, the one we believe killed Shane. We're calling on you to come testify about what you saw."

He handed me a piece of paper and all I read was YOU ARE COMMANDED TO APPEAR at the top, and a line with my name. And then below it his name, Jeremiah Wakefield. Patz said they were holding him for drinking out of an open bottle on the street, but that was just until they could get the details to charge him with murder. He said all I had to do was show up so they could make it official. He said not to let the summons scare me. They would hold a preliminary hearing next week to gather all the evidence and make sure they had a good case. That's where I would come in, telling them everything I'd seen. Then they could lock Jeremiah Wakefield up for a long time. Patz probably forgot that he could arrest all of us for drinking out of open bottles, carrying a blade or smoking weed on the street, for living and breathing out there. I stood there looking at the paper like it was the first thing I'd ever read in my life.

The day of the hearing it was raining and I felt bad leaving Root with Fleet, but she said she didn't mind. I thought Root might cheer her up. She was quieter since she'd gotten sick. She said she was thinking of getting a rabbit. Ash so far had talked her out of it, saying it would make every dog go crazy. It would be like putting out dinner on a big tray.

"Root wouldn't go after a rabbit," Fleet said, kneeling and putting an arm around his muscled neck. He licked her on the mouth.

It took us an hour to get to the courthouse, walking all the way down Haight to where the street was lined with new concrete and glass buildings that fit together like a giant puzzle. You could see people in their apartments, sitting on long couches, watching screens flickering light across the wall. We passed around the back of the gleaming gold dome at city hall.

A guy standing on the steps tapped out a dope dance, hopping from foot to foot while his hit took hold. The rain glued strands of his hair to his head.

We crossed under the freeway and walked past a row of tents on the sidewalk crowded with suitcases, bikes, and shopping carts. Ash nodded at a group sitting in canvas chairs.

"Pack up while you can," said a guy with a red knit cap pulled down to his eyebrows, his feet on a cardboard box. He pointed at a garbage truck parked a block away. "They say you'll get everything back if you tag it, but you won't. It'll all end up in the trash."

It happened every week, the guy said. He'd move around the corner, then come back after the truck went by. One week they put giant rocks on the sidewalk, like that was going to keep people away. The rocks actually blocked the wind that gusted under the freeway.

"Can you help us out?" said a lady with a long ponytail, sitting next to him. She had a pile of folded blankets on her lap.

Ash said he didn't have anything, that we were on our way to court. He pulled his pockets inside out to show her. Not money, the woman said. She needed us to carry her stuff over to the parking lot of a computer store across the street, where she could sit in peace. They didn't bother people over there. I told her maybe later, we had to go. I hoped Ash wasn't going to start talking about the guy in the park and how I had to be at a hearing.

"There won't be no later," said the woman.

The garbage truck started moving toward us. Two workers in yellow vests stood on a metal bumper in back, then jumped down when they reached the tents. They tossed mounds of cardboard, plastic jugs and clothes into the back of the truck, which opened like a giant mouth to accept it all. "Hello," one yelled into a deserted tent, before knocking it over. The woman put her blankets and bags into a shopping cart.

"I have grandkids your age," she said, looking at us. "They all moved back to Missouri to be with their mom." She pushed her cart away, down the street. The guy in the knit cap walked behind with his box.

Why did people keep asking me for things I couldn't do? I shouldn't have to go to court, not for someone I didn't even know. I'd put on a clean pair of pants from the shelter box that morning. I thought it might be better to show up looking fresh, but I couldn't figure out why I'd bothered.

There was a line of people waiting to get inside the courthouse, past a security gate. We inched our way up to the x-ray machines. There were two ladies in red and yellow saris, their heads draped with filmy scarves, some guys speaking in a language I didn't know, a teenage kid with the beginnings of fuzz and pimples, headphones stuck in his ears. Some of us would end up in jail and some of us would help send other people to jail. We dropped our packs on the conveyer belt and a sheriff waved a wand around our bodies, a little too close. Then we went to the cop station on the first floor, just like they'd told us, to find out where to go.

"People versus Jeremiah Wakefield," said the clerk. "Fifth floor. Wait outside until you're called."

We sat on a wood bench outside the courtroom, our packs against our knees. I tried to remember what Jeremiah looked like in the park but could only call up the picture in the line-up. Maybe I'd picked out the wrong guy. My mouth was dry. I would have trouble speaking with my tongue stuck up against my teeth. Was Jeremiah going to be in there? I pulled my hair back and wiped my face with my hands. Ash tugged on my ponytail and rubbed his thumb on my chin. We sat like that until the door opened and a guy in a beige uniform announced my full name, where it echoed down the hallway. "Miss Madlynne Donaldo."

I waved and he said Ash could come with me. I grabbed his hand, even though I'd avoided it when we were on the street, under the freeway where people were all wandering like ghosts. I was more scared of the room, the seating area that looked like a cheap movie theater where, raised on a platform, a lady judge in a black robe stared at me.

The man who'd led me in guided me to a seat on the platform by her side. He told me to raise my right hand and say my name and then spell it. He asked if I promised to tell the truth. I barely got out a whisper of an answer and he made me say it again. "Yes," I said. It came out a strange peep, but loud enough for the judge to hear.

She asked me if I knew why I was there. I nodded. She said it was a preliminary hearing to decide if the case would proceed.

She told me to answer out loud because the recorder couldn't pick up gestures and did I understand that? I said I did. She had a firm but soft voice, same as her face and hair, which was molded into a low bun. She said there was nothing to worry about, that I just had to tell the truth. I was breathing fast and my heart was pounding, like I was going to spew onto her desk. But I said yes to everything, as if I knew how what happened out in the park ended up in this room.

I searched the seating section for Ash and saw Dave and Marva, sitting in the middle. Dave smiled at me, but I ignored him. Ash was on the other side of the aisle from them. I breathed a little more slowly seeing him, his eyes fixed on me. I would pretend I was talking to him.

But then I saw Jeremiah Wakefield, up front at a table next to a woman in a suit as tight as a bandage. His hair was almost shaved off and his beard was gone. He looked skinnier and older, but it must have been him. Even sitting, hunched in his jumpsuit, he was hulking tall. His hands were pressed together in a knot on the table. He looked at me and blinked, but otherwise had no expression. I tried to look away, but I couldn't. This guy had put a knife through Shane's heart, even if I didn't see him do it. I'd only seen him standing next to Shane. Maybe Shane had done something to start a fight. How did I know?

"Good morning, Madlynne," said a man in a black suit standing at a microphone in front of the judge's platform. "Can I call you Maddy?"

I nodded and the judge told me I had to use my voice. "Yes," I said.

He said he was a lawyer for the people, and that he wanted to know what happened in the park the morning Shane Golden was killed. He pointed and asked if I'd seen the man in the orange jumpsuit before. I told him I had. Then he asked me where I'd seen him and I looked down.

"Don't be afraid," he said. "Tell the court where you saw the man you just identified, who, for the record, is Jeremiah Wakefield." He asked me where I'd been on some Wednesday, at some specific time. I looked down. How was I supposed to know that? I twisted in the chair, crossed and uncrossed my legs.

"I'm not sure what day it was or what time," I said.

"But you were in the park when you saw Mr. Wakefield, who is sitting here now?"

"Yeah," I said.

"Sorry, but can you speak more clearly?" he said.

"Yes," I shouted.

He said it was okay, not to worry, and asked me to explain how I happened to see Mr. Wakefield. I told him about running after Root and finding Shane lying on the ground. Actually, I didn't know if Shane was alive or dead. I couldn't see if he kept breathing. And, of course, I didn't know who Shane was then. He was just a kid in the park. But then I saw this guy standing there. He yelled at me and told me to control my dog, so I took off.

He kept asking me questions. How many steps away was Jeremiah Wakefield? Did I see a knife? Was it pointed up or down? I didn't know about any knife, I told him. Then he said he was done and the woman in the tight suit got up. She said she was Mr. Wakefield's lawyer and she looked at me like I was the saddest thing she'd ever seen. She asked me where I came from and how long I'd been in the park and if I associated with other homeless people there. The people's guy jumped up and said he objected, what difference did that make, and the judge told him to sit down. "Continue," she said to the woman, who kept asking me questions. She wanted to know how often I used drugs. How much did I drink? Was I high the day I saw Jeremiah Wakefield?

"Objection!" The people's guy yelled. The judge told me I didn't have to answer.

"Did you notice anything else about the defendant? Did he have any wounds?" said Jeremiah Wakefield's lawyer. "Was he bleeding?"

"There was a little blood on his face, but I didn't stick around long enough to see where it came from," I said.

"No, of course not," she said. "But you did see blood?"

"Yes," I said. "A little bit. And it seemed like he was out of it or wrecked. Or something. He said he knew where to find me, but I'd never seen him before."

I could hear Dave and Marva shifting in their chairs and then the sound of Dave crying. Jeremiah Wakefield looked at me again.

"Little shit didn't see anything." I knew the voice. That is something that doesn't change.

"Mr. Wakefield, you will refrain from speaking while the witness is in the box or I will hold you in contempt of court," said the judge.

Then she told me not to blurt anything out, to wait for the questions. I told her I would try. The judge said we were almost done and she thanked me again. Then a guy in a sheriff uniform snapped on a pair of plastic gloves and held up a knife. The lawyer in the tight suit wanted to know if I recognized it. I almost laughed. I picked Jeremiah Wakefield out after he'd cut off his hair, taken a shower, and changed clothes, but no way did I remember seeing a knife. It seemed like they wanted me to lie and say I did.

The sheriff dropped the knife in a plastic bag and made a big show of sealing it up. Jeremiah Wakefield's lawyer walked to the microphone. She asked me how I was doing, as if she hadn't heard my answer the first time. I looked up at the ceiling, small squares of off-white tiles covered with tiny black dots, all lined up. I could probably figure out how many there were. Count the number on one side, then the other and multiply.

"Your Honor," she said, in the most suck-up voice. "I'd like to point out the defendant had a defensive wound on his forehead and this witness can't even say if he had a knife. She did not see any confrontation. He was clearly acting to protect himself against Shane Golden, who attacked him with no provocation."

"Is that all for this witness?" said the judge.

She said it was and she sat down next to Jeremiah Wakefield. He ignored her and kept looking down at his hands. The judge told me I could go sit in the courtroom or leave, it was up to me. My part of the proceeding was over. I sat down next to Ash. "He looks guilty as shit," he whispered. The people's lawyer stood up and said he knew it was out of the ordinary for a preliminary hearing, but he was moving to admit into testimony a statement from Shane Golden's parents. Jeremiah's lawyer yelled out that she objected, but the judge said she'd allow it because it might shed light on Shane's state of mind. Dave walked to the front of the room and unfolded a sheet of paper from the pocket of his gray blazer, which looked brand new. You could see the lines of dried tears on his face.

"We did not know what Shane wanted or why he came here," he said. It was clear he hadn't shown his speech to Marva because he looked at her uncertainly while he read and then suddenly he stopped. "Excuse me," he said, and swallowed loud a few times as if he had something in his mouth that was about to choke him. The sheriff came over and gave him a small paper cone of water. Dave gulped it and held up a hand to the judge. She'd probably seen fathers lose it before.

"I'm okay," he mouthed silently and then he started again. "I know he got into trouble out here, he probably did things he shouldn't have. What I can tell you is that he had a good heart. He did not deserve to die. We loved him, even when he withdrew and wouldn't talk to us. And he loved his family, particularly his older brother and his two nephews, who will never get to know him. Our lives will never be the same. Whatever this fellow goes on and does," and he pointed at Jeremiah Wakefield, who still looked down at the table like he didn't hear, "Shane's life is over. And we are staring at a blank wall that will block out every last thing."

Dave kept reading, but I walked out, along with Ash, and sat on the bench next to the door. I couldn't take Dave going on about Shane and the holes in everyone's hearts. How was he going to explain why Shane was in the park? I felt cold and spacy. Ash leaned against the wall and shimmied back and forth, like he had an itch. He didn't say anything about Dave's speech, but I kept thinking how Dave must have written it at the kitchen table where he'd served me the chili, scribbling onto a piece of paper as pale as the rest of the room. Ash and I sat outside the courtroom for another half hour, until the door opened.

"He's going free," said Dave.

"What?" Ash balled his hands together and then he punched the wall.

Dave said the judge had given a speech about senseless loss of life, about people who prey on others and never face consequences, and then said there was nothing she could do because there were no witnesses to the death, besides Jeremiah Wakefield. She said something about reasonable doubt. And that it was plausible that he acted in self-defense. There was no way to build a credible case against him. Dave had his arm around Marva but looked like he might collapse.

He said the judge ordered that Jeremiah Wakefield could not come near me, that he would go to jail if he did. If anyone caught him before he stabbed me, I thought. He'd already been ordered to stay away from his ex-wife, Dave said, and he had violated that more than once. The judge said she had considered that, but there wasn't enough evidence to bring charges and she couldn't keep him in jail. He had already served his time for drinking out of an open container.

Marva looked blank, dried up inside. Dave was burning with anger. His cheeks were red and he kept clasping and relaxing his jaw. Each time his lips gave off a little popping sound, small explosions of fury. I wanted to get out of there before Dave said anything else.

"I'm sorry, Maddy," he said. "It's not your fault. But we're back to where we started. We have to get busy."

I didn't know what he meant. Shane was gone and his killer was free. There was not much else we could do, unless he was thinking we should kill Jeremiah Wakefield. No way was I getting into that, except that when I let myself think about it, I caught some of Dave's rage and it occurred to me that maybe I could kill him. Or help kill him.

"I have to make them appeal," Dave said, "so we'll need to know more about Jeremiah and what he was doing in the park. The lawyer told me the police aren't investigating any further. They have presented their findings and now they're dropping it. No one wants to know what really happened. We'll have to do it ourselves."

He started talking in a rush about inspecting records at the courthouse, hiring a private eye, coming to spend a few nights with us in the park, when Marva slumped against the wall and started sliding to the floor. Dave put his arms around Marva's back and pulled her over to the bench.

"I've got to get her home," he said. "Why don't you two come with us?"

"No one has to get me anywhere," said Marva. "Stop talking about me like I'm not here. There isn't anything we can do now."

I thought about the cabin and how I could not go there and listen to Dave and Marva talk about Shane. Then I thought about how I'd have to stay up all night looking out for Jeremiah if I went back to the park, even if the judge had ordered him not to bother me. Why would he pay attention to her? Maybe it would be a relief to lie down on the beige couch and stay there.

"We're going to bounce," said Ash.

We shouldered our packs and there was an awkward pause.

"At least let me put you up in a hotel for a few days, while we figure out what to do," said Dave. He leaned over and I thought he was going to hug me, but instead he took a card out of his wallet and handed it to me. HOTEL VALENCIA, A BRIDGE TO HOME.

"They'll help you find a place to live, if you want that," said Dave. "Or you can just stay for a few days. Your choice."

"That won't change anything," I said. "Jeremiah will still be out there."

But Ash said we'd check it out. He snapped the card between his thumb and finger a few times like it was a guitar pick and then put it in his pocket.

"We should go, at least for a night," he said when we got into the elevator. The floor was scuffed and the steel walls dented and stained from the millions of trips made by inmates and lawyers and people caught in the middle, trips that decided where they walked in life. They might think they had control over some small part of it, but in the end, decisions were made, they would go to jail or walk free. It would be fair or not, but all of it was out of their control.

"I guess," I said. I just wanted to sit, maybe get wasted. And sitting in a hotel room, with an actual bed, sounded comforting.

"Is that a yes?" said Ash. "Because I can't tell sometimes. You were amped up back there and now it's whatever. It pisses me off when you disappear like that."

I was about to slap him in the arm, but I knew he was right. I was going around with myself inside, where I was doing all the talking, as usual. Trying to tell myself what to do, until my mind got so busy that I couldn't do anything. It was like a flood coming into a house slowly, the furniture starting to float and drift around. It was violent, but in slow motion.

"Okay," I said. "Let's go to the hotel. But what about Root?"

"He'll be cool with Fleet for one night," Ash said. "We'll get him tomorrow. Maybe they take dogs at this place and we could all go there."

The Valencia was a skinny brick building next to a deli with a neon welcome sign and bars on the windows. A man sat on the sidewalk out front running a dumpster sale—coffee cups, a big chipped blue bowl, some pants and shirts. He said he'd been living at the Valencia for ten years, give or take. It wasn't bad. They let you alone if you didn't bother anyone. He'd worked as a guard at the drug store around the corner, but it folded so he set up his own business, like everyone else in the city.

"Welcome home," he said.

Inside the lobby there was a stand of drooping ferns against one wall. Ash went up to a small tinted window at the end of the room. A loud buzzer sounded and a guy inside asked what we wanted. Ash told him our names.

"Just a minute," he said, his voice tinny through the speaker, and we heard the door click open. He made us sign in, looked through our backpacks and then motioned us to a small round table in the middle of the room. The only light came from a bulb overhead. There were more forms on the table, in small piles. He pushed a sheet at each of us, but there weren't any questions I could answer, except my name. Social security number? Permanent address? Person to notify in case of emergency? Actually, that one I could fill in. But should I put Ash or Root? I laughed.

"What?" said Ash. I showed him my blank page, except for Root's name.

"I'll put him too," he said, and wrote it in big block letters that he shaded so they looked 3D.

"It's not a test," said the guy, whose pec muscles bulged from under his shirt. He told us his name was Mick and that he was the manager. He would set up a meeting where he would tell us about our options. For tonight we just had to pick up towels and sheets and a copy of the rules. No drinking or smoking inside. No drugs, unless they were from a doctor and even those he would have to keep locked up in his office. No loud noise after 10:00 p.m. No cooking or hotplates. No fighting with the other residents.

"Just promote peace and it will all be good," he said, holding up two fingers in a V.

"We're all about peace," said Ash and returned the sign.

"Good, we understand each other then," said Mick and handed Ash a key attached to a small plastic orange. "Your room is on the fourth floor. You got a shared bath down the hall."

The elevator was a cage, so small we had to squeeze together. It lurched up and stopped hard, and we banged into the side. I unlatched and folded back the door and we went down the hall. The door to our room was open, but it was stuffy inside. Gauze curtains that had once been white covered the streaked window. I could hear people talking on the street outside. There was a small bed along the wall, a dresser, and a lamp. When I lay down, the mattress felt like it was full of crackers. It crunched and then squeaked. All I wanted was to sleep, even though it was still light outside. Ash wanted food, but he couldn't just set up outside. No one out there was going to give him anything. I told him to go and I'd stay in the room.

But as soon as he left, I regretted it. I heard doors opening, water running in pipes overhead, thudding from the stairs. Someone was coughing and then spitting. I had to hit the window a few times to get it open.

Ash was too far down the street to hear me. "Wait up!" I yelled and then climbed out on the fire escape even though there was a sign telling me not to. But I couldn't stay in the room. There was no way I was going to fall asleep. I needed air, anything to get me away from what had happened at the court. In the alley below, a small group of guys sat in torn red vinyl chairs, smoking and passing a bottle. The one on the end was asleep with a pipe in his lap.

Jeremiah was out there somewhere. No one cared what he had done. What difference did anything make? No one was back in Los Angeles all worried about me, waiting for me to call. I stretched out my arms and leaned over the fire escape. No one would care if I stepped off it. The wind might carry me a few feet and I'd land in front of those guys in their chairs. It would give them a start, but they'd go back to normal soon. Everything would. I wasn't seriously thinking of falling, even though it would have been easy to slip. What would it feel like? There was an instant you could go too far. A few seconds of panic and then nothing or maybe terrible pain and then nothing. The important thing was that it ended in nothing.

That's what happened to Shane. He probably didn't feel much while the blood drained out of him, while his heart slowly stopped pumping.

"Get your crazy ass down here," yelled one of the guys, holding up the bottle. "We got a place for it here." He slapped a chair.

I dropped my arms as I climbed back in the window. Shane was gone and I was here. That was never going to change. I lay on the bed and turned on the lamp, which made a popping noise and went off. I would be glad when Ash came back, maybe with food, which he would spread on the floor. We would eat in the dark and then go to bed. I turned over, but it was too much trouble to take off my shoes. I kept thinking about Dave saying he would spend his life staring at a blank wall. I tossed around on the bed until Ash arrived, holding a bag of leftovers from a place down the street, and then tore into them, oblivious. I reached for some of the noodles before Ash devoured them all. Tomorrow, I told him, I was going back to the courthouse.

CHAPTER 18

The records room was down a long corridor in the courthouse basement. It looked small for a space that stored up everything bad that people had done. A lady at the counter said I could look up the records myself and that she would get me any I couldn't find in the computer system. Some people still had trouble getting used to electronic records. She said to let her know, then turned to a stack of folders on her desk. I was used to the computers at the library that went blank for no reason, but the one in front of me clicked and whirred when I typed in his name, taking its time to think. There were three Jeremiah Wakefields. I had to look up each one and wait while the computer searched, flickering, a circle of dots slowly turning around in the center until it finally spit up lines of gray print. I tapped my finger on the table, worried that I would get kicked off before the words came into focus. There was a thirty-minute time limit and people who'd walked in after me were waiting in chairs along the wall.

Ash and I had stayed two nights at the Valencia. Even with our own room, it was too loud to sleep. An old guy next door put on the same act every night, yelling "Police! Police!" until people came to check and then he would scream and beg them not to hurt him. As soon as it got dark, he forgot where he was. He had a daughter who paid his rent, but she didn't want him at her house. The man had miseries, like everyone else, the night manager said. Wait until we were his age and trying to get by. Then we'd understand. No one was coming for us.

Dave and Marva, it was clear, wanted us to stay there. They would know, at least, where we slept. We'd had to meet with a chaplain who invited us to a prayer meeting, and with Mick, who gave us power bars and water that tasted like blueberries and then questioned Ash while a lady social worker talked to me. She said she needed some information so she could find out what I needed. Where was I born she wanted to know. I said I was from New Orleans because Hope told me about how she wanted to go there and see people from all over the world, not just California. You'd be less warped when you saw people like that, she said. If you were there at a certain time of year, the whole city went in the street and got wasted and danced together all night. How long had I lived outside? When is the last time I had a medical check-up? A mental health one? How often did I drink or do drugs? When she started asking sex questions, I stopped listening. I wasn't going to tell the lady if I liked to have sex with girls or guys, what I knew about AIDS and where I got my condoms.

She said she could put me on a waiting list for a group house, where there would be counselors and people my age, but a quicker solution would be a bus ticket home if I wanted that. All I had to do was contact my relatives there and get the okay. The city would pay for it, something she called Greyhound therapy, which she knew sounded bad, but the city only had so much money. The thing was, Dave had made the same offer, to send me home, even though he didn't know where that was. They figured if I was gone I'd be someone else's problem or maybe I'd decide I wanted to go to school and learn how to cut hair. I told the social worker the same thing I told everyone else. I wasn't looking to go anywhere, there wasn't anywhere to go.

Dave came by the hotel the second day to check on us, like he was afraid we'd disappear. He looked wrung out and empty, the way my mother was the last time I saw her. Maybe he was breaking down. I was going to tell him to let me alone, we were done, but, instead, I felt bad for him. I said I had started to look up everything I could about Jeremiah Wakefield.

"Technically you're a digital native so it should be easier for you," he said, handing over a bag of bagels and fruit. There was a speck of hope in his voice. "I wish you'd let us get you a cell phone so we could stay in closer touch."

We didn't tell him about the hotel, but it would have made anyone freak out. And they didn't allow dogs, even though some people smuggled them in. One lady on our floor had two cats that yowled at night, adding a layer of noise to the guy shouting for the cops and the body noises, partying, the slamming doors and footsteps. Root was lucky he was staying at the shelter instead of trying to find a corner of peace at the hotel. He would not have closed his eyes there. And Dave, he would not have lasted.

The first Jeremiah Wakefield I looked up was the wrong one. He lived downtown and had a page worth of charges. There was a number that stood for each crime and you had to look those up, the secret codes – possession of substance, accessory to possession, assault with intent to commit bodily injury. It was plain and unemotional. None of it described exactly what had happened. I researched all of the first Jeremiah's run-ins. He'd been in county jail and sentenced to a drug diversion program. He was two years older than me.

The second one was the Jeremiah I was looking for, the one who was out, free. He was fifty-six, with his own list of charges, each with a different number. I wrote them all down, except the last one, filed a few weeks ago. I knew what that was. Drinking from an open container. It never mentioned what he'd done to Shane, as if it didn't happen. The other numbers I looked up one by one on the computer: misdemeanor theft, public urination, probation violation, violating a restraining order. The judge had ordered him not to bug his wife, but he couldn't stay away. So why would he stay away from me? I remembered when my mom had drawn an imaginary line around herself on the floor. I had stood right near the line waiting for her to change her mind. I might as well go and get snatched by a stranger, I told her. Maybe a stranger would pay attention to me. I kept poking my toe near her, but she didn't notice.

"I'm taking a time out," she said. "You can do anything you

want but don't cross into my space. I can't be held responsible for what I'd do if you come close right now."

I read the whole record on Jeremiah's restraining order. I could hear minutes being ticked off by the metal hands of an old wall clock. A lady tapped me hard on the shoulder. "I already gave you an extra five, but you can't monopolize the terminal here," she said. I gave her a look I hoped would make her feel bad and then I got up and sat in a chair along the wall, waiting for another turn so I could get back to where they drew a line around Jeremiah's wife.

It took me a while to look it up again. His file had so many pages it was like reading a book inside the computer. One of the pages was labeled POLICE REPORT and was filled out by someone with faint handwriting. I could read about every other word, but that was enough. It gave a date and address where police responded to a call by Laurel Wakefield. I wrote it down, looking over my shoulder to see if anyone was watching. I wasn't sure if they allowed you to copy things from the files.

Back at the shelter I showed Ash the address and told him about Jeremiah's wife. The court papers said he had ripped out the phone cord after she called the police and then beat her with his fists and tried to wrap the cord around her neck. She had marks on her face and neck. She said she didn't want to go to the hospital, but they took her anyway. And later she asked for a restraining order. She wanted Jeremiah to stay away. If the judge knew he'd hit his wife why did she let him go free after he knifed Shane?

"I'm going to find her," I said. "His wife. Maybe there's other stuff he did, things no one knows about."

Ash said he'd go with me, even though he thought it was a bad idea. She might think we were harassing her and call the police. Why would she want to talk to us? What was I going to figure out that the lawyers didn't know? At least, Ash said, we should get Dave to drive us there so we could make a fast escape if we needed to. I said that might scare her more. Some guy pulling up in his car, three people and a dog getting out, like we were hunting her down. We should go by ourselves.

She lived in the southern part of the city. I looked up directions in the library and wrote them down. It would take two bus rides and a long walk. Ash said I should be a detective because I seemed to get so jacked up thinking about finding Jeremiah's wife. He started calling me his private dick. I told him to shut up, but my mind felt smoothed out when it was fixed on finding her. I didn't feel as jumpy. I wasn't seeing Jeremiah's face every minute and thinking how he could show up and pull out his knife.

We waited an hour for the second bus and then walked what felt like miles before we got to Laurel Wakefield's small house, which was attached to the one next door. The roof was low and flat. The front window was closed and covered with a yellow bedspread. Ash and I had decided we'd wait if she didn't answer the door, maybe slip a note underneath telling her we'd been there and would come back. There was no buzzer outside, so I knocked. The paint on the door was chipped and scratched.

The bedspread curtain slid to the side and half a face appeared.

"What do you want?" said a woman's voice.

We had thought about how to find the house, how we'd get there in the late afternoon when she was home from work, if she worked. But we had not planned exactly what to say if she was there. If I'd been an actual detective, I would have known what to ask and what to look for. I'd know if it was normal business for a stranger to stand on someone's doorstep and wait. It wasn't like sitting on the sidewalk, which didn't belong to anyone. It was a house where people did whatever they wanted. Jeremiah could be there. Or maybe his wife had moved away and this was some other woman scared out of her head by us. She might already have called the cops. Or she was inside, with her gun pointed at us.

"We want to talk to you about Jeremiah Wakefield," I said, surprised by how steady my voice was.

She let go of the curtain and we heard the unclanking of locks. She opened the door about two inches and looked at us through the security chain. She was small and solid, with brass-colored hair twisted around a pencil and piled on her head.

"What about him?" she said, her head cocked to the side the way Root looks at me, when he is trying to understand.

I knew how she must be seeing us, in clothes from the free basket, Ash's hair in dreads, mine all tangled. She didn't look much better, but we were the ones knocking on her door. At least I was carrying a pad of paper, so I didn't look like I wasn't going to attack her.

"I am Maddy and this is Ash," I said. "We're here to talk to you, if you are Laurel Wakefield."

She shut the door. I don't know why I thought this would work. If it was so easy, the cops or lawyers might have done it.

"Just a minute," she said. "Let me get myself together."

We sat on the front step. She didn't have to tell us anything. Why should she? I folded the end of a piece of paper into a neat square and then unfolded it, over and over, until Ash stuffed it in his pocket.

When she reopened the door, she'd changed into harem pants and a T-shirt. She'd reassembled her hair, but it was still twisted around the pencil. She looked like some tiring things had happened to her.

"Laurel?" I said.

She had a deep raspy voice. "I used to be."

She sat down on the step next to me and lit up a cigarette. She didn't call herself Laurel anymore, she said. The smoke trailed out while she talked. Now it was Loretta, a name she'd been born with and never liked. But after splitting from her husband and getting a legal order for him to leave her alone, she went back to her original first and last name. No one called her Laurel anymore, unless they knew Jeremiah, in which case she didn't want to hear from them.

"What's he done this time?" she said. "He was one piece of bad news after another. I hear his name and I want to be sick."

I apologized all over the place and told her I knew exactly what she meant. She took another hit off her cigarette. If she'd had one thing to do over, she said, it would have been to press charges the first time he touched her, get him out of circulation. I asked her if she'd heard about the kid who was killed in Golden Gate Park. She said she never got over to the park. It was too far away. Enough kids were killed right there, in her own neighborhood, and no one ever heard about them either. I said that we lived in the park actually, but I could see how she wouldn't want to go there.

She said she didn't work and had been on disability pay ever since Jeremiah broke two of her ribs. They'd healed a long time ago, but she didn't feel like going outside most days, even though she hadn't seen him in years, thanks to the Lord. He had started out so sweet, always brought her something when he came around. He knew how much she liked orange roses because they didn't seem real, but they were. "He used to be," she lowered her head, "considerate. He paid attention, you know?" He had a car and he'd drive her to work and then wait for her to come home. He would be there sitting on the couch, not like most men, who go out all the time and pretty soon you can't trust them. But then he started telling her she couldn't go out with her girlfriends. She couldn't go out at all, except with him, and he didn't want to go out. He thought everyone was out to make him look bad, even her. There was nothing she could do that was right.

"I didn't say anything as long as he kept to himself and didn't bother me," she said. "That's all I hoped for, because when he turned the bad juice on me, there was no end."

"Did he ever go to the park?" I said.

She didn't know what he did. Whatever it was, it didn't make him easier to live with. He was hopped up on something. If she wasn't at her secretary job, he wanted her at home, where he could keep her safe. He got mad if she talked to the neighbors or the guy who delivered the mail. He went off on her all the time, slapped her, broke a tooth, but she didn't say anything, until the last time. Then she called the cops and they filed the report. He was supposed to get anger management counseling and go to AA meetings, but she didn't care what he did as long as she never had to see him again.

"I knew if he came back, he would kill me," she said. "I saw it in his eyes. And you want to know what's weird? After he left here, I felt bad for him. There was a time I dug Jeremiah. Things were past over for us, but I was torn up inside, thinking of him with nowhere to go. His own family, over in the Central Valley, wouldn't have anything to do with him. I wondered if I didn't cause what happened to us, a little bit. There is only so much a man can take. That's what he told me."

A few times he stood outside across the street and stared at the house and then sometimes he opened his pants and pissed, like he was marking his territory. Once he knocked on the door and she called the cops. They arrested him even though she said she didn't want him locked up. She thought maybe the cops would threaten him. She didn't want trouble, as long as he didn't come over and bother her. The look he gave her when they put on the cuffs was pure hatred. You can't shake that off.

I took a sharp breath. I knew that look. I told her how he had killed a kid who was staying in the park. She didn't seem surprised that the police didn't care one bit. They were not trying to figure out what happened. The kid was buried and Jeremiah was out there, free.

"They figure one less shit in this world is a good thing," she said. "I hope you're not expecting them to make it right."

"Shane was not a bad kid," I said. "His name was Shane."

"Well then you want to tell me why he was out there?" she said. "There are people in this city who think they have a right to live wherever they want. We got them here. I see them every day. You can't go to the grocery without them asking for your money. Anyone with half a brain can get some kind of handout. Just ask me."

"How would you know why anyone stays in the park?" I said. "You spend all your time hiding inside your house."

I moved closer to her, my voice louder. Maybe Shane didn't have a choice. Not everyone is looking for a handout.

"Whoa." She stood up and moved into the doorway. "This is my property and you are on it, in case you forgot."

She looked scared, which made me stop yelling.

Staying in the park was better than staying at a shelter most of the time, I said in a normal voice. I told her about Dave and Marva and how they needed to figure out what happened, which meant finding out about Jeremiah. I would have kept talking, but she gave me a look like either she didn't understand or she didn't want to know.

"As far as I know he never killed anyone, but now you say he did and got away with it," she said. "I can tell you, it doesn't surprise me one bit."

She put a hand on the door. "If I was you, I wouldn't look for him," she said. "Jeremiah feels like he can take whatever he wants. If you came here to warn me, you don't need to."

"We didn't come to scare you or warn you," I said. "We wanted to know what else he did, before he killed that kid. Shane."

"I can't help you with things I don't know about," she said. "He never answered to anyone. He must have had business with your friend at the park. You do business with Jeremiah, you come out on the wrong side. He never forgets what anyone owes him."

She half closed the door and then stopped. "You are better off with an animal than a man," she said, looking at Ash. "They don't hit you."

She left us standing on the porch. We could hear her inside, clicking the locks shut.

CHAPTER 19

A few days later Dave came by the shelter with a sack of bright green apples he'd picked at an organic farm near the cabin. Back in New York the trees would have lost their leaves already, he said. The ground would be half frozen. He handed me the sack awkwardly and I felt like I had to give him something in return, so I told him about the court records I'd found and how I'd gone to see Jeremiah's ex-wife. I thought he would be impressed that Ash and I had tracked her down and gotten her to talk. But he didn't ask me anything about her, so I didn't tell him that she was so done with Jeremiah she'd changed her name.

He looked ten years older. His hair was grayer and his skin was like pale tissue paper. He said Marva was thinking of going home, but he had to stay until he sorted things out. All I wanted was for him to leave me alone and now I was surprised to hear that Marva was giving up. Or maybe she was leaving him, going to live in a city where she would not be looking at Shane's closed up room.

He said he wanted me to keep looking for people who knew Shane, as if that was something I could do. I'd been to see Jeremiah's wife and that didn't do anything but make her want more locks on her door. What did he expect? As if I could go where Shane was killed and keep asking people if they'd seen anything or walk around with a picture and ask people if they knew him. It didn't make sense. Even Marva was quitting.

"It's just that—" Dave stopped mid-sentence and took my hand in both of his. "I need to see his life so I can walk part of this with him."

"What?" I took my hand back and held it close to my own chest. I should have been yelling at him, not Loretta. "It's not like I can see what his life was like."

"Or course not." He said he was sorry and then apologized for that too. "I just need to understand. Maybe I never will."

When he walked out of the shelter I could see he was emptied out of everything but sadness. I thought about running after him, but I didn't know how that would help.

I got used to half sleeping, being on alert so I could get up and run, especially if I was at the shelter. I felt safer outside, with Root on one side and Ash on the other. Hope was there, although more and more she was in Santa Cruz. She said she felt free sleeping on the beach and was learning to surf. Fleet perked up after she got a white rabbit that she called Robo and took around on a leash. She said someone on the street gave him to her, but I wondered if her mom sent her money and she went and bought him. No one was handing out rabbits.

We were sitting on the grass, Robo scraping around in the middle, when Dave walked up carrying a blue backpack a few shades too cheerful that said HAPPY TRAILS on the straps. He sat down next to me, no explaining. Root nosed his way into Dave's pack and pulled out a box of Milk-Bones. It didn't take him long to bite through the cardboard and scatter them on the ground. Dave tried to grab them up before Root finished them all. He said to carry on like he wasn't there, he was sorry to visit without warning, but he had to see for himself how Shane lived. He had gone over it in his mind and figured this was the only way. I wanted to tell him that Shane had never stayed with us, that we didn't know where he'd spent the night. Maybe he was out dealing or shooting up or waiting until the light came up and he could, at last, fall asleep. But I looked at Dave and I couldn't. In some weird way, he looked like one of us, scraggly hair, baggy jeans, fingernails bitten down raw. He sat against one of the short twisty trees and crossed his legs. "Coastal oak, nice tree, but I prefer cypress," he said. He couldn't help himself, reeling off tree facts the way he had about birds. Ash passed him a bottle of Wild Turkey and he took a small sip and swallowed loud, forcing it down. He turned down the joint, but Ash told him he should try it, if he really wanted to see how Shane lived. No one was going to come and arrest him for blazing a little weed, not here. So Dave took it, pinching the joint like was it was burning his fingers. He took a small hit, held it a long time, then breathed out and said he didn't feel a thing. Ash told him to go harder. Dave inhaled deep a few more times, blew out rings as if he knew what he was doing, coughed and said he still didn't notice much.

"Just a fullness, kind of a pressure in my forehead." He rubbed his temples, but his eyes were out of focus. His mouth was smiling on its own. We made a tight circle and Dave said we needed a talking piece. When Shane was in grade school his teacher had a plaster sculpture of a tiger paw that she passed around to each kid, which meant it was his turn to talk.

"Dave is so fucked up," said Ash. Dave laughed.

I said it wasn't a bad idea. Maybe we should use a talking piece and see what happened. Dave went looking around in the bushes for something we could use. He came out a few minutes later with a tennis ball covered in dirt.

"Better than nothing," he said. "I'll start." Root sat up and stared at the ball, waiting for Dave to throw it.

I was waiting for another story about Shane, but instead Dave looked around at all of us. He held the ball clenched in his fist.

"I feel that this is an important moment," he said. "Maybe it's impossible to really know another person, but I feel I'm understanding you better."

"It's called being baked," said Ash.

"No," said Dave. "I'm getting it. Getting you. Why you're here. You have found something here that maybe the rest of us lack."

"Sour Diesel," said Ash. "It's good shit." He put his arm around Dave and clenched his shoulder.

Dave passed the ball to me and it was like holding a half-cooked egg, slimy and firm at the same time. I was trying to come up with something to say, but I was afraid I'd laugh if I tried to talk. Dave was serious. Root pounced and grabbed the ball out of my hand. He bent down in front of me, whimpering, so I tossed it as far as I could.

"He wanted a turn," I said.

Dave smiled, but I could tell he was disappointed. Root ran back and forth with the ball, which was no longer the talking piece. Ash lit up again and handed the joint around. We all took long hits. Dave held it and took two in a row. "Quick learner," said Ash. I laughed and couldn't stop. I was so gone it burbled up out of me. After a while, we got up and walked, single file, to 40 Hill. Dave was at the end, not bothering to hold back the brush, which scraped against his pants. At the top, he felt the ground to make sure it was dry, crawled into his sleeping bag, rolled on his side and was out. He snored so loud that Hope collected some sticks and threw little pieces at his back. That shut him up for a few seconds and then he started in again, gulping air and grunting. He was an old guy, so of course he snored. I told her to leave him alone.

Ash got out his ukulele and Hope sang in her screechy voice, but that didn't wake up Dave either. Only Fleet was quiet. She was not all there since she got out of the hospital. She acted stoned when she was straight, and she talked in a hushed private voice to the rabbit. She stared at a book but didn't seem to be reading. Ash said to give her time, she would start acting normal.

Ash finally put the ukulele down and wiggled into the bags we rolled together to keep us warm. We'd fallen into this habit, like we had been together forever. We didn't talk about it. And we didn't get loud in front of other people. I wasn't going to put on a show if Fleet and Hope were there. And forget when Dave spent the night. It was like doing it in front of your dad. I kept my hands to myself.

Just before four, Ash's alarm sounded and Dave sat up, his hair scrambled. He didn't know where he was, but it came to him quickly when he looked at us, untwisting from our bags and stumbling onto the dirt. He walked with us to the bus stop, then to McDonald's and acted like it was a usual thing for him to file into the bathroom with Ash. He was lucky because early morning was the best time, before the toilets got stopped up and stinking, before paper was scattered on the floor and the sink filled with bits of food, dirt, and whatever else fell off a person during the day. Dave came out with water dripping off his face and hair, imitating Ash's quick sink bath. Then he bought us all breakfast sandwiches and extra-large coffees and watched us intently while we ate. But he wasn't any closer to knowing Shane. He was looking for something that could not be checked the way I looked up the court records. He could not see the secrets that were inside a person.

"What happens now?" he said, leaning back in the booth and crumpling up the empty sandwich wrapper. "Where you all headed?"

"Nowhere," I said.

"The shelter," said Ash. "It's almost time for breakfast."

I hoped he wasn't planning to follow us around all day. It turned out I didn't have to worry because he left us on the sidewalk outside McDonald's. He said he'd eaten enough and he waved, keeping his hand up in the air stiff as a talking piece, and walked away, back into the park.

CHAPTER 20

The rest of the world started to celebrate. The smoke shop threw strands of red and green tinsel over a turkey statue and the corner grocery hung little HAPPY THANKSGIVING tags on its faded plastic tree, turning it all into one giant holiday. Hope wore a green plastic tiara she found on the ground. She said people liked decoration, that it put them in the right state of mind. It might help me to try, she said.

Ash was tired of my research on Shane, which he said was changing my personality, and not in a good way. I was edgy and wiped out at the same time. He said to let it go, but he didn't get it. I couldn't stop thinking about Dave looking at a blank wall.

I found a poster with Shane's picture still attached to a light pole and had started showing it around the park. At first Ash went with me because he said you never know what people are going to do. They could act friendly and then rip you off. Everyone had a game. But there was no way anyone was getting over on me. I could take care of myself. No one was going to think I was an undercover cop, carrying a notebook and pulling Root next to me.

The first day I started on the grass near the lake. I forced myself to walk up to a group of guys sitting next to a pile of guitars and packs. They'd only been around a few days, they said, following some copycat Grateful Dead band, but I showed them Shane's picture anyway. They had no idea who he was.

"They don't know shit," said Ash. "And even if they did, why would they talk about it?" He walked off and sat on a far corner near the street while I talked to two girls who were throwing breadcrumbs into the lake. They said they worked at a used clothing store on the street and it was their personal goal to revive the fish. Neither one had ever seen Shane, but they said good luck. I told them good luck with the fish, which were probably already extinct. Then I went after every other person on the lawn. No one could remember seeing Shane.

That night I couldn't sleep, partly because I kept thinking about whether Ash was right, and also I itched so badly I wanted to rip open my skin and scratch underneath. Ash was next to me, completely out. I turned over and back again. My thighs started to tingle.

The next day I told Ash he didn't have to help me. I could do fine on my own. He trailed after me toward the shelter, not saying much. After breakfast, I went into the free clinic around the corner. I had been there once before, when I stepped on a thorn and it swelled so much I couldn't walk. I went to the window and signed my name on a waiting list. The lady at the desk said the doctor was running late so it would be a while unless I had an emergency. There were only a few other people in the room, but I wasn't going to tell her what was going on. She handed me a bottle of water and asked if I wanted to sign a petition.

"We'll have to close unless we get more support," she said. "It's not like it was fifty years ago. We get fewer people, but some of them need serious help."

I added my name, no address, and she smiled and said to let her know if I wanted a muffin. I sat down and looked at the faces that floated on a mural across the room. Pleading eyes, a hand holding a peace sign, a naked lady with her hair flowing out around her.

When it was my turn, the doctor, in jeans and a white coat, came out and invited me into the exam room. He reached over to shake my hand and asked me why I was there. I had a hard time saying it out loud, even though he must have seen it all before, every drug and disease a person could get. Nothing was going to surprise him. I told him in a matter of fact voice that I was going to die from some itch inside me.

"We won't let that happen," he said, writing in his record book, and I wondered if that's what he wrote: "girl says she is dying of an itch."

He handed me a paper blanket and called a lady nurse to come stand next to me while he looked around my crotch.

"I think I know what's going on, but I'll take a scraping here," he said, and rubbed something way up along my inner thigh, where I'd scratched until it bled. Then he went to a steel cupboard and pulled out a tube of lotion.

"Pubic lice," he said. I tried to find somewhere else to look besides his face. A small window faced the street where a kid was sitting, his dog's leash tied around his leg while he rearranged contents of a big duffle bag. "Crabs," said the doctor. "But the good news is that it's easily cured. Just make sure you tell your partners because they will need to be treated as well or we will have a circular situation."

I must have looked like I didn't understand. "Infection, treatment, and re-infection," he said. The nurse stood there, no expression.

I thought about the crabs I used to dig up at the beach, how they swam up in holes I hollowed out of the sand. Now there were millions of them, shrunk down in size, creeping on me. I left with a page of instructions, a bottle of vitamins for women, and a handful of purple condoms.

Ash popped two of the vitamins to see what happened. Maybe he'd wake up and be a woman. I blamed him for the infection, but he said he didn't itch and that I must have picked them up somewhere else. Whatever, I said, and took back the vitamins. I said I wasn't going to get with him again until he went in for his own lotion, even though I held tight to him that night. He turned away and let me hug him from behind, probably worried the bugs were going to crawl over on him.

The next day I went to the bookstore to look at one of their big maps of Golden Gate Park. The owner watched while I unfolded and studied it, then tried to put it back the right way.

"Just take it," he said. I told him I'd bring it back.

"No one borrows a map," he said.

Outside the store, I marked the park into sections, twenty even squares. It would take almost a month if I did one every day. But if I was going to find anyone who knew Shane I'd have to go everywhere. It was the same as one of my mom's chore lists. They'd kept us going, even though most of the chores were pointless.

I studied the names and places I had never been. The Rhododendron Dell, Stow Lake, Speedway Meadow. There was a boathouse, a rose garden, waterfalls and lakes, but no one had marked where we stayed. The park was so big you couldn't know everything that happened there. Ash and I once went all the way to the ocean, which was colder and rougher than it was in Los Angeles. The waves riffled out in front of us, frosted with white foam. We acted like we were going to jump in but we only took off our shoes and waded up to our knees. Hardly anyone swam there because there were signs, WARNING, with a stick figure person being swallowed by a wall of water.

I knew the Children's Playground because it was down the back corner from 40 Hill. At night, the horses on the carousel stood quiet, their prancing feet in the air. No one was in the sandboxes or swings, arranged in a line with seats for babies, then bigger and bigger kids, so you could move them down the line as they grew. When the park was closed, we would climb up the big spiderweb made of wood and rope and jump off. If you were whacked out enough it was easy to think there was a spider with killer poison waiting on top.

By the second or third day with the map I had a regular plan. I ate breakfast at the shelter and then went off with Root, the map, a notebook I'd taken from the crafts store, and my poster of Shane. It was torn and curled at the edges, but you could still see him smiling, looking straight into the camera. The picture was black-and-white so it didn't show the transparent blue color of his eyes. But anyone who had seen him would know that.

The first section was at a fenced-in lawn behind the playground. The rest of the park was full of wild gardens, flowers, trees, and creeping weeds, but that lawn looked like it was clipped every day. Six old men in white pants and hats stood at either end tossing a small black ball back and forth. I walked up to one of them and held the poster out in front of me.

"Interference on the green!" said one of the men, way in back. He was the tallest, a long white straw, and his pants were neatly creased. A broad canvas hat shaded his brown wrinkled skin.

"I'm not trying to interfere," I said. "I just wanted to ask a question."

"No dogs on the green," said the tall man and of course Root lifted his leg and peed. "No dogs!" The guy was yelling.

The nearest one waved me closer. He told the tall man to hang on a minute, see what the girl wants. I thanked him and showed him Shane's picture. He put his hand in his pocket like he was going to give us a handout and you couldn't blame him; he was probably thinking that if he gave us money, we'd go away. Root growled.

"I just want to know if you've ever seen this kid," I said.

The man took off his dark glasses and slipped on another pair so he could take a closer look. He examined it so long that I thought he recognized Shane.

"I've never seen the fellow," said the man. I explained how Shane had been killed close by and so I wanted to know if there was anyone who saw him around there. He shook his head and said he didn't know what happened in the park at night. It's why they bowled in the middle of the day although he didn't know if it was safe then either.

That night Ash said I should have shaken the guy for money. It was a waste of time if I came away with no information and no cash. What was that going to get me? I told him he could stay on the street with a sign if he wanted money. He said he could go live with his mother if I wanted to freak out on him all the time. She was on him and then I was on him. It was one thing he couldn't stand, he said.

"Shane is Dave's trip," he said, lying next to me between our sleeping bags. "This is eating up your brain."

"Whatever Shane was messed up with, it didn't mean he should end up dead," I said. I kicked him in the side of his knee to make the point.

"You're lucky I don't get up and leave your ass right now," he said. He sat up and crossed his legs.

I wanted to tell him that I didn't give up on things, unlike some people. But I didn't say anything. I was white-hot mad inside, the anger building up even though my face was stuck in a distant stare. I learned that back at Karen and Chip's house, when I let loose. Chip thought the best way to make me learn self-control was to wash my mouth out with Irish Spring soap, which had a burning stink more than a taste. The smell of it on someone still made me gag. I would try to throw up during the scrubbing to make him feel bad. Karen just shut me in the bedroom. She put a lock on the outside of the door so I couldn't get out until she said it was time. I usually turned the dresser upside down and scratched into it with a pen. I thought about what I would do to Karen later. Put nail polish in her coffee and bleach in her shampoo. When she unlocked the door, though, I was usually worn out from all the planning so I let it be. I'd act like everything was the same.

I'd never seen Ash go off on any of us before, but he got up and started yelling that everything I was doing was bullshit and I was going to keep obsessing on bullshit until the end of time. He grabbed a wad of my clothes tucked in the tree overhead and threw them on the ground. Then he stuffed his own clothes into his backpack and walked off. Root climbed into my lap.

I looked over at Fleet and Hope, hard in sleep. Ash had taken his clock and it was only a few hours before the police would come by to rouse us. I would not be going back to sleep. I pulled out my notebook, but realized I'd need a light to look at the map of where I was going to search for Shane the next day. I thought how Ash would be sorry if I got knifed after he left, but that only made me feel shaky.

I covered myself and Root with the sleeping bags. Instead of writing a list I called up a movie in my head, the way I did when I was at Karen and Chip's. I could tune in, like I was watching a channel on TV. I chose a time my mom and I went to the beach. She had brought home two little flowered bags, each with a bathing suit inside because the store near Safeway had a two-for-one special.

"I had to buy these," she'd said. "Even though yours is a bit loud."

Hers was a light pink bikini outlined in hot pink, which looked good, for a mom. It tied behind her neck and had little crossed bands on her hips. When she turned around it looked as if her butt was hanging inside a hammock. Mine was one piece, bright pink with little black anchors. My mom smeared on scarlet lipstick and we headed out to the beach in Santa Monica. We sat on a towel and my mom unhooked the top of her bikini so she wouldn't get tan lines. People looked at her when they walked by, but she didn't care. She told me how the women in other countries walked around topless and no one cared. I should have asked her how she knew that, but of course I didn't think of that. It bothered me now, and it interrupted my memory watching. Even though it was cold in the park, I was getting hot under the sleeping bags, partly from the heat that Root was giving off next to me, along with his dog smell.

I forced myself back to the beach, where my mom was propped up on her elbows, watching me play in the water. Little birds scrambled down to the water next to me and took off before it could wash over their feet. I pretended I was one of them, running down to the edge of the ripples and then flapping my arms and running away. When I got back to my towel, my mom told me that she used to play sandpiper too when she was my age. We had a picnic of hotdogs and French fries that day. Usually she brought home packages of almost-expired fruit, peanut butter, and wheat bread from the Safeway. She said no daughter of hers was going to eat the junk she saw coming down the aisles at work.

I parceled out the memory, trying to make it last, at least until it was light enough to get up. My mind took turns, went down small alleys. How could my mother have been related to Karen and Chip, the most practical people in the world? They never thought about where food came from, or at least they never mentioned it. Dinner showed up on the table every night at the same time. Monday was spaghetti and meat sauce, Tuesday chicken legs, and on down the week. I could tell what day it was by what they served. Karen marked the cookie package so we didn't steal any between meals. If cookies went missing, no one got any that day. After dinner, we each got two and no more, unless it was a birthday. Then we got seconds.

It was full-on morning when I threw off the top sleeping bag to gulp some cool air. Sweat was running down my face. I could feel it trickle past the small of my back into my pants. Root was lying on the dirt by my feet, head on his paws, watching me.

"Why did you let me sleep so long?" I said, putting my hand on his head. Fleet and Hope were gone and the cops, for some reason, hadn't bugged us.

Even my spare clothes were damp, lying on the ground where Ash had tossed them. I walked to the shelter, T-shirt stuck to my back, pants feeling like I'd taken a leak in them. I went straight in, even though breakfast was almost finished, and picked through the free box for a dry shirt and pants. Fleet took a look at me and gave me her place in line for a shower. I turned my face to the water, letting it rinse off the sweat.

At the breakfast table Fleet had saved me a plate of runny eggs, with a handful of Cheerios on the side. Grease from the eggs oozed toward the small discs of cereal. I ate half and took the rest outside for Root, who slurped it and then started eating the paper plate. He growled when I wrestled it out of his mouth. I gave him a look that said he was never getting anything more out of me. "Maybe tomorrow you won't get breakfast," I said.

I left, without looking for Ash. I thought about sleeping alone at night in the circle of trees without him and my throat closed up and my head pounded. Forget him, I told myself, which made my head throb more. It was clear but cold and the pavement was still wet even though it hadn't rained in a few days. I pulled up the hood of my sweatshirt and zipped my jacket. The chill seemed to give Root more energy. He pulled on the leash, nose to the ground, tail in the air, taking in the scent of whatever had gone before us.

The Rhododendron Dell was across a street from 40 Hill and past a patch of hillside covered with bushes and spiky weeds. Inside the dell each plant looked like it had a fresh haircut, stems and branches chopped in a neat line. There wasn't much to see, no flowers or visitors. But it was a spot on the map and I had to walk it end to end, to mark it off even if I didn't find anyone to look at Shane's picture. It was the schedule and I had to keep to it. At the end of the last row I drew my marker in a satisfying streak through the dell.

Root pulled me back across the street, but once he was on the other side he turned the opposite way, lunging forward and stopping next to three people snugged up against a stubby tree near the lake. He sniffed at a pile of wrappers and empty weed bags. Two guys nodded a what's up and the girl stayed bent over a red and blue thread bracelet, weaving and tying little knots. She had a mound of others that she'd finished and set on a dirty square of fabric next to her. Artsy girls could be the worst, spaced out and hopeful, thinking they had something all superior to the rest of us with only our handmade signs.

"You want to make some?" she said, not looking up. She was a swirl of color, red and green felt hat, sun-yellow sweater, a skirt with all of them melted together. I didn't answer because I was not going to weave bracelets.

"What happened to your man?" she said.

How did she know anything about Ash? "What a pig douche," Hope had said, when I told her that he'd walked off because I was talking to people about Shane. Now this girl was trying to figure how she could work me. She probably had seen me before, even if I didn't recognize her. Root was not looking fierce right then. He pushed his nose into the top of her backpack so he could get a full idea of what was inside. She could be crazy or just crazy high. I held him back and she laughed.

"Kid on his way to school gave me his lunch," she said. "He wanted a bracelet for his girlfriend but he didn't have money so he dropped a smelly tuna sandwich in there that his mother probably made him. I love private school kids. They are so guilty and you kind of have to go with it."

She took the sandwich out of her pack, unwrapped it, and threw it on the grass for Root. I started breathing again and remembered why we were there. I took out the poster of Shane, sat down next to her and asked her if she'd ever seen him. That started her off. She'd been here last spring, but things had changed since then. Now the cops were all over. She had two warrants from up in Eureka, but why would anyone check on them? They were only for disturbing the peace. Who goes to jail for that? What kind of a place would send you to jail for making art all day and singing all night anyway? Were the cops here like that now? I told her she'd get roused at a shithole hour if she stayed in the park. I asked her to look at the poster. She put down the bracelet and reached for it.

"Merlin," she said, turning to one of the guys next to her. "You seen this dude?"

"This is the first time I've been here," he said, looking at me.

Merlin reached in the backpack, took out another sandwich and threw it to Root, who ate it quickly.

"Asshole, that was your lunch," said the girl, but she laughed. Root walked over to Merlin and sat next to him.

"So have you ever seen this guy?" I said, pointing to the poster.

"He got attacked near here?" the girl said. "I think I saw that poster on the street. What I heard was that it was over some girl. It always is, right?"

"What?" I said. How could it be over some girl? Jeremiah was old. Shane was a kid. No way would they be hooking up with the same girl.

"I'm just saying, it's what I heard, that Pops didn't want him hitting on some chick," said the girl, starting in on a red and green bracelet, twining the two strings together. "I saw that kid the last time I was here. I love every single person in this city. It's all love, you know?"

"Pops?" I repeated like I couldn't hear.

"Right," she said. "I saw him the other day, so if he did it, you know, killed that kid, then the kid must have started something."

"Shane," I said. "That was his name."

"I can't remember calling him anything," she said. "But he was hanging around a chick and that, if you want to know, is where the problem started."

"What problem?" I said.

She shrugged. "I hung with Pops a few times. He was super mellow. I never talked to the kid. But I saw him around. I don't think he was here that long."

Merlin took a guitar propped against the tree and started tuning it, tightening strings and plucking them, then readjusting the knobs. He was strumming and I half recognized the melody, up and down, grindingly low, and back to up and down.

"Merlin, stop," said the girl with the bracelets. Then to me, "I can't stand him playing unless I'm totally out of it."

Merlin played louder and started pacing with the guitar. He put down a paper cup for change, even though we were in the park and no one was around. I was going to tell her it didn't bother me, but Merlin paused. He looked pissed off and then he started jamming on the strings again, until one popped. I watched him bunch his mouth up tight. He put down the guitar, stomped over to the girl and hit her in the face with the back of his arm. One long quick smack.

"Maniac creep," she said. "Get off me."

"Bitch broke my string with her negative energy," he said, and turned to me like I was going to back him up. She crouched low over her bracelets. Root growled.

"Hey," I said. "I got money for another string."

He turned to face me, eyes empty, like he didn't remember me being there.

"There you are," he said.

He slung the guitar around his back and I handed him a few ones and fives that Dave had carefully folded and given me last time I saw him. I regretted it as soon as he shoved the money in his pocket. Why was I acting like I was going to save everyone? But the girl, who was wrapping up her bracelets in the scrap of fabric, looked relieved.

"I should leave his ass," she said, after he walked off toward the street. "Let him go back up north. He's good in the woods, but he's a freak around people."

"Hey, Sara Moon," Hope called from across the grass. She sat next to me, her spikey hair twisted into sharp points. "She knows everyone. We worked a harvest last year."

Sara Moon leaned over and hugged Hope, and then started arranging the bracelets in a row. A bruise was getting ripe under her left eye, but she seemed to have forgotten about Merlin's outburst.

"She knows about Shane," I said to Hope.

"I just told her what I heard," said Sara Moon. "You had the guy staring at you from those posters and everything."

I'd been combing through the park, marking off every inch where Shane might have stayed. I'd talked to everyone and gotten nothing. I'd been to the playground and the dell, the botanical garden, even to the pen where they kept the bison, which looked like cows in freak costumes. They stood there in the field watching me with their hooded eyes and I'd watched back. They were living in the park, same as me, and they knew about as much.

"Who was the chick, the one with Shane?" I said.

"She's obsessed," said Hope, nodding toward me. "You don't have to pay attention."

"How much for the one on the end?" said a man walking toward us, holding a bag from the smoke shop with a foot-high bong poking out the top. "Just got this for myself, but I need something for my girlfriend."

Sara Moon picked up the bracelet, which was red, blue, purple and yellow, and held it out to him. "Usually ten dollars, but five for you," she said.

He pulled a bill out of his wallet and passed it to her. "Tie-dyed, like the neighborhood," he said, pocketing the bracelet. "I'm digging it."

"I have no idea who the chick was," said Sara Moon. "I'm just saying what I heard, which is that he hung around her. She was really young, which is always creepy. But like I said, I didn't know him. Why are you so into his business?"

"She saw that kid killed, over in the park," said Hope, like it was part of her tour guide talk.

"Is it possible to keep you from blabbing about everything in the world that doesn't have anything to do with you?" I said.

"She's been crazy since it happened," Hope said to Sara Moon. "But basically she's cool."

"Thanks," I snapped. Why was Hope taking up with Sara Moon? She was supposed to be on the same side as me.

....

CHAPTER 21

Ash ran up the hill a week later, a pink stuffed monkey sticking out of his pack. His smile was exaggerated, but I could see he was glad I was there. He handed the monkey to me, which couldn't make up for him blowing up and disappearing. I stood with my hands on my hips. He held it out to me, but I didn't take it. He tossed it to Root, who shook it back and forth, like he'd caught a gopher or a raccoon and was trying to say, look here, see what I can do. I tried to take it away, but he ran away. He circled back and dropped it to tease me, then picked it up and took off again. Ash held out a string of red licorice so Root would let go.

"Don't give him that shit," I said.

Ash laughed. He was wearing a fresh white T-shirt that said DELL on the front and had a new nose ring. "At least *he* hasn't changed," he said.

He said he'd gone to Arizona and visited his mom, which only lasted two days. He couldn't take it there. He'd thought maybe things had changed. In Wyoming, they'd told him his mom was trying to do her best. Not everything had to do with him. But she was the same. Or worse. She said he could stay and she'd give him an allowance while he looked for a job. She didn't pay for him to go to wilderness camp and then come dragging home like the world owed him. Why couldn't he ever finish anything? He would have to cut his hair and take a drug test every week or else go back to Wyoming. She never asked him what he wanted to do.

"You still playing detective?" he said. Root was running in circles again. "Sorry," he said. "I know. I'm a jerk."

I told him I'd worked through all the squares on my map and hadn't found anyone who'd seen Shane, except for the kids from Eureka. I left off the part about Sara Moon because no one knew if she was telling the truth. She had stayed around until Merlin got busted for shoplifting. Then she took off to visit friends in Santa Cruz. Hope went with her and came back a few days ago so strung out that someone had called 911 and the cops gave her a choice, the hospital or a trip back up north. You'd think she would want to go visit her kid, chill with her parents, and they'd want to see her. But she called them and they'd gotten her into a halfway house. She had been sleeping there at night but hung with us and worked tourists during the day. That left me with Fleet, who was behind me all the time, waiting to see where I'd go. It seemed like all the bad parts of having a kid.

I set the pink monkey in the lowest branch of the tree where I'd tied a bag with my extra clothes and that seemed to make

Ash happy. "King Pink," he said. It had already lost half its yarn mouth. We took Root around the Children's Playground and then to the shelter for dinner, even though I could tell Ash wanted to stay outside with me. I wasn't going for that, not yet.

"I missed you," he said, while we stood in line for dinner. "Honest."

I knew what he wanted, but I wasn't going to say it back. I reached for a plate and moved forward in the food line. He sat next to me at a table on the far side of the room. We were the only two until Hope and Fleet, who was carrying the rabbit, sat down, followed by the group from Colorado. I could see Hope's T-shirt, even though she kept trying to cover it up under her sweatshirt. Jay House.

"I'm starting a class at City College after Christmas," she said.

"What? Introduction to halfway house?" said Ash.

Hope flashed him a fuck-you, but she laughed. "Well, close," she said. "The psychology of addiction."

"I want into that," said one of the Colorado guys. "But I'm not sure where I'll be after Christmas."

Hope said to screw us all, that she'd be learning about what happens in the brain to make people crave drugs. Her caseworker told her that it was a disease, that people didn't become addicted randomly. If you tried something and your brain was up for it, you didn't have a chance. "It's not like some moral flaw," said Hope. Someone should tell his mom that, Ash said. The caseworker also told Hope that maybe she could go to college and be a psychologist. Help other kids on the street. Break the pattern. Fleet sat next to her, quietly eating dinner, cubes of meat and potatoes in a yellow sauce. She looked like she was thinking about something, maybe counting the number of times she chewed.

"Well, I will be here," said Ash, putting out an arm and smashing me in next to him.

"We're having Thanksgiving dinner at the house and I can invite two guests," said Hope. "I guess they're thinking we could invite our parents. But who would want to do that? Mine are up in Mendocino with their turkey. They pay more attention to it than they did to me. Or my kid. They write down what it eats every day and how much weight it's gained."

"Then they kill it and eat it?" said Ash. "That's perverted. Make friends and then eat them. It would be like feeding Robo," and he put his hand on the rabbit's head, "and then eating him."

Fleet laughed, one long snort, and then she was snuffling and carrying on like it was the funniest thing she'd ever heard. Ash slapped her on the back, but she kept laughing until the tears started pooling in her eyes and running down her face. She was crying and laughing and it sounded like she was choking. I passed her my cup of water. She took a sip and coughed, the mist shooting out on all of us.

"There's still something wrong with my kidney so I don't even think I could eat turkey," said Fleet. "They said to watch how much protein I eat. But I could eat everything else on Thanksgiving."

"Weed and potato chips," said Ash.

"I'm not doing that again," I said.

Last year we'd waited in line for hours to get into dinner at the church downtown. First there was a long sermon and choir music that filled up every space in my head. The preacher wanted us to thank god and then everyone in our family, then everyone in the room, until we were hugging on people next to us, most of them we'd never seen before. When we finally got to dinner, I was on overload. There were trays of meat, potatoes, and green beans that went on forever. Girl Scouts quietly handed out tiny pumpkin pies at the end of the tables. They all deserved a badge because there were hundreds of us there, one giant room of need. We sat down and said grace with everyone and yelled "Praise God" before eating. We were not total bums. The food might have been good, but we ate so fast I couldn't tell. There were people behind us, waiting with their plates. When we left, volunteers handed each of us a can of Pringles, which, suddenly starved, I ate back at our spot. Happy Thanksgiving, Ash had said, and pulled out a joint as big around as his thumb.

"Maybe you want to take that class with me," said Hope.

She dropped her empty plate in the compost and waved over her shoulder at us without turning her head, saying she had to get back before curfew. It didn't sound like Hope. I picked up my pack and got in line for a bed at the shelter. Fleet followed me, holding Robo. She was quiet again, like she didn't want anyone to try and talk to her.

"Let's get out of here," said Ash, nodding toward the door.

"I'm staying tonight," I said. Fleet, flush up behind me, half smiled.

"Catch you tomorrow, if that exists, along the continuum." Ash reached out and took the end of Root's leash and walked out with him.

I wanted to jump on his back and pound him, but I didn't want to lose my place in line, which stretched across the room. No one was going to let me cut, even if they could see what Ash was doing, stealing my dog. The worst part was watching Root bobbing along beside Ash, as if that was where he belonged. What was the point of letting someone inside the circle you drew around yourself? This was always what happened. If I'd had a small knife, one I could use to slice between Ash's ribs, into his heart, I might have used it.

CHAPTER 22

Marva fussed over a long table in the living room that she'd covered with a bright orange tablecloth and matching napkins. "I couldn't resist this," she said, pointing to a gravy bowl shaped like a pumpkin. "I thought that's exactly what we need, but now I realize it looks all wrong." She smoothed out fake fall leaves she'd scattered around the pumpkin.

I sat on the minimalist couch wondering why I'd agreed to come. Dave had pleaded with me, said Marva was back for Thanksgiving and wanted me to meet their oldest kid and his family. They had heard all about me, he said. Marva was cooking, which was a good sign. She hadn't been in the kitchen since they'd gotten the news about Shane. He was hoping we would all show up. I told him I was going to Jay House to be with Hope, but he wouldn't give up. "Just for a while?" he said. He would bring me back early and I could go to Hope's later, with leftovers. I found myself getting into his car with Root, who must have remembered he'd been there before. He burrowed into the back seat and went to sleep.

"At home, I have a ceramic turkey the size of an actual bird," said Marva. "My grandmother used it every year and she's passed it down. We'll just have to imagine it this year."

Dave put his hand on her arm, thinking he could turn the channel, but Marva kept going about how she usually decorated the Thanksgiving table, with the giant turkey in the center of everything.

"You probably had your own traditions growing up," said Marva, sitting down next to me on the couch. "Everyone gets used to what they have at home and then that's what they want. Sometimes they don't think about it, but then they're disappointed if it's not the same way, over and over. Tell me how your family spent Thanksgiving."

I told her we didn't make a big deal about it. Sometimes my mom had to work at Safeway early that morning, so we'd eat when she got home. I didn't say that Karen and Chip didn't care about Thanksgiving; it was on a Thursday so we had hamburgers and baked beans. And I didn't say that I liked how my mom brought part of a cooked turkey home the day after Thanksgiving when she got it half price. She opened a can of cranberry sauce that sat on a plate, shining, still in the shape of the can, and some mashed potatoes from the deli counter. She could afford turkey on Thanksgiving, but she didn't like the idea that they marked up the price right before. It was a crime. But people were sheep, she said, so let them pay a premium. On Thanksgiving, we ate TV dinners sitting side by side on the living room couch watching whatever was on, with our little trays of fried shrimp or chicken strips. Honestly, I liked those more than turkey, but I wasn't going to tell Marva that I wished I could heat up a frozen dinner.

"You must miss your family," she said. "I hope you'll like being with us." She wiped her face, which was pink from cooking, and went back into the kitchen. The whole room smelled like turkey.

Marcus's two boys ran in from the back bedroom, chasing each other and scooting under the table. They were four and six, with identical blond bowl-shaped haircuts, light blue button-down shirts, and red clip-on ties. "Mana," the younger one cried, in escalating bleats. "Mana. Mana."

Marva peered out from the kitchen, closed the oven door and rushed to the table. The kid was underneath it, tears running down his face. "My head," he whined.

"You bumped it?" She reached for him.

"Here." He pointed to the top of his head. Marva patted his hair and kissed him. "Can you read me a story?"

"But who will take care of the turkey in there?" Marva said. "Your mom and dad have gone to get more firewood."

"I will," said the six-year-old. "Where's Grandpa?"

"He is going to take Root for a walk," she said. Both boys looked at me for the first time but were more interested in Root. He showed his teeth to strangers on the street if they made a move on me, but he was backing up like he was scared. They didn't seem to notice that I was in jeans and a clean but stained T-shirt, which I'd grabbed at the shelter when I thought I was headed to Jay House with Hope. At least I would have looked like I fit in there.

"It might take him a while to get used to you," said Dave. "But not her." He turned to me. "This is Maddy. She knew Uncle Shane."

"I didn't really know your uncle," I said to them, my back to Dave, in a voice that only a kid could hear. "Your grandpa made that up." The kids looked at me like they didn't get it. Or maybe they didn't care.

"Can you read to us?" said the older one.

"How about if we let Maddy get settled," said Dave. He showed them how to hold out their hands under Root's nose so he could get used to them, but neither boy did it. Dave took Root by the collar and led him out the front door.

"You know how to make gravy?" Marva said, holding out her arms for the boys.

"That's silly," the smaller one said. "Gravy."

He ran into the back room and came out with a book. Marva sat back down on the cream-colored sofa and read a story about a green caterpillar that ate too much fruit and still turned into a butterfly. She held them, one on each side of her lap. The trees blew back and forth against the big picture windows.

"Mana, read more," said the younger one. He had one hand on her wrist. She covered his hand with hers. It was like I wasn't there. Marva forgot she'd invited me. The kids forgot they'd asked me to read. I half listened to the story. I thought about the bird that Dave had shown me, the one that had forced the fish down its throat. Did it fly home for the winter or was it out there in the wind? Either way, it was where it was supposed to be. It was born in a nest and stayed there until nature meant for it to leave. What would that be like? It didn't seem like there was any place I fit, not here, not with Ash or at Hope's halfway house.

....

The older kid slipped off Marva's lap. "You run and I'll catch you," he said.

"How about you catch your brother?" she said. "But not under the table. Let me go take care of the turkey and then we can play."

She looked over at me. "You want to come?"

From the kitchen, we could hear waves of giggling in the back room. The turkey was brown on the outside and Marva covered it with tinfoil and put it back in the oven above a cookie sheet filled with vegetables. A basket of fresh rolls sat on the counter.

"I think this is my favorite holiday," she said. "Or it used to be. You must have a favorite."

I was going to say how I didn't have one, but Marva looked so happy right that minute, focused on the roasting vegetables and the pumpkin and pecan pies that sat cooling. For one second everything was the way it should be.

"Maybe we could all drive back with you, show the boys San Francisco," she said. Her face was still flushed and she pushed back her hair. She said she'd already told the boys about the sea lions at the wharf, the penguins at the science museum, and the lake in the park where they could ride in paddleboats while ducks trailed behind them begging for bread.

"You could be our guide," said Marva.

She should hire Hope. I wasn't a tour guide. All I knew was the park, and not the way they'd want to see it. They didn't know how I'd marched through every part, looking for Shane. But I let myself think about going with them. I'd sit in the back of the car with the kids pressed up against me. We could go out in a boat and I'd paddle because their legs would be too short. Dave would buy popcorn so we could throw it on the water, let the ducks chase behind. I felt drugged by the smells in the kitchen. Maybe I could be part of all of this, take up some of what Shane left behind. It wasn't like my mom would even mind.

I could see Dave outside in the driveway as the car with Marcus and his wife pulled up. He had a hand on Root's back and seemed to be talking to him. Marcus and his wife, each holding a carton of wood, got out and walked toward the front door. Dave was behind, holding a round package topped with a huge orange bow.

"I figured you had to have this," he said, handing it to Marva. "I had it hidden away in the trunk."

She sat on the couch and unwrapped the package slowly, unsticking each piece of tape and folding back the paper. She frowned at a life size ceramic turkey.

"What?" said Dave, watching her expression. "I thought it was festive. It's like a cousin of the one we have back home."

Marva took the turkey and carried it to the back bedroom. "Nothing will ever be the same," she said. "You can't try to make it the same."

"Hey, it's Thanksgiving," said Marcus. "Let's try."

He came over to me and stuck out his hand. "Maddy?"

Small chips of wood stuck to the front of his sweater. He had the same blond hair as his kids and the same transparent blue eyes as his dad and Shane. I shook his hand, but of course he already knew who I was. I wondered what Marva and Dave had told him. Here's the homeless girl who saw your brother last.

It was only the middle of the day when we sat down to eat. Dave pointed to a chair and pulled it out for me. The kids sat on either side of me. Marva put her hands on the table and reached for Dave's hand. The kids each grabbed one of mine and then we were sitting there at the orange table, connected with the chain of hands.

"Sometimes it's hard to find anything to be thankful about," she said. "Believe me, I've had a hard time lately."

Her voice got so low it was hard to hear. She said she'd been waking up blaming God for everything, but today it was time to show gratitude. There was some healing power in that.

"I'll start," she said, her voice normal again. "I'm grateful that we have Maddy here to share our beautiful feast." She reached over and patted my hand.

Dave said he was grateful for Marva who cooked all the food. I didn't catch what Marcus or his wife said because I kept thinking about what I'd do when it was my turn. The older kid said he was grateful for his soccer team that was going to kick butt.

"That's stupid," said the younger one.

"Guys," said Marcus. "It's Thanksgiving." He turned to me. "Maddy?"

I didn't say anything. "Can I go? Can I go?" said the littler kid.

"Can we let our guest speak?" said Marcus.

"It's okay," I said.

I didn't want to have to say how I was grateful that my mom got us TV dinners so we didn't have to sit around and think up things to be grateful for. Saying nothing was fine. I was relieved when Dave tapped his knife on a glass and bowed his head. "Bless us, oh Lord, for your gifts which we are about to receive from your bounty," he said, and then looked up and told us we could start eating.

Marva and Marcus's wife brought the food over to the table and we ate like it was a race and someone had just shouted, "Go!" Root had his own plate, on the floor, filled with turkey and potatoes, which he finished in a few gulps. Dave talked about the birds in the lagoon and Marcus said he'd like to go duck hunting there. Marva kept getting up to refill platters, until all the clattering stopped. Everyone said they were full, they thought they'd die if they ate one more thing. Marva said we could take a break and eat the pies later. The kids and their parents went outside for a walk and Dave and Marva lay down on the living room carpet. Dave patted the ground next to him.

"Come on," he said. "It's what we do. Forced digestion and a nap."

I sat down next to him, knees to chest. "Are you going to tell her?" said Marva, like I wasn't there in the room.

"I was going to wait," said Dave. "Until we'd finished dessert. But, well . . ." He breathed in sharply and let out the air in small spurts. "Marva and I drove down to Los Angeles last week. We met your dad."

I could feel blood rush to my head. I swallowed hard. I hadn't seen my father in more than fifteen years. It was easier to think he was dead. I had started believing that.

"If you were our daughter we'd want to know where you were," said Marva.

"Why would you go see my dad?" I said.

"I thought he'd want to know where you are," said Dave.

He told me how it had been easy to find him, even with his primitive computer skills. They had looked up my birth records in Los Angeles, then searched online for his address. You had to work hard if you wanted to hide. George Donaldo lived in Culver City, on the west side of Los Angeles.

I was thinking about how I'd busted in on Jeremiah's wife, which was different. She didn't want to be found, but Jeremiah had killed someone. My dad was only guilty of not wanting his kid. He hadn't killed anyone. "What makes you think I'd want to know about him?"

Marva pulled her sweater tighter. She looked thinner than a few weeks ago. She was a small woman and she was disappearing more every day.

"What did he say, when you told him why you were there?" I said. Dave had probably already arranged for me to go down there and live with my dad. I tried to think where Culver City was, but I could only see the place where we used to live, the pullout couch and yellow tile counters in the kitchen.

Dave said my dad had seemed confused at first. He looked at the ceiling like he was trying to pick out how he might have a kid. Maybe he thought he could lie about it. But then he'd opened the door for them. The inside was a wreck. The paint was peeling and there was hardly any furniture. He looked as if he spent a lot of his time drinking. His face was puffy and his gut hung out.

"But I could see you in him," said Dave. "The eyes, the shape of your face."

"I bet he was dying to know about me," I said. "If he even remembers me."

"I'm sorry," said Dave. "I wasn't even going to tell you, but Marva insisted. She said it wasn't right to keep it from you. But now I'm not so sure."

Dave said my father had had a rough time. He had diabetes and was sick from alcohol and hadn't worked as a truck driver in a long time. My dad figured I'd be better off with my mother even though she had fits. But then she'd kicked him out. He never saw that coming.

"He left *us*," I said. And *fits?*" I said. "That's what he called it?"

"He wanted to know how you'd turned out," Dave said. "We told him you were living in San Francisco, homeless, but that you were a remarkable, intelligent young woman."

"Yeah, I'm sure he believed that," I said.

"He said he didn't have any control of you," said Dave. "There was nothing he could do. He didn't have anything when you were born, and he still didn't have anything. He wanted to know what exactly we wanted out of him. Half of zero is zero. Then he walked over and stood too close, like he was fixing to clock me in the face. Were we going to try and blackmail him? He'd heard of cases like that. I told him we wanted nothing. Absolutely nothing. It was a piece of the puzzle we had to know."

"My puzzle," I said.

"I wish I had more to tell you, but he threw us out," said Dave. "Physically pushed me out the door."

"He doesn't deserve to know you," said Marva. "There is no excuse for him."

Dave said that before they drove away, they folded up a poster with Shane's picture and wrote, "This is our son" on it and then shoved it under his door.

"This is your kid? Killed in the park up there?" my dad had shouted out the window, as they walked to their car. "Like you know anything about raising up kids. If that isn't the pot calling the kettle black."

"We should make him pay," said Marva, "for all those years he wasn't there. For all he did to your family."

"I don't think anyone can make him pay," said Dave.

"Not with money," said Marva. "But your dad owes you." I put my face into Root's fur so I didn't have to look at her. She wasn't really talking about my dad. It was all about Shane. She would never know what she owed.

CHAPTER 23

"Snap," Ash said, and we clinked our bottles together.

He patted his pocket and I could hear the pipe rattling in there. I should've brought more from Dave's house, but all I had was a bottle of wine from the kitchen counter. The pumpkin pie, its shiny hard crust decorated along the edges with pricks from a fork, I threw in the trees on my way out. Let the birds get it. "Remember the pies," Marva had said before she and Dave fell asleep on the living room floor. "We always eat in two parts. I forgot to tell you that."

Ash didn't seem surprised when Root and I showed up, even though I must have looked wiped out. It had taken me two rides and a walk all the way from the bridge to get back. I reached for a torn bedspread that had been looped around a tree and spread it on the ground. Ash put the soggy pink monkey in the middle. It kept falling over so he propped it against his pack. Fleet's rabbit was leashed to the bottom of the tree, curled in a ball, nose quivering. Root flopped on an opposite corner of the bedspread with his head on his paws and stared at the rabbit. Ash said Fleet was off dumpster diving at a grocery store a few blocks away. I wondered if Fleet would score anything on Thanksgiving when a lot more people would be there. Even on normal days you had to go early, ready to push people out of the way to get at what was on top. I was relieved to see her walk back with a full pack. She turned it over and dumped out bruised apples and bananas, a package of sweet rolls, and two cans of pinto beans onto the bedspread. Ash took out his knife and started jabbing the top of a can. I closed my eyes and held its edges.

"That is stupid." I looked up and Hope was there, in a faded black sweatshirt that said GOD IS BUSY. Over her shoulder she had a mesh bag full of plastic containers. Jay House had given her a Thanksgiving dinner to take with her after I was a no show and she decided to leave. What was the point of sitting around there with people she didn't know? Ash said that was how he felt when he was at home with his mom. He held the knife, still attached to the top of the can, liquid oozing out the side. He wiggled it until he had the top partly peeled away.

"May be stupid, but it worked," he said.

Hope high-fived him and took a slug of the wine. "I've been too straight too long," she said. She drank another sip and then said she was heading to Haight Street. Tourists would be out thick on Thanksgiving afternoon, she said, ready to give. Leftovers, socks, change. A last few moments for generosity and redemption.

"Whatever," said Ash, sounding hurt. "There will be more for us."

"I'll be back. Keep your pants on," said Hope.

Fleet lined up the fruit, from smallest to biggest, and sat cross-legged next to her rabbit. Ash lit his pipe, took a hit, and passed it to her. I shook my head when Fleet handed it to me and she sucked in another deep one. Ash turned his back to me and puffed, like he didn't want me to see.

He took his guitar and started playing a riff I didn't recognize. I leaned against a tree and closed my eyes, listened to how it went along steady and then got faster, on its way to connecting to something before Ash lost control, the way he always did. The sun was almost down but still warmed my lap. Fleet seemed more together than she'd been in a long time. When I opened my eyes she was smiling, scratching Root's ear with one hand and the rabbit's head with the other. Root was sleeping and sighing. I put a bruised apple in the blue soap dish I'd taken from the cabin and set it next to the monkey. We had a centerpiece.

"Sweet," said Ash. He put down his guitar and sat next to me, trying to get his arm between my back and the tree. I didn't give him any help. It felt like I'd dreamed about going to Dave and Marva's. Marcus and his wife, their little blond kids, even the story about my dad, didn't seem real.

The trees were covered in shadow by the time Hope reappeared, holding packages of sliced meat and a half-eaten pumpkin pie. "Plus this," she said, pulling out a small stack of dollar bills, with a ten on top. "I told you. I knew people would be out there and they'd want to give extra. Someone bought me a crepe already, which I had to eat because I didn't want to look like a douche, taking it to go. I practically got adopted."

Root jumped up, alert and smelling the meat, even though he'd already eaten enough at the cabin for a whole week.

"Are we going to pray or some shit before we eat?" said Ash.

I thought about last year at the church when we all had to hug and pray, and then about Dave and Marva's, where we had to say what we were grateful for. They may have felt his absence every single minute, but no one had even mentioned Shane.

"In Wyoming, we had to say a prayer before we ate. Every time," said Ash. "It kind of freaked me out because I'd do it, but then I'd be thinking of something else when I said it and then I was sure I'd die, get hit by lightning or fall off the mountain, because God knew I was praying for show."

"But if you don't believe in God, then what's he going to do?" I said.

"I know," he said. "It's where my head took me. I couldn't help it."

Fleet was still sitting in her corner, petting her rabbit. Hope put her hands together and pressed them high on her chest. "Namaste." I wondered if she was thinking about her kid, up with her parents, eating little pieces of the pet turkey they cut up for him. She stood in the center of the bedspread, next to the tilting monkey, her hands still against her chest, her eyes closed. "I am so fucking happy I'm here now." She took a deep breath and let it out slowly.

Ash stood and copied Hope's arms. He bent a leg and balanced it on his other knee, like people we saw doing yoga in the park. I couldn't tell if he was serious or showing off, but he held still in the position, his skinny athletic arms flexed under his sweatshirt.

"I am here now and it's good, better than," he said, and at first I thought he lost his footing or was searching for what to say next. I couldn't see what knocked him forward, tumbling onto the bedspread.

When I turned, I saw Jeremiah, his face sunken, his cheeks almost gone. His beard had grown out since I saw him in court. Ash rolled over before Jeremiah could hit him in the back of the head. He took the punch in his chest and then kicked Jeremiah below the waist, but he must have missed because Jeremiah kept coming at him. Ash was younger, could move faster, but he was wrecked. Jeremiah was swinging with his full weight.

I wanted to kick him from behind, but I couldn't move, just like the first time I saw him in the park. He had a power to make me freeze up. Any minute he could pull out his knife and turn it on me. Fleet put the rabbit in her lap and held her arms around him like a cage. But Hope's voice was loosened up.

"Get the fuck off him," she yelled.

Jeremiah turned from Ash and looked at me. "There you are," he said. "Miss Holier Than Everyone. Right here. But you're not any different."

"He's out of his head," said Hope. "Watch out."

"You don't know anything," Jeremiah said. "And talking to Laurel. My wife." He said her name like she was the most important person in the world. I wanted to tell him that she wasn't his wife anymore, that she changed her name so no one would know she'd been his family. No one in this world wanted to be related to him. If he disappeared no one would care.

"That kid was a real sicko," Jeremiah said. "He was whacking off in the bushes. Maybe he pulled some girls in there. How do I know? There were little babies on the swings, going down the slide, right next to him. I told him he was going to burn in hell. He had it coming."

He grabbed for my arm, but I yanked it back. He dug into his waistband like he was going for the knife. Or worse.

"You should know about burning in hell," I screamed. Root started barking on full alert, every muscle stretched tight. Jeremiah took a step back and Root leaped and bit deep into his calf. Jeremiah looked startled, maybe because it was the first time he got what was coming to him. He yelled and punched down hard on Root's head. Ash kicked his other leg, knocking him to the ground, where he curled up to protect himself from Root.

"Root, off," I yelled. He stopped, his eyes moving from me to Jeremiah, who was splattered in squashed fruit and blood. Root trotted over and sat down in front of me, growling but leaving Jeremiah, who held onto his leg, the centerpiece in our circle of gratitude.

CHAPTER 24

....

It seemed like the park had settled into a funk of mud and leaves. Even the birds were quiet, except the seagulls that flew from the ocean before a storm, circling and screaming overhead. Jeremiah had gone to the hospital for stitches to sew up Root's tattoo of teeth marks. Then they took him to jail, but only for two weeks, for breaking the order to stay away from me. They didn't want him there either. Root got as much time as Jeremiah. He was locked up because he didn't have tags or proof that he had all his shots. They could have checked with the animal control office, but they said it was my responsibility to get him licensed. The cops said he had to wear a muzzle, that if he bit anyone else they would take him away and destroy him, which sounded like a big reaction against a dog that was trying to protect me. But they said a dog in the city is not allowed to bite anyone, no matter what. You can't have your own private guard dog. What you can do is keep a knife in your pocket and use it to take someone out. No one punishes you for that.

Jeremiah had told the cops that Ash jumped him for no reason, and then I ordered Root to attack.

"And you think that's true?" I asked Officer Patz, who was doing foot patrol on the street.

"I don't think I'm in the business of truth," he said. "We do the best we can. We could find a reason to lock up Jeremiah Wakefield, but I could say that about a lot of people."

"Maybe no one should call the cops, ever," Ash said, "if they didn't know what was true."

Patz said it was more complicated than that. Stories were hard to decipher because they were filtered through people.

"Who you can't trust," said Ash.

Patz took off his cap and rubbed his head. He turned to walk down the street, but then stopped and came back. "I don't know sometimes, is all I'm saying. There are more sides than you think. Jeremiah came to the station one day last fall to tell us that Shane was hanging around with an underage girl. We did what we always do. We checked it out. We found him with a girl who was thirteen, but there was no evidence of any abuse or molestation. They were smoking marijuana, there was an open bottle. She agreed, not with enthusiasm, to go home. We didn't have much of a case, but Wakefield was yelling at us, followed me all the way back to the station."

"Shane was creeping on little girls?" I said. "Why didn't anyone say that at the hearing?"

"We had no evidence of anything," Patz said. "If we went out and arrested someone after a game of he-said, she-said, that's all we'd do. Some cases we leave to the judge and jury in the sky." He looked up at the gray clouds and the birds floating overhead in formation.

I had to work off the fine for blocking the sidewalk, which they said had escalated because I never showed up in court to pay it. Everyone had told me I was free to sit where I wanted, but it turned out I wasn't. They made me pay by wearing a yellow vest and cleaning trash off the street for two weeks. I didn't mind the job, walking around with a long metal pincher and picking up needles, food cartons, bottles, piles of shit. It was people who bugged me. "You forgot this," said one of the guys from ES EF, kicking over a jar of pee that someone had left by a pile of boxes on the sidewalk. Other people I knew on the street nodded, said what's up, and I tried not to catch their eyes, because they would want to know what happened and I didn't want to go over it all again. The worst was the ones who stopped and thanked me for taking care of the street, like I was some kid suddenly arriving on the right side of life. "No problem," I said quickly, so they couldn't see my face. You get what you pay for. Whatever happens, you asked for it, one way or another. At dinner, I tried to act normal, as if I hadn't spent the day bending over on the street picking up what everyone left behind.

I knew Dave would be back because he always found his way. One night he walked in while we were eating dinner. I hadn't seen him since Thanksgiving, and I wondered if he was mad that I'd snuck out of the cabin while he and Marva were sleeping on the floor. He looked as washed out as when he stayed in the park. No one gave him a second glance. He knew where he was going, straight to me. The security guard who stood by the door didn't say anything to him.

"I wanted to see you before I leave for home," Dave said. "Can we go somewhere one more time and talk?" Root wriggled out from under the table and jumped on him. Dave put his hand on Root's head and we both followed him outside. I was shivering in my T-shirt and jeans, but I told him I didn't want his coat.

"Marva went back already, but she wants me to ask you something," he said.

There it was. He was going to ask if I'd found out anything new about Shane, like it was all I had to think about. No one was talking about Shane anymore, at least not here. A kid from Oregon fell off his board riding down Haight and survived after he split his brains open on the curb. Some dude was beaten up, then half drowned in the lake near us and now two cops parked their motorcycles next to the water all day. A coyote was living at the meth park a few blocks away so ES EF and everyone else moved out to the street, like that wild thing wanted their nasty asses. But Dave didn't know any of that. The movie he had in his head was never going to stop. I understand how he couldn't get rid of that. But the world, it was different.

"Marva wants to know if you'd like to come and stay with us," said Dave, his hands in his back pockets. "You can bring your boyfriend if you want. We have room."

I didn't answer.

"Partner, boyfriend. I don't know what you call it these days," said Dave. "I'm sorry. Everything is more fluid with your generation. It seemed like you two are together. I'm thinking like a dad. I can't help it."

"Not like *my* dad," I said.

Dave's lips tightened into a line. He looked hurt, but we both knew it was true. My dad wasn't thinking about me and he never would. Nothing was going to change that. Dave said he planned to go home, at least for Christmas, and after that he wasn't sure. He said he wasn't sure of anything anymore, even if he'd stay back east with Marva. Maybe they could find somewhere else to live that wouldn't remind them of Shane. She wanted one thing and he wanted another after Shane died, he said. Then he apologized for telling me too much and I said it was TMI, which I had to explain to him, too much information. He smiled and thanked me for the translation, which he said I'd done more of than I realized. Why was he trying to get me to come with him if he was going to turn around and leave Marva? He told me he never had a daughter, but he always wanted one. He'd be lucky to have someone like me, he said. Then it looked like he was going to hug me, and part of me wanted to be there, against his chest, with his arms around me. But I scrunched up so he restrained himself.

"I don't know what to tell her," he said, and we stood there like two kids at school who don't have anything to say to each other.

"At least walk with me for a bit?" said Dave.

I went inside to get my sweatshirt and Ash wanted to know what was up. Did Dave offer me money? I should take it if he did, Ash said, and gave me the rap again about how people like it when you take a gift. It makes them feel important. The person who gave the gift actually got more than the person who took it. Do it for Dave, he said. I told him I'd be back at 40 Hill later.

The lights were already on inside stores on the street and up on Twin Peaks, where a giant radio tower glowed like a bright red tooth. Dave said he'd given up the cabin in Marin and was staying at some inn nearby called the Palace. Despite the name, it wasn't fancy, he said, probably because he didn't want me to think he was staying at a mansion. He told me how the Victorian bathroom was moldy and the floors sloped to one side. It made him dizzy. The man who owned it said it had once been a big flophouse, with padlocks on every door and a drug lab in the basement. He'd bought it for nothing, fixed it up, and slapped it with an aspirational name. The one thing Dave liked was the view. He could see the bay, the sailboats gliding by and the buildings trimmed like presents in green and red Christmas lights.

"But it doesn't seem like Christmas," he said. "I wonder if I'd ever get used to that. No snow. I don't know how you can tell the season is changing. I guess you don't think about that, growing up in California."

"We can tell what time of the year it is," I said. "We don't need snow for that."

"Of course not," said Dave. "And I like the idea of no snow, no days when it's twenty below zero and your face feels numb."

I'd only seen snow once, when we'd had a cold snap in LA. It felt like it fell all at once from a trapdoor in the sky, turning the yard into a snow globe for about half an hour. Then it melted before we could play with it. I couldn't remember if it was even near Christmas because it wasn't what we used to tell time. Stores knew when to put out decorations, schools knew when to close. And my mom knew what to do. She'd put out a plastic tree a few days before Christmas, and stockings for both of us. It didn't occur to me until I was older and living with Chip and Karen that she must have filled her own stocking and bought a neatly wrapped present for herself. She'd open it and say it was exactly what she wanted. I'd say the same thing.

Two mannequins in Santa suits looked like they were kissing in a window of a used clothes store. Bottles of flavored vodka sat on top of mounds of fake snow in the liquor store window next to it. This was how you could be sure it was Christmas, I wanted to tell Dave, but he'd stopped next to a small group gathered outside the liquor store. He dropped change in a pot in front of one guy who had a sign, CHRISTMAS HERE. A banjo player sat next to him, strumming. He looked expectantly at Dave, who fingered through the bills in his wallet for a few ones.

"How about a Hamilton?" said the banjo player. His ears were dotted with silver loops and studs. "This isn't going to buy anything."

"What do you want?" said Dave. "I can get you a sandwich or two."

"Sick," he said. "How about extra cheese?"

I followed him around, through the aisles of bottles to the deli counter. "Joy to the World" blasted on the store speakers. Dave ordered the sandwiches, extra-large, with everything. *And heaven and nature sing.* The counter guy layered on meat and cheese and then covered it all with slabs of mustard and mayonnaise. Dave paid, walked out and handed the sandwiches to the kid with the banjo. I wondered how we'd get down the street if he kept stopping to buy food. Could the guy not give it up?

"I hate mustard," said the banjo player, looking at one of the sandwiches as he slapped a red beanie up and down on his head. "Now what?"

Dave laughed.

"Sorry. I tried," he said as we walked away.

"I wonder if someone ever stopped to buy food for Shane. Did anyone try to help him or ask where he came from," he said. "But Shane probably wouldn't have told the truth. He didn't want to be found." Dave hunched over, wrapped his arms around his middle. "I spent so much time with my boys, taking them to soccer games, baseball practice, tossing a ball in the yard, making sure they knew how to say please and thank you. We had dinner every night. Marva sat with them if I was off at the firehouse and watched that they did their homework. I always thought everything was a phase. It would all work out the way it was supposed to. That's what I told Marva because it was how my life had gone."

We kept walking and he was looking at me. When he was in high school, he said, he'd stolen a bottle of his father's rum and driven around all night with his friends, one of them lying on top of the hood yelling directions on the windy roads.

"I hate to say this, but I was so drunk I might have killed someone or ended up in jail," he said. "But I made it through to the other side. Shane would too, I always thought. He was a normal kid doing what he had to in order to grow up. What should I have known? There must have been evidence of what was wrong and I missed it. We both did."

Down the street Sara Moon sat with her legs crossed, bright colored bracelets scattered around her. I raised a hand to say hi. Root nuzzled her thigh and then her pack. She looked up and I could see the bruise under her eye had disappeared. Merlin lay sprawled nearby, one arm overhead, like he'd been reaching for something before he passed out. The air around them was a fog of dirty clothes, weed and beer that worked its way through every breath.

"They are five dollars each," said Sara Moon, holding one up to Dave to take a closer look. "Maddy, tell him."

"He's not here for that," I said.

"You could have them all for twenty," said Sara Moon.

"Seriously," I said. I wanted to say he was only there for me, because he wanted me to be his kid, that he didn't have any use for bracelets. He'd throw them away. That's how pointless they were. Merlin stretched and rolled over but didn't open his eyes.

"It's okay," said Dave. "Here." He pulled out a twenty and handed it to her.

"Cool," she said, and gave him the handful of bracelets.

Dave took them and stuffed them in his pocket. The grass at the edge of the park was empty except for a drum circle tatting on an overturned plastic container, a pair of bongos, a metal barrel topped with cowhide, banged up congas. The drumming got louder and then softer, the beats chasing one another. We sat on a bench and Dave tossed a pinecone for Root, who ran after it and pounced, bringing it back for more until it broke into pieces. He rested his chin on the remains and closed his eyes. No one would know how we were related, me in a dirty blue hooded sweatshirt and Dave in his sagging jeans and feathery gray hair. I wondered if Shane had ever sat here, listening to the drummers. Maybe Jeremiah was right and he came there to watch girls at the playground.

"I don't think you'll ever know what it was like for us," said Dave. "But since we found you, it's like we have a way to go forward. Maybe it's meant to be."

I moved away from him on the bench because I could just as easily have climbed closer.

"And there is one more thing I should tell you," Dave said. "I should have said it earlier, but I'm not perfect. You already know that."

I stared at the drummers and promised myself not to look at him.

"Marva and I, we found your father," he said. "But we couldn't figure out how to locate your mother, and we couldn't give up on it. On you. So we hired someone."

I felt heat rising into my face. My mom was no one else's business. My dad, he was out there living in his house and he didn't know anything about me. But my mom still knew more about me than Dave ever would.

"She is in a small boarding home near Venice Beach," he said. "The door was locked and no one answered when we knocked. We never got to see her." He stared out at the drummers, along with me, so at least I didn't have to look in his eyes.

"The thing is, we'd like to have you live with us. Back east or wherever we wind up, for as long as you want."

"Like I'd be some replacement?" I said.

"No," said Dave. "That's not it. But we would like to give you what you need to move on with your life. We're not asking to adopt you formally or change your name. You don't have to change anything. You're an adult and it's your decision to make."

I couldn't answer. All I could think about was that he'd gone to where my mom was. How could he have done that? At least he hadn't seen her. I wasn't sure I wanted to know if she was better or if she still sat there all day, staring.

"Don't you want to know what I found out?" I said. "Why didn't you even ask me? You wanted me to talk to people about

Shane. I spent weeks walking through the park, all the way down to the beach. You don't know how many people I asked."

"I thought you'd tell us if you heard something," said Dave. "I know you showed Shane's picture around here and looked up the court records. I should have paid you for all that work. That's what Marva said."

"What are you talking about?" I said, getting up off the bench. "You think I wanted money? You think I did it to get something off you, while you were out there secretly tracking down my parents?"

I was going to tell him, how Shane was perverted, how he followed little girls around in the park, while Marva was home washing his clothes over and over. Who knows what he did in the bushes. Maybe Jeremiah was saving those girls when he went after Shane. Dave needed to know who his kid was before he tried to make me his daughter. I started to talk, but the drums got louder, a jumble of banging, all of it moving together in a growing wave.

"I guess it's not possible to ask them to pipe it down a little?" Dave said.

A guy with the metal barrel threw his drumsticks in the air and caught them with a single hand, nodded at the others, one by one, and then each took a turn playing solo until they all joined in. It was an earsplitting clanging catfight of noise, but it fit together like the weird random way I had ended up where I was.

"Did you say something?" said Dave. I stared at him and he looked so uncomfortable and sad. I swallowed what I was about to tell him and listened to the drums. They drowned out whatever I could say that was true. My mom was locked in a boarding house and my dad was useless, but that didn't mean I needed Dave. Shane was more of a mess than I ever was. I would never be Dave's kid.

"I didn't say anything," I said loudly because I didn't think he could hear over the explosion of drumbeats. And then I made my way over to the drum circle and I started jumping up and down and spinning. It seemed to give the drummers a blast of new energy, a strange girl under the spell of their rhythm. They swayed back and forth and played like one huge instrument. Someone handed me a conga and I banged on it so hard that my hands ached and nothing mattered. I rocketed between the drummers until I was dripping with sweat and then I fell over on the grass and lay still. I stared up at the stars and they kept playing.

I could see Dave, walking out of the park, back toward Haight. "Shane was fucked up," I yelled as loud as I could. "You don't know how fucked up he was." But Dave was too far away to hear me.

On the bench, he'd left his phone on top of a folded-up note. "Maddy," it said, "use this to call us whenever you want. No matter what you think, we care about you. But we both know this: you don't get to pick your children any more than you get to pick your parents. You will be in my prayers every night when I close my eyes."

CHAPTER 25

I started writing the letters the next day. I was never going to mail them, even though I wrote the first one sitting outside the post office, next to a row of chipped blue mailboxes. They creaked when anyone opened them and dropped in mail. I sat chewing on the end of a pen I'd gotten from the library. "Dear Mom," I wrote, but that sounded too light, like I was gone for the weekend and there was something I wanted her to remember. What could I say to someone who didn't know anything about me? I'd never called her Mother. Maybe I should have used her first name. Dear Hannah. That sounded wrong too, so I went back to where I'd started. Dear Mom, wherever you are, if you can still understand words on a page.

I told her how I was in San Francisco and that I was okay, still trying to figure things out. It sounded lame so I drew a picture of Root with his mouth open like he was smiling and wrote "your other kid." I thought about the last time I'd seen her, how she didn't seem to recognize me. How would she now? She hadn't seen the outside of me for a long time. I wondered if I'd know her either. She would be different than she was all those years ago. But if anyone saw her, it should be me. Dave should not be the one who told her about me. That was mine. I crossed out Mom and settled on Hey. If I didn't use her name then I could be as mean as I wanted. Even if I mailed them, she might be so off in her head that she wouldn't understand them.

I wrote the next few letters in the library. It was warmer there and the librarian said I could have as much paper as I wanted. She showed me her drawer, which had dividers for pens, paper clips, and animal-shaped erasers. "I'm overly organized, right?" she said. She told me she'd give me free stamps if I wanted to mail anything, that writing a letter was one of the most meaningful things that could happen between two human beings. I wondered what it would be like to have a place where everything belonged. What if I'd gone with Dave? His house would be like that. I could have forgotten that I ever had a mom who couldn't get out of bed and take me to school.

"Maybe you never should have had a kid," I wrote. "You couldn't take care of anyone, even yourself. It was good someone came and took me away." I kept going on that way and the words spilled out of me fast. I boiled with nastiness until I got so tired I had to put my head down on the desk and stare at a shelf of books across from me. There was so much to tell her, but I couldn't figure out how to say it. Most of what I'd written she already knew.

One day the next week I sat at a table in a corner of the library, away from the line of people waiting to use the computers. "Hey,"

I wrote, "I'm here in the library, and you'd think it would be the best place to figure out what to do. I could look up what it's like to be a vet or a teacher. It seems that the library is what I like. I always have. It used to be my favorite part of going to school. I would sit in there so I didn't have to talk to anyone. Then I'd start in telling the other kids weird random facts. Did you know I was good at that? There are nine planets in the solar system. Spiders aren't related to beetles." I kept writing until I had a few pages and I went and took more out of the librarian's drawer. She was sitting with a group of kids, helping them with homework.

Ash asked what I was writing and I didn't answer. I didn't want him or anyone else reading the letters so I'd wait until he was gone to take them out of my pack and bury them near where we slept, another small part of me hidden away. He wanted to know why I hadn't told Dave anything more about Shane. I said I didn't actually know anything about Shane. I had heard things, but they probably weren't even true. Why would I trust anything that Jeremiah said? If you went across the park and showed people my picture, they would say they didn't know me either. Or that I was a slut or a tweaker with a weird ass dog and I hung out with three other kids.

"Dave wanted to take me home, make me into his own kid," I told Ash. "I wasn't going to tell him that his real kid might have deserved what he got."

"I'd want to know what my kid was like," Ash said, and he looked at me in the way he had, like he could see into the center of me.

"You could have told him," I said. "Free country."

I wanted to say that maybe it wasn't just Shane. We all got what we had coming. Could anything change that?

"I wish I thought people got born into other lives, based on what shit they did to other people," I said. "Then maybe I'd have a normal family. Or maybe that's why I'm here. Maybe I did something so bad that I got fucked up parents."

"Reincarnation," said Ash. "I'd probably be a worm or a fish."

"You'd be a millionaire who lives in a castle on the beach and takes in strangers who will then probably kill you."

"Thanks. I don't even like the beach," Ash said. "But I'm down with castles."

I held out the phone Dave left with me. "Sell this," I said. "We can stay in a room downtown for a few nights."

I thought it would make him happy, but Ash said it was stupid to sell the phone because Dave was paying for it and we could use it to do whatever we wanted. He said he was going to take some classes and he would use the phone to get a job.

"The city is crazy with computer jobs," he said. "Why shouldn't I have one?"

"Because you dropped out of college? And you live out here? And what is the point?" I said. "Plus, you better hope they don't give you a drug test at your job like your mom wanted to."

Ash put his arms around me and picked me up like I was a little kid, then set me down. We walked down the street, Root following. At the smoke shop Ash pulled out cardboard for a sign. $$ FOR SCHOOL. People walked by, but no one dropped change. So he turned over the cardboard and wrote BEER FUND. Underneath he drew a smile and two big eyes. People started leaving quarters and a few bills. Being real got them, plus it was the week before Christmas. Ash left the money out in a used paper coffee cup where everyone could see. He said no one wanted to be the first to give, or to do anything. As soon as he had enough, he bought a handle of vodka and put it down in my lap. I drank a few gulps and passed it to Ash. He stashed the rest of his change in the pocket of his shirt, a soft flannel that looked like he'd lifted it from the army surplus place.

"Nice," I said, fingering it. "Where'd you get those?" I pointed at an almost new pair of tan desert boots on his feet. "Are those for your computer job?"

It hit me almost before he said anything. "They're Shane's," he said. "Turns out I'm about the same size so Dave gave me a box of his stuff before he left. He said his wife shipped it out and that he liked to think of me wearing it. He left a pile at the shelter too."

I looked at him but didn't say anything. "What?" he said. "I was supposed to wait for everyone else to take them? Why does it matter?"

It wasn't that he was wearing a dead guy's clothes. Maybe we all were. Who knows why stuff got left in the giveaway box. Everything started somewhere, then ended up in a place you couldn't have pictured. It was that now Ash also had some weird connection with Shane. My own dad didn't want to know me. I would never write him letters. And there was Dave, so attached to Shane that he'd saved his boots. Maybe Ash was going to replace Shane. They didn't need me.

"You better take care of those boots," I said. "They'll get trashed."

"He would have given them to you," he said. "But they fit me."

On Christmas, someone left a stack of pizzas and a half-gallon of orange juice on the lawn. Hardly anyone was out, so we had them to ourselves. Most people had taken off to where it was warmer, maybe south along with flocks of Dave's birds. We slept outside unless it was raining hard. The shelter would be open until April, the end of what passed for a season here even though the fog and wind blasted all year. Hope was back at Jay House. They kicked her out for a week for missing curfew and showing up in the morning, trashed. But then they said she could stay if she promised to stop hanging with her old crowd, like that was going to happen. She said they expected slip-ups and called us a trigger to her past. "Bang," she said, making her hand into a gun shape, pointed at her head.

At the end of February tiny pale pink flowers sprouted on the trees around the lake. They were all you could see, glowing at night. Then, just as suddenly, they dropped off into the leaves and mud. We sat on piles of cardboard to keep dry. Ash found a refrigerator box someone left on the curb and dragged it over. It was big enough to hold our sleeping bags and Root, who spread out across the bottom. Ash said he was going to make a built-in bed and then we could rent it out. We stayed in there until it got too soggy and collapsed on top of us.

I kept thinking about what happened to Shane, even though no one talked about it anymore. There was nothing left of him here. Sometimes I passed the green metal bench where Dave and I had sat. I didn't notice that day that it had a plaque in memory of some guy who died, with writing in raised letters. "He found peace in this spot." It was like we'd been sitting on the guy's lap while Dave was trying to adopt me. Ash said not to look at the bench. Forget it existed. How hard was that? But it seemed that something had shifted, my world was falling in on itself. I sat on the bench, that spot of peace, and listened to the drummers who showed up even when the park was thick with fog and drizzle, a never-ending chorus.

Ash couldn't take it so he'd go look for the neighborhood kids who let him hang in their basement and play video games, until their mom showed up. She was happy to give him a space to get warm, no kid should be out on the street, she said, but he could not sleep down there. I stayed in the park or went to the library, where I kept writing letters. The librarian said I was a faithful correspondent, but never asked who I was writing to, which was fine. I wouldn't have said.

I told my mom about Root and Hope and Fleet, then, because of Marva, about where we stayed. Maybe she would want to know where I put down my head at night. So I wrote about the circle of trees at 40 Hill, the bed of leaves where we slept. I couldn't tell her about Shane or that Dave and Marva had found where she lived. Writing about Ash was hard enough. I didn't know what I thought about him lately. He kept wanting to hang around with me, but he had a problem with everything I did. "Do you think there are people in the world who are part of your orbit?" I wrote. "That's what he says. You are meant to find them and then you circle around one another, like planets." I didn't say we had fights because of his weird ideas. "Sometimes," I wrote, "I want to know what you'd think."

....

CHAPTER 26

We could hear the bushes crackling before we saw her. I snapped a leash on Root, who'd been asleep, folded over on his side. He picked up his head and put it back down when he saw her. She was small, with eggplant purple hair and black glasses sitting midway down her nose.

"I'm looking for Maddy Donaldo?" She pushed the glasses up with her index finger. How would she know where I stayed? No one but us came up to 40 Hill.

"I'm here to check in with you," she said, then started in on a talk she must have planned and tried out on herself. Dave had contacted her, said that I'd been in the park for two years and needed to get inside. Anything we spoke about would be confidential. Just between us, she said, like I didn't know what she meant. She said her name was Cade and she could point me to resources, or we could just stay here and talk about anything I wanted. And then, no invitation, she sat down in the damp leaves and leaned back against a tree.

"I had to give my dog away," she said, "because he kept

getting into it with every other dog he saw, which was not good for what I was doing. What I am doing."

I told her that Root usually knew who to trust. Then for some reason I told her how I found Root, that I basically rescued him and he had my back. She said she got that, her dog had had the same instinct. He'd been abused, which is why anything triggered him. She missed him, but she got her fix when her roommate came home with foster dogs. She was all over them, spoiled them with table food and let them sleep on her bed. She said she'd been a foster kid for a while so she could relate. When she got up to leave, she asked if I wanted to come with her on the bus to her office so we could talk more. I said no and she handed me a card, saying she'd be back, if I didn't mind. I couldn't say anything. I didn't own the park.

I carried the card in my pocket, even though I knew I wasn't going to call her. Ash said she might trap me into a cult. Maybe the next time he saw me I'd be wearing an orange robe, chanting "Hare Krishna" or waving incense and talking in a secret language. But he said I could do whatever I wanted. He said he might check out Mendocino with Hope, come back in the spring. The corners of his mouth turned up in a fake smile and I tried to ignore him. I might not be there when he got back. Maybe I'd be living with Cade and her rescued dogs. How much coming and going, tearing up a heart, could anyone take?

I took the card out one day after breakfast, mostly to make him mad.

"What the hell, Maddy." He grabbed it and ripped it up. I punched him in the arm, not hard enough to make Root get worked up.

Cade came by every week, the top of her head stripey where the black roots were growing out. She said she'd planned to do a different color every month, but she got tired of it. She used to set little goals for herself the first time she moved inside. It helped clear her head. She grew up in the city, out near the beach, and she'd stayed in the park twice, the second time for most of a year. She still wasn't sure what was going to happen, even though she worked for a program now and was taking college classes at night. She didn't think about dope every second, but she thought about it every day. That hadn't changed. If you stopped to think about it, a lot of people were addicted to something, whether it was dope or booze or approval. She didn't have any answers, or at least not one that she could give everyone.

We'd see her on the street, talking to Jax or handing her card to kids on the sidewalk. The pouch that Jax hung on the back of his chair bulged with power bars and juice boxes whenever she left. Some of her cards usually ended up in the dirt around the street tree, along with the weeds and cigarette butts. Someone had put a fence around the tree, like it was in jail.

Whenever Cade came by she talked to me like she'd known me a long time. I had no idea what Dave and Marva had told her, but she didn't ask questions. She didn't have to. She'd lived in the park with a guy named Toledo, who still slept out near the windmill and worked at a gym where he showered and worked out. She said it wasn't her job to change him. Besides she never wanted to live with a guy. Dogs were all she could handle. "Right," I said, not because I agreed, but because she knew that well enough to say it out loud.

I didn't talk to her about Ash, who kept saying he was leaving. He couldn't stand for me to talk about Cade, even though she seemed to be in my orbit. "Forget I ever made that up," he said. When some guys from Portland showed up, he said he was going up there. Don't bother, they told him. Portland was over.

"What isn't over?" said Ash. "This is over." He was in front of the smoke shop with a sign, DONATE HERE. Fleet was next to him, with Robo. Root was still muzzled but that didn't stop him from checking out a small black dog in a red bandana with the guys from Portland. One of them opened a guitar case, the inside a faded blue velvet, and put it on the sidewalk. He started picking a blues tune and singing in a deep voice, something about going home to his baby right now. People leaned over to drop change as they walked by. A few stopped and listened until the blast of a revving engine drowned him out. We all looked down the street at a black sports car, its motor full on racing while it sat there. No one moved. Time stopped, the way it does when you know your life might change in a quick second. And then the car took off and skidded into the intersection, where it spun out in front of us in fast swerving circles. Fleet, who usually clammed up, screamed like it was aiming at her. We backed up against the wall while it made a final turn, ending with its front wheels up against the curb.

Ash and the guys from Portland ran to the driver's window and banged hard. It was tinted so dark they couldn't see inside. I held tight to Root, who was trying to bark and break from his leash. They kept it up until the driver rolled the window down a few inches and shouted that he was practicing doughnuts for a movie shoot. Get the fuck away or he'd call the cops. Then the kids were shouting back at him, who did he think he was, he was going to get his ass kicked. He had the door locked, but they were pulling on that too when two cop cars pulled up, sirens and lights on.

The cops ordered the guy out of his car, while we watched from the sidewalk. A crowd gathered around us and started to ask what happened.

"He tried to get away," said Ash, pointing to the man, who was surrounded by cops. "But a group of us pulled him out of the car."

I turned to find Fleet, but she had already left. I couldn't keep standing there. I wasn't thinking how lucky we were that the car stopped in the street, instead of hurtling onto the sidewalk. That's what you think later. I just wanted to get away. The crowd stayed on the corner and murmured. Ash kept talking and gesturing, everyone pushed up around him.

"He could have fucking killed us," he said. "Or her." He pointed at a lady pushing a stroller on the other side of the street.

The next day I pulled out one of Cade's cards I'd found on the sidewalk and called. I didn't want to use Dave's phone because Ash had it with him, stashed in the bottom of his pack. I waited until dinner and called from the shelter. No one noticed because Ash was still telling his story. He'd even told it to a news station, which was putting it on TV, he said. They were going to call him and the kids from Portland the homeless heroes.

CHAPTER 27

The room had a single bed, a dresser, and a miniature refrigerator. The uneven wooden floor was painted pale blue. Root snuffled around the edges of the room and climbed onto the bed. Cade said the room was mine, I could stay as long as I wanted. I probably looked like I didn't believe her because she said that yes, it was a two-way street. I had to demonstrate that I could make good choices and, eventually, I'd have to pay some rent. The program could only go so far. I could live in the room forever, but there were rules. Everyone had to be in school or rehab or have a job. And there would be chores and a mandatory support group. I told her it seemed like a lot. It wasn't that bad, she said.

"Did she use the line about giving people fishing poles instead of fish," Ash said, when I went to 40 Hill to pick up some of my stuff. "It's what they told us in Wyoming. You give people tools instead of a handout and then they can take care of themselves."

He said go ahead if I wanted, he was not signing on for another program where people were checking on him every day. When did I become the kind of person who'd go for that? I didn't tell him that it was when that guy in the car pushed his pedal all the way down and drove straight at us. I had no idea what was going to happen. I felt that way all the time. Something was coming for me and would never stop. Maybe the car had nothing to do with it and I was mixing everything together. But I could not keep jumping out of the way.

He headed off to the shelter for dinner and I almost yelled at him to wait for me. Root and I trailed behind, all the way to the bus stop. I stood there, holding a bag of dog food, my jacket and extra sweatshirt. Ash didn't turn to look back, so I sat and waited for the bus.

I said I would move in for a month, which is how long you had to stay if you took a room. They said it was part of the investment you had to make. I filled out the forms with fake information, the same way I did at the Valencia. Cade said not to worry, that no one was checking. There were some secrets I was not ready to give up, so I wrote what I wanted.

Father: deceased

Mother: unknown

Last address: the world.

I left the sections on goals and job experience empty. *Who do you want us to contact in case of emergency?* I left that blank too.

Ash pretended nothing had happened when I came by the park. Sometimes I spent the day with him. I told him he could come by my room and check it out. I wasn't going to trick him into living there. The program didn't have a curfew like Jay House. No one hassled me about when I got back. I had my own set of keys and I could come and go when I wanted. There was a guy downstairs in a gray uniform and badge, but he acted like they were paying him to play games on his phone. He seemed to know me by sight; he never asked for my ID card before hitting a button under his desk and letting me in.

For two years I'd never slept all through the night, not even when I stayed in the shelter. I thought it would be different when I moved inside. I would sink into a bed in a room that was my own and the next thing I knew it would be morning. I liked the room, the color of the floor and the bed pushed against the wall, the way you like something because it's yours. But I couldn't get used to it. I thought someone was going to bust in the door so I'd lie there, listening, or I woke up sweating and didn't know where I was. One night I dreamed I was back at Karen and Chip's hiding under my bed, waiting for Karen to find me, and I woke up shouting. Then I lay in bed, hearing car tires whisking along the street, music from a boom box. Red and green lights from the street signal flashed against the blinds. I heard doors opening and shutting, the weird ticking and breathing of the room, but otherwise it was quiet. It should have comforted me, but it didn't. I couldn't stay in one position long. I turned on my side, then on my back. It didn't seem right to look up and see a blank ceiling instead of trees outlined on the night sky or to roll over without feeling the warm slight body of Ash.

Every week I had to go to a meeting downstairs. Cade sometimes came to lead it. She'd go around the room and ask everyone how they were doing. You could skip your turn and go meet with her later, which is usually what I did. You were supposed to say what had happened since last time, but she had a rule about including one good thing. If there was nothing good that had happened, you could use something from a few weeks, or even years ago. It was important to leave positive energy behind, she said. You could talk about slipping up and using again or being too bummed to get out of bed or look for a job, but then you had to offer up something good. My first week, the guy who lived next door to me said he came out to his mother and she said she never wanted to see him again and then he missed a meeting with his probation officer, so he was on double probation. But he ended by saying that there was an opening at the bakery around the corner and after he applied, the owner said she was going to see what she could do. She'd hugged him on the way out.

When it came to me, I said I didn't have anything, but everyone piled on. "Come on, Maddy, step up." Root lay by my feet, like he was the only one on my side.

Cade told them to give me time, which made me want to tell her to stay out of it. She didn't know me as well as she thought. I said that a friend kept giving me a hard time and I didn't know what to do about that. But I was in my old neighborhood the other day and people said hey, like I'd never left. I could go back there any time. What I didn't say out loud was I wasn't sure anymore. I hadn't even seen Fleet or Hope. The people in the room looked at me like they already knew who I was. Maybe I could get used to that.

"Thanks, Maddy," they said.

When everyone else left the room, Cade came over and told me good going, that it would get easier. She said I reminded her of the way she used to be, which she thought might not be fair.

"Easier how?" I said. It seemed like everyone tried to take up all the space, at the support group then the house meeting, where we had to decide everything by consensus and if one person disagreed, we had to start in again on finding a solution. We had to agree on what tea to buy, how to stack the plastic chairs, where we should store the extra toilet paper, how often we'd clean the shared kitchens on each floor. I couldn't make myself join in.

"It was easier after I made myself tell the truth," said Cade.

I walked back to my room and sat on the floor, looking out the window. No wonder Ash didn't want to live here. He didn't want to be told what to do. Cold air seeped in from outside so I put on another sweatshirt and then I started pacing around the room to get warm but also, I could not stay still because even I had to see that Cade was right. Except I wasn't like her. I didn't know what was true.

Ash came over the next day and said he'd signed up for a biology class. If he was going to take three buses for an hour and sit in a classroom, he wanted to learn something that wasn't obvious, that he couldn't teach himself. He said he could figure out computer coding at the library. He'd smoked so much that the smell came into the room before him. I'd have to tell the group that it wasn't me, even though they wouldn't rat me out. No one cared. I almost wished I could go to the biology class so I wouldn't have to pick an activity. Technically I had to do something. I could not go sit in a library, which would have been my first choice. There was a list of classes at the front desk, which took place all over the city. Easy Cooking, Mindful De-stress, Money Matters. I signed up for a photography class because it met downstairs. I didn't want to hike across town with Root to the community college. I'd stopped making him wear the muzzle they'd put on him at the dog jail, but he'd need it over there. I couldn't stand to look at him, shaking his head and rubbing the muzzle against the wall. And he barked if I wasn't with him in my room. He used to sit next to Fleet's rabbit and do nothing, but he went crazy if he was alone and heard someone outside in the hallway. Cade said that was normal, that he would adjust. She'd started taking him to her office while I was in the photography class. Maybe he'd end up being a therapy dog and help people recover from trauma, she said. That was fine as long as he remembered when he needed to protect me, I told her. I didn't want him forgetting that.

The first day of class the teacher asked how many of us had experience taking pictures. "Even with one of these." She pulled a cell phone out of a square canvas bag on her desk. "These are fast becoming the tool anyone can use." I was one of the only people who didn't raise a hand. She said she used to carry heavy cameras all over the world and was angry when everything went digital. No, actually, she was insulted, she said. It meant anyone could use a camera and the art of photography was lost. But then she started thinking the opposite. Film was expensive. New cameras were lighter. If they were more democratic, maybe that was a good thing. She turned off the lights and projected some of her pictures on the wall so we could see for ourselves, she said.

The first pictures, in black-and-white, showed people and the things they owned. Someone had paid her to go around California and document people standing outside with their furniture and clothes and dishes and cooking pots. I wondered how she convinced them to haul it all outside, to make those trips back and forth for someone they didn't know. She said she learned that possessions were important, but they weren't what defined people. When I looked at the people in her pictures, I thought they seemed annoyed that some lady with a camera had made them act like a moving company. Not many of them were smiling. One man stood with his hands on his wife's shoulders, his two little boys in shorts and bare feet, in front of a table and chairs, two mattresses on a frame made from thick ropes, stacks of plastic bins full of rice bags, cereal boxes, powdered milk, and canned food. He was looking right at the camera, proud, like he was daring the photographer to try and take it away.

Then she showed us pictures of people who lived outside, posed next to their stuff. She had asked them to arrange it however they wanted. Some piled everything in carts and others sat in the middle of a mess of sleeping bags and blankets and clothes. They didn't seem to notice she was there or they were thinking who cares, one more person seeing what they want. She said she felt more intrusive with people who lived outside, so she started handing out cameras and asking them to take their own pictures.

The guy who lived in the room next to me stood in the hallway, craning his head to watch. The teacher asked him if he wanted to come in and he sat down loudly in a chair near the door. When she turned on the lights, it took a minute to see clearly. The eyes were slow to adjust, she said, while cameras could change in an instant, which should be a reminder. They were not interchangeable. Don't forget that, she said, while she began handing out small black cameras to all of us.

She said we were going to spend the first week learning how to use them. She snapped a picture of us sitting around the room, then walked around and showed it to us. You might not recognize yourself, she said, but this shows the beginning of our relationship. People don't know what they look like on film. They are always surprised. She told us to take pictures of whatever we wanted. Don't think too much or censor yourself, she said. Everyone started to mob her with questions: What were the two buttons on the side for? Where were the batteries? Could we just use cell phones if we had them? She held up a hand to shut us up. We didn't need to know anything technical, she said. Push the button on the top right to take a shot whenever we felt like it. Start off like that. Concentrate on what was in front of us instead of what was in our head.

There was only one big rule, she said. We could keep the cameras if we showed up and completed the class. Miss a class without permission and you have to give up your camera. They'd been donated by some company downtown, so try not to lose them, she said. The guy from next door was turning his over in his hands like he was figuring out how fast he could sell it on the street.

I hid my camera under my sweatshirt when I went outside and took it out to take pictures in the neighborhood. At one corner, there were six signs jammed on a single pole saying where the freeway entrance was, what time you could park, when the street would get cleaned, all yelling different directions like someone too mixed up to make up his mind. I pointed the camera sideways, then straight on, trying to catch it all. I told myself not to think but I wasn't sure how to do that, to stop talking to myself.

I could not take pictures of people. I knew what that felt like, someone coming up and aiming a camera at you. People believed what they saw, but it was not the same as what was really there. The teacher said I should try to get out of my comfort zone. I should introduce myself, I'd be surprised how many people wanted to be open. If only she knew. There were so many people who had my face stored on their phones. Homeless girl. Gave her money on Haight Street. Told her not to spend it on drugs. I didn't talk to them, but I took their quarters and dimes and dollars, their quick sorry looks.

One day I went over near the park and took a photo of Jax. I thought it might be easier than going up to strangers. He was parked on the sidewalk outside the corner grocery with two of his buddies sitting against the wall. He was halfway through a bottle of vodka, but he looked like someone had taken him inside and given him a bath. His face was sunburned and swollen. "Girlfriend," he said. "Is the world getting better or worse?"

"Still rotating," I said and took the bottle he offered. The gulp of vodka tasted like acid. I held up the camera so he'd see it before I started snapping pictures. I thought he would say something, but he acted like he didn't notice. I took shots of his face from where I was standing and then close up. His eyes were crinkled into slits. There was a long scar along one of his ears.

"Am I going to be on the news?" he said. "Because it wouldn't be the first time. You know I was in Vietnam. That's how I hurt my foot." Then he laughed and started coughing. "But you know I'm a liar."

"We all are," I said, and I took another few pictures.

"But he's a hero just for going over there," said one of the guys sitting against the wall. "Unlike a lot of other people."

"Don't listen to him," said Jax. "He drinks." I couldn't remember if his bad leg was always bandaged. The wrapping was partway off, covered in dirt. He saw me looking at the hospital band on his wrist.

"Reminds me who I am," he said, jiggling it. "I had an infection, but they cleared it up."

I kept my camera up in front of me, so he'd have a chance to tell me not to take more pictures. He argued with the other guys about who was going to buy the next bottle.

"You want to get a round?" he said.

I told him sorry, I didn't have any money either. He and the guys kept talking, and I stood close and took more pictures like I was one of the tourists who couldn't stop. I had planned to erase all the pictures of him as soon as I got back to my room, but I kept them so I could show Ash. He was already giving me a hard time about taking the photo class because where was it going to lead? But he would get how it felt to watch Jax and know what he was thinking, which was that he was taking care of getting what he needed. He wasn't thinking about me.

The next week, the teacher told us to take pictures in our own rooms. She walked up and down the hallway, making suggestions. Lie on your stomach and look up while you're shooting. Stand and look down. Look away and then turn and shoot quickly. Try and look at all your possessions and see them for the first time. Spread them around the room, then put them in a neat pile. Decide for yourself, she said, if you want to be in the picture.

I didn't have much, but I piled all of it on my bed next to Root: clothes from the free box, packages of ramen noodles, Root's food dish, one of Ash's signs, NEED FOOD. I took pictures from every side of the room. I went out to the hallway and looked at the mess of my things and then sat on the edge of the window, until the teacher came in and told me to stop, I was going to fall. She put her arms around my waist and gently led me away from the window, but I hadn't even looked down at the street. I was too focused on my stuff and how, when I saw it through the camera, I wasn't sure I recognized it. Even Root, staring at me, looked different, a medium-size dog, mismatched eyes, an expression that said he was not surprised.

"Don't get disoriented," said the teacher, loosening her arms. "Everything looks strange when you hold up a camera. You don't see what's there. You see your take on what's there."

I went to the park and brought back what I'd left there and took pictures of that too, still in plastic bags, except for the letters to my mom. I spread those on top of the rest of my things like bread you'd throw out to birds. You couldn't read what I'd written. It was out of focus, so no one would know what it said. I took more pictures while Root found and ate a power bar with the wrapper still on it. I caught a photo of him with it hanging out of his mouth, full of drool. He was looking me in the eyes—you caught me, you know me, guilty as shit.

The next day in class the teacher held my photo of Root up for everyone to see. When she asked who liked it, everyone raised their hands.

"Why is this so good?" she said. She didn't wait for answers. "Because you can see this person's relationship to her belongings, especially the dog. You feel like you know her in some small way."

I kept looking at the picture, asking myself what had been in my head. How could they know me? They couldn't tell if I was thinking about the letters to my mother, about what she'd do if she saw them. You can't know someone from a picture. I had taken Shane's picture around in Golden Gate Park and no one knew him.

The last week of class the teacher put up fliers in the building inviting everyone to a party. "Come meet the artists," it said. She chose one photo from each of us and tacked them all on the wall, with little tags that had titles and our names. My picture was the one of Root, caught in the act. It had no title because I didn't know what to call it.

The day of the party the teacher wore a long black dress and black scarf with dangling threads. She put out grape juice, pretzels and cheese cubes, and a book where people could write comments. I wore a clean shirt and jeans because I had found the washing machine, in a small room behind the kitchen. Cade came over and congratulated me. She probably was relieved I was still there, taking a class like I was supposed to. I stood next to my picture while she went to look around.

Ash came and stuck with me when he wasn't grabbing handfuls of food. I'd taken so many pictures of him, straight and stoned, in front of the smoke shop, up at 40 Hill, lying on the grass when he didn't know I had the camera, but I hadn't shown those to anyone. I was trying to figure them out. I thought if I looked closely enough, I could understand what was going on with him and why he wanted to keep moving from one place to another. At night I stared at them, especially the ones where he was looking at the camera. I could tell he liked the photographer enough to stare right at her, looking uncomfortable and needy.

"Your picture is the best one," he said, and put his arm around me. It wasn't true because everyone had taken pictures that showed things about themselves that they weren't saying out loud. Ash wanted to know why I hadn't given it a title. I said it was because I still didn't know what the picture said about me.

Ash tore a piece of paper out of the comment book and held it against my back while he wrote, like I was a table. I could feel the tickle through my shirt, but I couldn't tell what he was writing. Ash taped the paper underneath my picture, a title in the blocky black letters he used for his signs. GIRL WITH FAMILY. I looked away from him.

"You're sure not in there," I said.

"It's just a picture, Maddy." He put a finger through a loop on the waist of my jeans.

The teacher tapped her hand on the wall a few times to get our attention and started in on a speech about how well we'd done, that it was a process of exploration that she hoped we'd continue. The pictures showed tiny moments that would ripple out through time. She went on like that. I missed the rest because I was thinking how I didn't know anything about the future. That was left for me to figure out.

Ash helped clean up, even though I could tell he was ready to go. Every time he looked at me, he nodded his head in the direction of my room, like he couldn't wait for the party to end so we could go up to my room and get into bed. The teacher came over and asked if she could keep my picture and enter it in an art show at the airport. If I won, I'd get a little bit of money. I couldn't imagine people getting off planes and stopping to look at Root standing on my bed eating a power bar. They might think of me like those people the teacher had photographed with everything they owned piled in front of them.

"I guess so" was all I could get out because I had too many thoughts going on at the same time. She shook my hand and told me I should consider taking another photo class.

Back at my room, Ash lit a joint and handed it to me. Root, lying on the floor near the bed, raised his head like we were going to pass it to him. Ash sank on the bed. I fell back on his lap and kissed the small tattoo loop in the crease of his arm.

"Infinity," he said. "My mother would shit if she knew she paid for it. But it kind of makes sense. Everything keeps moving forever, then goes back on itself. You can't get away from that." He took another hit and looked up at the ceiling. "I don't know what I'm saying." I took the joint and stubbed it out on the floor, where it left a burn spot that was probably going to get me in trouble. I didn't want to be high right then.

"I'm going to Los Angeles. Root and I are." As soon as I heard myself, I knew I meant it. I'd spent all that time writing to her, but I had to see her.

Ash sat up fast and put his arms around my waist. I rested my face against his neck. I said my mom was still in Los Angeles. Dave and Marva found the place where she lived, but they didn't see her. I was talking into his chest so I couldn't tell what he was thinking. Maybe he couldn't hear. I said my mom had something wrong with her brain. It happened so slowly I almost didn't notice, until one day she could hardly get out of bed. They took her to the hospital and the last time I visited she was too hollowed out to talk to me.

I talked quickly, hoping that would make me seem less hopeless. I said I might wake up and be like her. No warning. One minute I'd make sense and then I would be off somewhere in my head, psychotic. I thought about the map of the park I'd divided into sections. This one would be bigger, less knowable.

"We'll come back. They'll let me keep my room if I'm just gone for a week." I wasn't sure, but I didn't tell him that.

Ash said he could go with me, like it was no big deal I had a mom who was out of her mind. But I told him I had to go alone. He became still, the way he was when he was hurt and didn't want anyone to notice. I told him he could stay in the room while I was gone. He said that was not going to happen. Then he pulled me up and said we should take a walk.

Downstairs, everything was cleaned up. The security man, staring at his phone, didn't look at us when we left. Most of the stores on the street were dark, but a few blocks away a blue neon sign glowed on the door. A bell tinkled when Ash opened the door. He slapped shoulders with the guy at the front desk, who asked us what we wanted.

"I can draw her name right on your heart," he said. "Or on your arm. Some guys don't like it on the heart. You tell me. All my work is custom. You won't go out looking like anyone else."

I told Ash it was stupid, having my name on him. I didn't want to have to think of it there, forever. How did I know what was going to happen? And why would he spend money on something like that? Ash said not to get worked up, he didn't plan to put my name on his heart. He wanted to know why I always tried to ruin everything. I didn't try, I said, it just happened. Ash went over and picked up a thick notebook with pictures of tattoos.

"You see something you like, let me know," the guy said.

I turned to him and held out my arm. "Same as his," I said.

Ash looked like he didn't believe me, but he held Root's leash while the guy settled me in a chair and angled it back.

"Tell me about your tolerance for pain," he said. He told me I'd need to take some deep breaths when he started with the needle. Some people jumped out of the chair or fainted. But that was rare, in his experience. Most people were up for the hurt. Every spot on his arms was covered, a huge ruby rose, a woman's head with hair made of snakes, a field of black crosses, all shimmering under the bright light. I closed my eyes while he got ready and Karen's words kept repeating in my head. *You will be damaged goods.*

"No," I said, sitting up. "I'm not up for hurt."

The guy's goatee was right above my arm, where he was sketching the tattoo with a marker. He stopped and pushed his chair away.

"You get another one, if that's what you want," I said to Ash.

"You're not coming back from Los Angeles," he said.

"This is going to make me want to?" I climbed out of the chair and took Root's leash from him. "Besides, it's your tattoo. It has nothing to do with me."

"I got it when my grandfather died," he said. "He had cuff links in the same shape. I wasn't ever going to wear those."

The guy went to the front desk and said to come back when we figured out what we wanted. Ash rolled his sleeve back down over his tattoo and I felt a small ache that he could see a sign of his grandfather every day. The guy stood by the door and crossed his illustrated arms in front of his chest when we walked out.

Ash said we should walk the whole way to Los Angeles. He knew people who'd done that. You could follow the freeway or, if it was too hot, you could hike along the ocean. It might be possible to swim the rest. Once you got halfway there, the water would be warm. He kept talking, as if he thought we were already on our way.

When we got to my room, I reminded him that he was not coming with us. He sat on the bed with his back against the wall, watching me stuff extra clothes and food for Root in my pack. I'd tell him in the morning that Cade already bought me a bus ticket, both ways. It had nothing to do with him. Ash got under the covers.

"Wake me up when you finish packing," he said.

Then he was out, like he'd turned off a switch. I thought about taking the letters, dumping them in my mom's lap, here's the truth about the twelve years you missed. But I knew I'd leave them hidden. I'd written them for myself. I put my pack by the door, climbed in bed next to Ash and held on to him, telling myself, for one minute, let this feel like home.

Acknowledgments

Over years of living and working in San Francisco, I've watched several cycles of boom and bust, each one carving a deeper economic divide. This is a work of fiction, not based on actual persons, but I want to acknowledge individuals on the city's streets, in the park, and in shelters who spoke with me, as well as people working to help them. Certain facts and events are true: It has gotten harder to afford a stable life in the city. In California, a state with the world's fifth-largest economy, the number of unsheltered people reportedly grew by 16 percent from 2018 to 2019. When community groups gathered one chilly December night in 2019 for a yearly vigil to remember those who died homeless or in marginal housing, they called out 275 names. And all of this was before the COVID-19 pandemic, which landed more people on the streets.

I am deeply grateful to Barbara Kingsolver and the judges of the PEN/Bellwether prize for believing in this book. And huge thanks to my editor, Kathy Pories, for her invaluable insights, to the whole team at Algonquin Books, and to my agent Danielle Bukowski.

Thank you to Fenton Johnson and Jo Kaufman for reading early versions of the book, and to Candy Cooper and Bob Weisbuch, who listened to the first chapter around their kitchen table many years ago. I am grateful to the many colleagues, editors, and longtime friends who have supported me along the way. Thank you also to the wonderful community at the Writers Grotto in San Francisco, which made me feel like I wasn't alone. And I will always be grateful to John L'Heureux, a legendary teacher who was the head of Stanford's Creative Writing Program.

Thank you to my parents, Dorothy and Ewing Seligman, my sister Ginny, Rich Strock and the entire Heiden family for all their support. And, above all, thank you to Matthew and Halle for inspiring me every day, and to David Heiden, whose words and love give me hope.

AT THE EDGE OF THE HAIGHT

A Place to Hide
An Essay by Katherine Seligman

Questions for Discussion

A PLACE TO HIDE
An Essay by Katherine Seligman

It was the Fourth of July, too foggy to see fireworks over the bay, so we headed home through Golden Gate Park. I drove slowly even though I knew every curve of the road, how it threaded by a windmill, a herd of bison that looked like furry boulders, then a meadow and a rose garden. But at night, in the mist, it was hard to make out what was real. Trees creaked and swayed. There were shadows that could have been skunks, raccoons, or coyotes.

As we neared the edge of the park, a man ran into the road, waving his arms and pleading for us to stop. "Please, don't leave me," he shouted. "Someone is trying to kill me." He pointed to the bushes, but we couldn't see anything. When he got closer, I noticed a trickle of blood on his forehead.

Minutes later the police arrived and aimed a spotlight on a body lying motionless on the grass. My husband, a doctor, rushed over to help, but what he saw was a young man gasping his final breath. The man who'd stopped us sat on the curb, handcuffed. I couldn't tell if he was high, confused, or just agitated.

That's what I would say later, when I was called to testify. I had no idea what had happened. The man, who was in his sixties, claimed he was defending himself. No one was there to speak for the man who had died, at twenty-five, from a single stab wound to his heart. Both had been living in the park, but beyond that, nothing was presented. There were only two real witnesses and one was dead. "Neither one of them was up to any good," a police officer told me, after the man was released.

I couldn't stop thinking about his words. How did he know what they were up to? Was he going to say that to the young man's parents? And what about the man who killed him? I kept expecting to see him around the neighborhood, but I didn't. He'd vanished, or he lived in the park, hidden. I looked through court records and talked to kids on the street, but that didn't bring me closer to knowing the truth. Waves of dislocated young people, drifters, and seekers passed through the park every year. They followed rock bands, dreams, weed harvests, or they'd been kicked out or abused. They had nowhere else to go; more than a few died there.

When we stumbled across the murder, I'd lived in Haight-Ashbury, alongside the park, for more than twenty years. I'd written stories about it, but mostly I melted into life there and it worked its way into me in a way I never could have expected. Relatives—and sometimes friends in other zip codes—asked me why we stayed. Didn't the street scene and the noise bother me? Didn't people on the street try to sell our kids drugs?

Those are probably the same questions people asked more than fifty years ago when the Summer of Love blew in, transforming the worn neighborhood into a center of hippie counterculture. Kids flooded the streets, drugs flowed, and music blared all night. The crowds were so big that volunteer groups organized to provide free food and medical care.

Not everyone was happy, although there would be no turning back. The Haight would be known for its legacy of tolerance. Since then, there have been many cycles of boom and bust. The price of housing rose and fell. Rival neighborhood associations formed. Small businesses opened and closed, replaced by vintage stores, souvenir and smoke shops. Through it all, tourists kept coming. And so did kids, who sat in front of rainbow-colored murals, panhandling, busking, and doing what they needed to survive.

A while after we moved in, the owner of a building next door evicted all his tenants so he could sell. But he ran out of money to fix up the building, so he let people squat there. First it was people he knew, then people they knew. One guy with a teenage daughter always began the morning on the steps, drinking a tall beer, carrying his ancient chihuahua that could only pee propped up against a tree. Often, we'd talk. Later in the day, the guy fixed cars in the garage. He didn't pay rent, but every week he made a pot of chili that he handed out to the homeless. Then one night the police stopped his car and, because of his prior felony record, arrested him for having a gun and no driver's license. Neighbors took up a collection so his daughter would have enough to eat.

There was always something happening next door—a party where people dressed as elves ended up on our roof or someone who threw all his belongings out the window in the middle of the night or rang our doorbell at dawn so we wouldn't get a ticket on street cleaning day.

Then, during the latest pre-pandemic Gold Rush, the squatters got kicked out. In their place, the owner rented to founders of a medication app and a start-up that flew drones to discover who needed a new roof. No one threw anything out the window, but, somehow, I missed my old neighbors.

Now, the Haight, like much of the city, has fewer hourly workers, nurses, and musicians, and more lawyers, private equity investors, and unhoused people. In the former epicenter of free love, residents argue over the fairness of a law that bans sleeping and lying on the sidewalk and whether to support a low-income housing project.

Against this backdrop, I kept imagining the lives of two men who happened to be in the park that Fourth of July. They lived in close proximity to each other—and to me. How many people near me, living outside or right next door, led secret lives? Even in families, proximity is not a guarantee of intimacy. There are limits to how well we can know our children, and how well they know us.

At the Edge of the Haight is about a girl who flees her past and ends up in the park with her dog and a makeshift family. She wants to stay hidden, until she witnesses a murder and no longer can. The book is a story about both coming of age and what is happening when we aren't looking, in San Francisco, and around the country, where more people are ending up on the street. There is no one reason, just as there is no one answer. But there is a place to start, which is to open our eyes.

QUESTIONS FOR DISCUSSION

1. Maddy comes to San Francisco alone and quickly forms bonds with others who stay in Golden Gate Park. In what ways are they Maddy's family, rather than the one she was born into? How much of Maddy's history does Ash know? Do they keep more secrets than other kinds of families?

2. Animals play a key role in the book. Why does Maddy take Root and then feel as though he belongs to her? Does she treat him differently than other members of her chosen family? In what ways are Root and Fleet's rat, Tiny, like and unlike traditional family pets? What might be the significance of Root's name and how it fits with Maddy's history?

3. Why does Maddy want to stay unseen? Can you think of times in your life when you wished that no one knew your history or where you were?

4. What do Shane Golden's parents, Dave and Marva, want from Maddy? Is it because she might know more about their

son, or is it something else? How well do you think they knew Shane? How did you feel about their need to know Maddy?

5. How might being present when someone dies create a kind of bond or obligation? In what ways does that drive Maddy's quest to find out about Shane, or is she motivated for other reasons?

6. How does the Haight-Ashbury neighborhood, as well as the park and San Francisco itself, function as a character in the book? Could this story have happened in any American city that has a lot of unhoused people? In what ways were the residents in the neighborhood tolerant of or conflicted about their district being a magnet for drifters and the displaced?

7. Maddy and Ash come from different backgrounds; Maddy couldn't rely on her family, and Ash has a mother who seems to care, even if she doesn't know him very well. What do you think draws them together? In what ways is their bond real, and in what ways forged by circumstance?

8. Maddy sees a car barreling down the street, headed for where she's standing on the sidewalk, and in an instant she sees the need to change. What factors go into making such a huge decision? Why didn't Maddy make up her mind earlier to move off the street? Can you think of a time when you made a major life change based on something that seemed to happen in a split second?

9. Maddy learns to see herself more clearly partly by taking photographs. Why do the pictures Maddy takes bring her closer to seeing the reality of her life and her relationship to others?

10. Living outside requires a lot of work. Each day people have to rummage for food and money, find a safe, dry place to sleep, and then do it again the next day. Maddy and her friends carved out space for themselves in the park, gathering and hiding supplies. In what ways did their spot in the park replicate the feeling of a home? What surprised you about their strategies to survive outside?

11. Many young people run away and return home after a brief time. Has there ever been a time when you thought of running away—or did?

12. Readers often identify with characters who are like them in some way. Is it possible to see things through the eyes of someone whose life is so different? Talk about times when you worried about, empathized with, or distrusted any of the characters or wished they'd make a different choice. How did that affect the way you related to them?

13. The police in the book play a cat-and-mouse game with the homeless, forcing them to move off the sidewalk and to get up at dawn but then grudgingly allowing them to stay. How does the relationship between the police and the kids reveal the city's

attitude toward the homeless? Do you think the police showed compassion, or were they dismissive and resigned?

14. How did the book change how you feel about the issue of homelessness? Why do you think so many young people end up living outside in Haight-Ashbury? Why do some of them have such a hard time finding or accepting help, and to what extent is that in their control? Is homelessness part of a bigger, systemic issue? What do you think are some of the solutions?

15. What do you think the future holds for Maddy? Are there opportunities for her? Will she go to Los Angeles and try to reunite with her mother or stay and try to make things work in San Francisco? Will she return to the street, go to school, or become a photographer? Will she stay with Ash? Should she?

PENNI GLADSTONE

KATHERINE SELIGMAN has been a writer at the *San Francisco Chronicle Magazine*, a reporter at the *San Francisco Examiner*, and a correspondent at *USA Today*. Her work has appeared in *Redbook*, *Life*, *Money*, the *Sun* magazine, the anthology *Fresh Takes*, and other publications. She lives in San Francisco.